ZOO

PHIL PRICE

For my Father
Who watches down on us
From the stars

For small creatures such as we the vastness is only bearable through love.....

CARL SAGAN

PROLOGUE

EARTH

THE CRISP AUTUMN SUNLIGHT BATHED THE LANDSCAPE IN A gentle yellow hue. The summer had been long and warm, its heat melding seamlessly into the latter stages of the year. Cars traversed the small village of Belbroughton, slowly heading along the country lanes as children climbed slides and laughed as their parents pushed them on swings in the communal playground. Mums sat chatting on wooden benches, coffee cups in hands as they kept an eye on the little ones who were foraging and finding adventure in the gated play area. As the morning headed into the afternoon, a stout man unlocked the front doors of his public house, the carved pumpkins that adorned his frontage a welcoming sight for the dark nights that were to follow. A young family stopped to look at the seasonal decorations, two little boys pointing and exclaiming at the macabre sight as their parents looked on adoringly. All was calm in the cosy village, with its butcher's shop and the scattering of pubs that lined the sleepy streets. At the far end of Belbroughton, a large field stood empty, save for a few locals that had begun work on the annual fete. Two scarecrows stood motionless at the entrance to the grassy expanse, keeping watch over the comings and goings. Their eyes gazing blankly ahead, looking for trouble. Sometimes though, trouble does not appear straight ahead. Sometimes, it comes from above. From the stars.

ONE

THE SHIP HUNG IN A PERPETUAL ORBIT, SLOWLY CIRCLING THE gas giant beneath it. Flashes of light from planetary storms crackled across the ionosphere. Far off, a dying star lit the ship's metallic hull, its beacon casting its stark light across the ancient solar system. Inside the vessel in a low-slung room, six figures sat. The room offered no windows. No vista or daylight to distract any of them. Dust motes floated in the air as the light gently pulsed, reflecting off the shiny alloy of the figures' suits. They were all humanoid. All male. Their pathetic, withered bodies were ridiculously emaciated, titanium shells encasing them. The metal pinched their skin, holding them firmly in place, their limbs powered by the suits. The suits, in turn, were powered by a neural link from their engorged brains. Brains that bulged against their paper-thin skulls, dark veins crisscrossing their mottled skin. They were effectively cyborgs. Machines with a humanoid core. The lights in the confined space lit the tops of their faces, obscuring features that were flat and nondescript. The figure at the head of the table gestured with a metal hand, a metallic whirr echoing off the walls. "We don't have much time. We know what has been finalised. This chairing is just to clarify a few points." His mouth remained shut, their communication on another level.

———————

After an hour the humanoid at the head of the table spoke again. "The war is all but won. Just two systems remain where the rebels are holed-up. We will hunt them down and make martyrs of them all. Barajan, their leader, will have a very public execution. It will send a message to all."

"Agreed," a collective voice said in unison.

"Can trade recommence?" another voice said.

"Certainly. We will send out a pulse-message to all systems. It will take time for normality to return. We must recoup the costs of this skirmish."

"How are preparations for the attraction?" another figure asked.

"On course. We have identified a thousand potential systems to plunder. Terraforming is underway. Once complete we can send them out. We hope to have the attraction up and running in one moon cycle."

"Do we have a name?"

"Not yet. We will put our more creative thinkers on this task. They have been busy, finding outposts for us to scout. They tell me that we'll have a very diverse attraction that will draw visitors from far and wide. This venture will be a sure-fire way to replenish our funds. I will be in touch. Safe travels back to your stations."

TWO

BIFLUX

HALF A MOON CYCLE LATER TWO FIGURES LOOKED OUT AT their binary sunset. The larger yellow star seemed to engulf the brown dwarf in front of it. The orbs seemed stuck together, although almost half a light year of space separated them. The two figures watched the giant balls of hydrogen slowly sink beneath the horizon, the spectacle holding their attention for the countless time. They looked down at the plaza and the clutch of buildings below them. Folk were dispersing after the event. A few still milled around, hoping for more excitement. Most were heading home before the storm on the horizon engulfed them.

"It all went off without incident. No rebel spies trying a last-minute rescue." Ark Ramkle sat cross-legged with a large bottle of corn beer in his hand. He was young for a pilot. He had only recently sprouted growth on his chin. His red hair sprang out in tufts on top of his head. He had mischievous eyes that were constantly looking for something to do or something that could make him crack a joke or poke fun. His life had been one long adventure so far. Nothing critical had befallen him.

"They probably knew better. That's if there's any left.

They are probably huddled together in a cave on Svikan, shitting themselves. All their plans for domination lie in tatters in a puddle of piss." Torben Fraken sat next to the younger man. His eyes were heavy set, framed by a mono-brow. His hair was dark and closely cropped. He had the look of a man whose woes lay heavily on his shoulders. He too held a beer in his hand. His arms were uncovered, revealing intricate ink work from cuff to shoulder. The artwork was of star systems that wound themselves around his arms. Torben would never reveal to anyone that he'd almost blacked out from the pain. That would have been a show of weakness. Torben was not weak. He was a badass pilot. A loner, with no family. He took a swig of beer, savouring the cold aftertaste. "I've read about the evolution of execution Ark. From the dawn of time when people were stoned, eaten, and chopped up. Then it evolved into things like acid melt, supernova impact, black hole ingestion." He took another swig. "All you really need is a strong arm and a sword to get the job done. Barajan is just as dead now that his head has been cut off. Forget the fancy ways. Death is death. Maybe we've come full circle."

"Maybe. Or maybe our masters are running low on funds. It must cost a great deal to fire someone into a black hole. A good sharp sword costs about fifty dunars."

"You may be right, my ugly friend."

"Ugly! Fuck you! This face gets me laid every weekend."

"With what. Rats from the sewers or stray dogs? No humanoid female would want a piece of that," he pointed to the young pilot's groin.

"You kidding? Many a female has sampled my delights. Beautiful ones. Green ones. Furry ones. You name it. Let's hope that someone out their in the cosmos will get to try it out too."

"Exactly where are you heading? Out of a thousand ships to be deployed, let's hope we're not at the bottom of the pecking order. I don't want to end up on some forlorn rock rounding up some fluffy pack animals."

"Me neither," Ark said in between swigs. "I want some fun." They both pressed a button on their wrist pilots, and a double ping indicated that a message had arrived. Two holographic images blinked into view in front of them. The setting sun's light had diminished enough to make the star maps very clear.

"Wow!" Ark said. "Looks like we both got lucky."

"Hmmm. You may be right, my friend." They both rotated their own displays, looking at the systems and the surrounding voids of space.

"This is a long way from here. Not our galaxy. Not even close. Galaxy Mj486. Spiral galaxy thirteen billion lights from here."

"Same as mine," Torben said in wonder as he looked at his own map along with his friends. "You're about seven hundred lights from my planet. Quite close. You could almost call in and say hi." Both men laughed. The older pilot pulled up a page of text relating to his destination. "I'm to round up humanoids and a few indigenous creatures that live amongst them. The planet is referred to as Earth by its inhabitants. Should be relatively easy. They are a very primitive species. Not as nearly evolved as we are. How about you?"

"The planet is called Lokash. Sixty percent land, forty percent water. The dominant species is a hominid." A picture of a large hairy mammal appeared in front of Ark's eyes. It looked a formidable target. "Wow. These guys are three metres tall and weigh five hundred key-grams. Tackling them will be fun." He scrolled through the rest of the text, looking at the other creatures on his itinerary. "Hmm. Humanoids are on my list too. Although they are bottom of the food chain. A large cat, reptile, and hybrid make up the list. So, humanoid must be the prey of the other four. Interesting. Very unevolved." The two men sat pondering their missions.

The older man turned to the younger. "Ten years ago, we'd never have thought this possible. It was only our alliance with the Lomogs that led us to this." Ark nodded, remembering how an advanced race had turned up at their planet with a proposal. Their own planet, in a far-off corner of space, was being threatened by a red giant and they needed a new place to call home. Their home planet of Biflux and the neighbouring moon offered these strange robot-like humanoids the nourishing atmosphere they so craved. In return, the Lomogs shared their technology with the Biflex people. It had started out as a perfect match. Nourishing air in return for untold advances in technology. The ability to reach beyond their own galaxy. Weaponry and medical treasures too. It had all seemed too good to be true. And it was. A splinter group opposed to such alliances was formed. Their leader Barajan waged a war on his own people, along with the Lomogs. Millions were killed. Cities decimated. It even raged away from the planet. Two orbital stations had been destroyed by nuclear weaponry, just as they were being populated. Countless thousands were sucked out into the vacuum of space. A silent crushing death for them all. The Lomogs, although weak in body, were strong in retaliation. Along with the Biflex, they'd chased and obliterated the rebels wherever they'd found them. In the end, it was Barajan's head hitting the plaza steps that would end the war. Others would one day oppose the new alliance. But for now, exciting times lay ahead. As the war raged, the Lomogs had upgraded the Biflex's Warp Drive spacecraft with their own advances. The new Singularity Drives were installed, with the Biflex people amazed at the results. They could leave the confines of their own galaxy. A galaxy that would normally take them years to traverse. Now they could venture to the very corners of the cosmos in days. It gave people like Ark and Torben new challenges. Like the ones that sat in their lap as the suns set on the rocky horizon.

"Let's go to the Sars club and have a few more drinks and talk about our mission," Ark said as a warm gust of wind ruffled his red locks.

"Why not," Torben said as the first drops of rain started to fall from the leaden skies above.

As they walked through the doors of the bar the rains unloaded on the street outside. People of all races, creeds, and species took cover as it would rain solidly for many hours. The two pilots slid onto two barstools and waited for the tender to serve them. The tender tonight was Vrolakian. New to Biflux. They were a tall race with bright blue skin. She smiled at both men as she placed two tall glasses on the bar. The suds spilled over the rim and down over her blue fingers, making them sparkle under the down-lighters. Both men watched as she shimmied off to serve another customer.

"I bet you ten kren that I nail her tonight," Ark said, as he wiped froth from his top lip.

"I'm not betting on you populating the cosmos, bartender by bartender. Keep your money. You may need it one day."

"What for?"

"Duh. Your own ship. Your brains are firmly rooted in your crotch tonight, my young friend."

The younger man made a play of smacking his ear a few times. "You're right. My mind is firmly on intergalactic love."

Torben looked around the bar, surveying the clientele. Some were revellers from the execution. Others were pilots, traders, and travellers. He spotted two pilots in a booth studying their respective wrist pilots. His mind returned to their mission. Torben motioned the younger man over to a quiet booth and flicked on his pilot. He scrolled through a few holographic screens, his brow knitted. "Hmm. We fly in three days. Fifty craft at a time. It looks like we're in the third group of departures. Just after midday." He read on for a few seconds. "Two days manned flight out to safe zone 784. Then, who knows. I can't wait to pass through, Ark, to think that we'd be able to do this in our lifetimes." He scanned the image. "Once on the other side it will take another two days to get to our planet." They watched fascinated as a series of planets appeared and passed out of view. The first two were a beautiful blue. One was slightly darker with a deep blue spot on its southern hemisphere. Then came two huge gas giants. One was surrounded by stunning discs. The other's surface looked an angry roiling collage. A solitary red planet came next. Torben noticed a deep ridge like a crooked smile, running along its surface. Space shot by for a few seconds before a blue and green planet came into view.

"Whoa!" Ark said. "She's a beauty."

"You're not wrong there," Torben said, mesmerized. They looked at oceans and land, framed by white clouds. They could almost reach out and touch it. "I can't wait to see that for real. It's beautiful." He read the coordinates that would pinpoint the spot on the planet where they would make their landing. "We have a ten-hour window. Sunset to sunrise. Should be easy."

The younger pilot leaned closer to get a better look. He smiled. "If you find any hot humanoid females, don't forget about your old friend, Ark."

THREE

THREE DAYS LATER TORBEN SAT AT THE CONTROLS OF HIS NEW ship, Shimmer050. It was just shy of seven hundred feet long, its dark grey exterior giving it a subdued appearance. She sat low to the ground, barely fifty feet tall, with a triangular fantail that housed the twin ion drives that was the primary propulsion system for the ship. The singularity drive was housed mid-way along its length, a fattening of the hull towards the rear the only anomaly in the cylindrically shaped hull. Torben watched through the cockpit window as figures came and went from the vessel. He had several crew members, who were making final preparations to disembark. Torben had flown with most of them several times. Some of the other staff were travelling with him for the first time. His co-pilot was a short hairy hominid called Rex. His green hair was trimmed neatly, covering his whole body, save for a hexagon on his chest. Darker green skin lurked there, dappled with raised symbols. Torben's three landing party were all humanoid, but from a far-off planet unlike his own. They were all taller than he, with reptilian eyes and bad breath. They were called En, Ko and Shaa. They liked to be called all at once as they never left each other's sides. He turned to Rex. "Okay, take us out."

Torben sat as the co-pilot deftly handled the ship through the cloud layers until the sky around turned dark. He could see the horizon of his world as they broke orbit. Torben could see the clear blue sea below where it kissed the sky in the distance. Ten minutes later they were nearing the planet's only satellite.

"Okay, Rex, I'll take over now. You've had enough fun for a while."

"Okay, skipper. Do you fancy some graff from the kitchen?" Graff was a hot drink, made from the leaves of the graffa plant that grew on the mountainous slopes not far from the launch site. It was faintly herbal and would relax them both.

"Two cubes please," Torben said as he bypassed the moon they called Lundell. Ten minutes later they were sat at their controls, sipping piping hot graff. The ship was cruising along at a steady 300,000 miles-per-hour. They barely felt the Ion-drive as it pulsed at the back of the ship, propelling them forward. Everything felt comfortable and serene. They knew that would change soon enough. Torben set his lidded mug in the holder to his left and gripped the throttle with one hand, the paddle with the other. He looked at the heads-up display in front of him and worked out the next part of the course. "Okay, we increase to eighty percent drive for forty-six hours. That should take us out to the safe zone. Rex, take over. Switch us to autopilot in two hours. I will go check in the stores. I need to make sure all inventory is accounted for and that they are behaving themselves. If not, I will jettison their hides into the void."

"Okay, skipper."

As Torben exited the bridge he felt the ship increase its speed. By the time he'd reached the stores, they would be travelling at a little over 5,000,000 miles-per-hour. He walked towards the room at the midpoint of the ship, his footsteps echoing down the narrow corridor that led out into a round chamber. Torben had quickly looked inside the confined space when he'd first entered the ship. However, the room had been empty. Now as he stepped off the walkway, down half a dozen steps, a small man with steel eye-glasses approached. "Captain Fraken," he said. "Welcome to the Singularity drive."

Torben nodded, noting the nameplate stitched into the man's tunic. "It looks impressive, Jonas" he said, taking in the chamber around him. The walls were a dull grey, studded with oddly shaped cones that were evenly spaced from floor to ceiling. In the centre of the room, a large metal ball hung between three rotating rings, also studded with symmetrical shapes that looked like mini pyramids.

"It certainly is. Are you familiar with the workings?"

"Somewhat," he replied carefully. "I have read up on this kind of technology. Bending space to create a dimensional gateway."

"Yes. The singularity is, in essence a mini black hole."

"Which is achieved by using the magnetic rings to focus a narrow beam of gravitons."

"Which in turn allows us to fold spacetime until a Singularity is created. Once that happens, the ship will pass through the Event Horizon, coming out at another point in space. Exciting stuff."

"It certainly is. This would have seemed impossible only a few years ago."

"Indeed," the smaller man said, his clammy complexion and facial tick making Torben feel slightly uneasy. "We once thought that warp drive was the be all and end all of interstellar propulsion. How wrong we were."

"Is it safe? And will it work?"

"Absolutely. I have already been on a ship that has made the jump. We started with a minor leap, just a few light years. This thing works seamlessly. When you execute the jump, it will take only a few seconds for the ship to pass through the gateway. And by then, we'll be on the other side of the known universe."

"What do you know about the system that we will be travelling to?"

"Enough. The solar system is approximately 4,000,000,000 years old," Jonas said enthusiastically. "There are eight planets, orbiting a yellow star that is known as the Sun. The first two planets closest to the stars are devoid of life, constantly blasted by the star. Then we have Earth, which lies nearly 100,000,000 miles from the host star. Beyond that, there is a red planet that we believe once harboured life, followed by two gas giants and two ice giants. This type of solar system is fairly common."

"And the inhabitants of Earth?"

"They are an intelligent species, but young in their development. They have only recently started understanding how the universe works. Our reconnaissance drones have picked up enough information about the human species. They have visited their satellite and are now planning more ambitious expeditions. But it will take them another generation before they discover the technology and the means to take them to their closest star, which is just over four light-years from their planet."

"Hmm. Maybe we could leave them the blueprints for that," he said, pointing at the metal structure in the centre of the room, a dull humming drone emanating from it.

"I'm sure that they are beginning to think about this kind of technology. But they have time on their side. Their system is stable, located on the outer fringes of the galaxy. I am sure that they will begin their voyage to the stars one day, possibly soon."

"Okay, Jonas. Thank you for taking the time to brief me, and I'm glad to have you aboard."

"It's my pleasure, Captain Fraken. It was nice meeting you too," he said before Torben excused himself, needing some fresher air and familiar surroundings. He headed out of the chamber, pleased by the mood lighting that the long corridors emitted. The changing colours at the floor and ceiling seemed to slow his pulse, calming him somewhat as he headed for the next stop on his round. He checked the stores, pleased that all provisions were accounted for. Torben chatted with the crew, enjoying the feelings of trepidation and excitement they gave off. He almost showed similar excitement, reigning it in slightly, maintaining his authority. By the time he entered the technician's lab, he was almost skipping. The dour-faced scientists took the edge off his good mood. They gave him a detailed update of the composition of the Earth's atmosphere and topography. Torben cared not. As long as he could either breathe freely or by regulator, he was happy. He nodded sagely, pretending to listen until he made his excuses and left. He popped back to the cockpit to check on Rex. The little hominid would not move for the best part of two days. He was happiest sat at the controls and Torben trusted him implicitly. The captain made his way to his cabin along white corridors whose ceilings and floors gently pulsed in ever-changing hues. Once inside his spacious quarters, he stripped naked and took a long, hot shower. His favourite folken music was piped in through overhead speakers, making all his stresses and worries wash away down the drain. He anointed his tattooed torso with oils to make it shine. His muscled arms looked impressive to him as he dressed for dinner. He knew who he wanted to impress too. Kyra, the medical officer. The captain had not known her long. She was tall and dark like him. She was Biflex like him too. He knew the country she hailed from. It was high up in the tundra. Her voice was melodious and light and made him feel like an awkward adolescent. He sensed a mutual attraction, although as Chief Medical Officer, Kyra, would of course be too professional to show any feelings towards him. *Unless I get her drunk and.* His thoughts were interrupted by a knock at the door. Torben nodded, the white partition opening. *Oh fuck*, he thought as Kyra stood uncertain in the doorway. He was still only dressed in cargos and a singlet. His feet were bare and his chest exposed. He quickly zipped up his top, snagging a few hairs in the process. He mentally swore as he tried to remain cool and collected. "Can I help you, Officer Zakx?"

"Yes, Captain Fraken. We have a medical emergency. Well, we did have a few moments ago. One of the porter staff has died."

"Oh no! How?"

"Heart failure. Totally unexpected. His name was Elion."

"Shit, I knew him. He lived in the same town that I did. His mother knew my mentor. Sorry for the bad language." He looked down at the floor and blushed.

"No offence taken, Captain."

"Please, call me Torben. This isn't a military craft. I prefer a degree of familiarity."

"Done. Only if you call me Kyra."

"Deal, Kyra. Okay, could you take me to see Elion? We won't have time now to send him home. He can stay in cold storage until our return." Kyra waited while Torben pulled his boots on and gave himself the once over in the mirror. He caught Kyra looking at him out of the corner of his eye. Now it was her turn to blush. Torben smiled inside. He was enjoying this twist to his mission, even if one of his crew had died. They walked in silence for a few moments before Kyra, for once at a loss for words, piped up.

"So, you're from Walvak." Kyra said. It wasn't a question. It was a statement.

"Yes. And I believe you're from neighbouring Cantis. A beautiful place. The glaciers are stunning. I have spent many a happy time there."

"Are you one of the adrenaline junkies who try the Cantis-Ebris challenge?"

"I am. I even came second a few years ago. That was the last time I was there."

"Really? Where did you stay? Kyra was becoming chatty. Unusually so for her with a man.

"At Mrs Alto's camp. We pitched next to the waterfall. It was amazing."

"Ah. Slumming it with the rabble. I'd expect a pilot, especially a captain, to have stayed at the Fazal."

"Not me. I'm more a rough and ready kind of guy. A bottle of suds and a hard floor are okay with me." He suddenly regretted that last statement. He didn't want Kyra thinking he was a lowlife. *Shit.*

"I'd probably join you in that view. Although occasionally a girl does like to be pampered." He chuckled as they rounded a corner, arriving at the double doors of the med-wing. "Follow me, Torben," Kyra said as the doors opened with barely a whisper. The med bay was like the rest of the ship. White walls were gently subdued into various colours that floated up from the recesses by the ceilings and floors. All surfaces were spotlessly clean. In the centre of the room, a large egg-shaped table lay beneath a holographic display. On it, Torben could see an X-ray of his dead porter. He suddenly felt all happiness and brevity leave him.

"Such a shame," he said, as he followed Kyra to a single door in a far corner of the room. It too opened silently, leading them into a long narrow room with several small square doors set alongside one wall. One door had been opened and a long chrome shelf jutted out of the doorway. On it, covered in a white sheet, was Elion. His skin was a mix of grey and blue. Torben noticed that his face had already sunk somewhat. "Poor guy. He was the same age as me, there or thereabouts. So much to live for."

"He would have felt nothing. He has a nasty lump on the back of his head. Probably from the impact after he'd died. Shame." Kyra covered the body and ushered Torben back into the lab. "I will fill out a D.O.A report. I will brief our operations on Biflux so they can contact his family. I'm glad someone else has that job instead of me."

"Yes, I agree," Torben said as he stood looking around the lab.

"Would you like to join me for dinner this evening, Torben?" It was out before Kyra even had time to think about it. She looked at the pilot with a mixture of expectancy and embarrassment. Torben noticed that the woman had a lock of red hair. It was a nice contrast to her darker hair, drawing his eyes to it easily. He'd never noticed it before. She nervously tucked it behind her left ear, the overhead lights catching the colour for a split second, making it shimmer.

Torben looked into her deep brown eyes, noticing a few freckles on her nose. She was impossibly good looking. "Of course. That would be nice," the captain said, feeling a swell of happiness and awkwardness wash over him.

"Okay, great. Shall I meet you in the foyer in an hour?"

"Yes. See you then. It should be a good choice tonight. First dinner and all."

"I look forward to it." Torben could see that the skin around Kyra's neck was flushed like she'd been on a taxing run. He diverted his gaze before excusing himself. He made his way back to the bridge. Rex was sitting casually in his seat, his drink finished in the holder next to him. He turned around to see Torben. "Hey, Captain. Everything's five-by-five."

"Great." Torben sat down next to the hominid, looking out at the black void around him. "One of the porters died not long after take-off. Heart attack. Completely out of the blue."

"That's too bad. Have you been down to see the body?"

"Yes. Kyra, I mean, Officer Zakx informed me and escorted me to the med bay." Torben could see Rex looking at him.

"So, you're on first name terms with Officer Zakx. You didn't waste any time."

"Knock it off. It's not like that. Although she did ask me to join her for dinner later."

Rex whistled through his shiny blue teeth. "Maybe she will invite you back to her cabin for dessert. She's very attractive, for a humanoid."

"I'm sure it will just be dinner. Nice and formal. I am Captain after all."

"Well, you enjoy. I have my lunch here. That will keep me going until tomorrow."

Torben placed his hand on Rex's shoulder. "Thanks, Rex. I don't know what I'd do without you." As Torben left the bridge, Rex sat in silence as the cosmos sped past him. A serene smile framing his furry face.

FOUR

HE ROUNDED THE LAST TURN BEFORE THE SHIP'S MESS HALL, spotting Kyra looking at a series of pictures adorning the wall of the foyer. They were galaxies, placed there at Torben's request. They were as varied as they were beautiful. They were all holographic pictures. The galaxies and nebula moved slowly in each frame, captivating the viewer with the promise of far-off wonders and mysteries. He noticed she was fidgeting. She had her hands on her hips for a brief moment, before chewing on a thumb. Then back on the hips before she seemed to slap her thighs. She sensed someone was looking at her and turned to see the ship's captain appraising her. Kyra fidgeted some more, shifting her weight from one foot to the other. Torben approached her. "Nice artwork," she said, instantly regretting how lame that sounded.

"My indulgence. I think they give an otherwise sparse ship a bit of character." He motioned towards the mess hall, "Shall we?"

She made a slight bow of her head and walked alongside him through the doorway. A few minutes later they were seated in a far corner of the hall, away from most of the other occupants. "So, are you okay with the mission that you are about to undertake?"

Torben looked up from his plate of Makamaka, a local Biflux delicacy. Large cuts of dark meat, drizzled with sauce, served on a bed of red rice. "I think so. Why do you ask?"

"Well, we're about to travel to a far-off corner of the universe to abduct members of another civilization."

"Hmm. When you say it like that it does sound kinda bad. To be honest, I knew what the parameters of the mission were, but I got so excited about travelling to that far corner of space that I forgot about the actual task." He looked at Kyra, who was pushing her food around her oval plate with a fork. "How about you? Are you okay with what we're about to do?"

"Not totally. But I needed this mission. I needed to put some distance between myself and the wars."

Torben could see that there was more that could be gleaned from her statement. "I don't mean to pry, but how so?"

Kyra put down her fork, took a swig from her glass of beer and dabbed her mouth with a towel. "I lost someone. My partner, Relkon. He was a pilot." She composed herself, trying to remain in control. "He was shot down on the eve of the last battle. His body was never found as he'd crashed down in the tundra."

Torben nodded sadly. He knew that the tundra of Biflux was a place filled with predators. Even if Relkon had survived the crash, without weapons or rescue he would have lasted less than an hour. "I'm very sorry, Kyra." He thought about placing his hand over hers, then dismissed the idea. *That's too much too soon. It might spook her*, he thought.

Kyra regained her composure as she continued. "So I decided to take on a mission. No, I'm not totally happy about the task in hand, although under the current circumstances I can turn a blind eye to it. Does that sound heartless?"

"No. What if the people of Earth are living a horrible

existence themselves? We may be giving some of them a chance of a new start."

She smiled at him as her face softened. The smile reached her eyes and seemed to transform her already beautiful face. "I like your optimistic outlook, Torben." She reached across the table and briefly squeezed his hand. The static in that fleeting contact was almost audible.

He smiled back. It also reached his eyes, smoothing out his serious face. "Believe me, I'm not normally that optimistic."

Members of the crew came and went. The noise around them was enough to keep their conversation private. It also made them lean close to each other as they spoke, which they both seemed to enjoy. They were oblivious to anything or anyone. Kyra told Torben about her childhood, even adding the embarrassing moments that she'd never thought she would share with a relative stranger. She sensed a deepness within him. A sorrow that bubbled under the surface, never quite showing itself. He spoke about his childhood too. She sensed, though, that he omitted certain things from the conversation. Maybe they would come in the fullness of time, she hoped. She was attracted to him. Kyra sensed it was mutual, although her confidence had taken a battering over the last few months. She tried to play it as cool as possible. As plates were taken from them and beer glasses replenished, Kyra became aware that she was under the influence. She needed to be careful. Alcohol had a habit of letting the truth come out. She needed to come up with an excuse to head back to her quarters. The woman glowed inside when she saw a brief flash of disappointment as she tried to wrap up the evening.

"Oh," said Torben. Shall I walk you back to your quarters?"

"That would be nice," Kyra said, almost too eagerly. The journey only took a few minutes. They walked in silence for most of the way. Their swaying hands almost touching. Torben could almost feel the static crackle as they swished passed, to and fro. She turned and addressed him as they reached her door. "Thank you for a pleasant evening Torben. It was nice to finally get to meet you properly."

"Yes, it was," he said, also a little too quickly. He sensed that he sounded too keen. "I'm sure we'll bump into each other soon."

"I hope so." *Damn that beer*, she thought. She flushed before extending her hand. He took it, matching her grip, liking the cool firm feel of her skin.

"Goodnight, Kyra," he said.

"Have a pleasant evening, Torben," she demurred before turning and entering her cabin. Torben stood there for a moment, lost in his thoughts. He walked back slowly to his cabin, a warm smile on his usually serious face.

FIVE

THEY DID INDEED BUMP INTO EACH OTHER OVER THE NEXT DAY and a half, although they both had company when the moment arrived. They mentally swore inside, wishing that their crew would evaporate into the air so they could converse some more. Kyra liked watching him fidget like a boy when they tried to exchange pleasantries. She thought about this as she lay in her quarters, a thin blanket draped over her long body. She let warm thoughts combine with the thrum of the ion drives to send her off into a deep, dreamless sleep.

Torben checked in regularly with Rex to plot their progress through the solar system. They would be slowing down in a few hours and the Hominid told his captain to retire for the evening. Tomorrow was a big day. As Torben stood in the shower, letting the hot water pepper his torso, his mind was not on what it should have been. Here he was, a pilot. A badass. On the verge of the greatest moment of his life and the lives of his people. And yet as he stood under the torrent, his thoughts were of Kyra. Thoughts of far off civilisations were hidden under the warm, fuzzy thoughts of Officer Zakx.

Was he getting feelings for her? *Impossible.* He hardly knew her. Yet she was always in his thoughts. He mentally made his brain move her to one side as he tried to focus on tomorrow's tasks. Torben was still trying to think of the itinerary as he lay under the silk blanket. However, he was fighting a losing battle. A tall dark beauty kept knocking his flight plans to one side. Eventually, he relented as he drifted off to sleep. The last sound he heard was the throttle of the Ions falling away. By the time he woke, they would be in position.

"Okay, Rex. Slight reverse thrust. Slow us down to a standstill." The hominid deftly handled the controls of the ship. Hardly any inertia could be felt as they slowed from a few thousand miles per hour to just a crawl. Finally, they were drifting in deep space. Ahead of them, they could see the galactic core a few lights away. It had a faintly purple tinge. A large plume of blue light rose into the heavens on the horizon. They knew it was Pulsar. It was magnificent. But deadly. They were glad that they were several trillion miles away from its death grip. Would they see anything so spectacular in the next few days? Torben slapped Rex on the shoulder. "I'll go and get us some graff and a few snacks to see us through the next few hours." He looked down at his furry co-pilot. "Get her ready for the jump. Like we did in training. You, my friend, have the honour of taking us into the void."

Rex drew in a sharp breath. "Me! Really, Captain? This should be your moment."

"And it will be. Being captain of this ship is honour enough. You deserve this, Rex. I will be back in a bit." As Torben left the cockpit the little green hominid sat gently coaxing the controls, salty blue tears streaking his face.

· · ·

"Torben," Kyra called out as she spotted the captain heading back to the cockpit, laden with provisions.

"Kyra. Hello. How is everything?" She was dressed in civilian clothing. A blue all-in-one with leather boots that fell just shy of her knees.

"Fine. Although my captain is about to burn himself or spill food all over his ship. Here let me help." She took a beaker of graff out of his hands and a long sandwich that was perched precariously in the crook of his arm. He could almost hear the crackle of static as they touched.

"Thanks. I'm glad you came along. I can be quite clumsy."

She smiled evenly at him. "So, are we all set for departure?"

"Yes. I was about to give a ten-minute warning to all personnel to strap in." He looked at her, a plan forming in his mind. "Would you like to accompany me back to the bridge? We have a spare co-pilot's chair. You could be with us when we make the jump."

"Really!" she exclaimed. "I'd love to. I don't have anything else I need to do that is pressing. Thank you, Torben." Before Kyra realised what she was doing, she kissed him on the cheek. Not a peck. Her lips lingered on his stubbly skin for what seemed like minutes. Her heart rate increased as she reluctantly pulled away.

Torben blushed a deep crimson. "People will talk."

"About what?"

"You and me."

"Is there a 'you and me' to talk about?"

"I don't know." He hesitated, smiling. "I hadn't thought that far ahead."

She smiled, cocking her head to one side, a move that made her red lock glimmer in the under-lighters. "Maybe you should start thinking far ahead."

"Really!" he said as a voice crackled through the ship's communication system, relaying a ten-minute warning.

She took his free arm, guiding him to the bridge. "Really. You men only think as far as the next beer."

Rex looked up from the controls as Kyra and Torben entered. He was momentarily at a loss for words. He looked at their lunch.

"Is there enough for three?"

"We'll make do." Torben turned to Kyra. "Allow me to introduce Rex. The best pilot in the galaxy, and the worst graff maker. Rex, this is Kyra."

Rex stood up from the console and extended his furry arm. Kyra took it, matching his considerable grip.

"Pleasure to meet you, Rex. Is your graff really that bad?"

"Likewise, Kyra. Our Captain is far too fussy in his tastes. This little hominid likes his graff rough and ready."

She smiled, liking him instantly. They all settled into their respective seats. All food and drink in holders and trays. Rex turned to Torben.

"All crew have been given their instructions."

"Okay, Rex, initiate heads up."

Rex punched a command into the display, his green fingers delicate and precise. Kyra almost gasped as the cockpit came alive. Above them was a miniature reconstruction of their position. She could see the galaxy slowly moving and pulsing in the dark confines. A moment later another galaxy appeared underneath. It was a spiral galaxy, beautifully rotating.

"That sure is something," Rex said, to no one in particular.

"It sure is," Torben added. "Zoom."

The little hominid drew his hands apart in front of his face in three quick movements until their position and destination were visible. Kyra sat slightly behind them, a wide-eyed expression on her face.

"Position locked. Are we ready, skipper?"

Torben nodded. "Just like we practised, Rex. Execute."

Rex reached across the control panel and pressed a red button that pulsed in unison with the rest of the cockpit. There was a shift in the ship's position as if the space around them had been disturbed.

"Hull camera on. Heads up," Rex said. Another holographic image appeared next to their position that showed what was happening a few hundred feet under their ship. To Rex, it looked like a giant black whirlpool was forming. The stars seemed to start travelling in an anti-clockwise direction. The three of them were gently buffeted around in their seats as Shimmer050 started to turn from the unseen force below. Torben could see what looked like blue lightning around the cockpit. He was about to turn around to look at Kyra when he felt a cool, firm hand grip his. He turned his chair to see her, beautiful in the shimmering strobing light of the cockpit. She smiled at him, tears forming at the corners of her eyes. He smiled back, fighting to keep his own tears hidden.

"Okay. Here we go," said Rex, who was watching a holographic countdown display. The lightning seemed to intensify and grow brighter as the ship rotated faster. The hominid flicked his eyes to their position, captivated by the funnel that was making its way from the bottom galaxy towards them. They suddenly felt the inertia as they were pulled downwards, towards the great unknown.

SIX

EARTH, 2017: BELBROUGHTON, UK

"Have you seen my watch, babe?" The woman paced the kitchen, her stockinged feet making barely a noise as they glided over the quarry tiled floor.

"Try next to the bread bin. In the coin mug," a muted voice said as it filtered its way into the square kitchen. She walked over, picking up the large chipped mug. The woman smiled when she saw her retro wristwatch. She clipped it onto her wrist, liking the cool feeling of the wide leather strap on her skin. As she left the kitchen she paused to look in the large mirror, flicking her chestnut hair behind her ear. Satisfied that all was as it should be, the woman walked through the house, turning left into a small lounge. A man sat slouched in a leather recliner, his watery eyes watching the plasma television that sat perched in the corner of the cosy room. Two young boys lay together on a brown sofa, a blue blanket covering their bodies. Only their heads peeked out as they too watched television from watery eyes. "I'll take them up for a bath in a minute, babe," the man said, shifting in his seat.

"I can stay here and take care of them," she mildly protested.

"No. You need to be at the fete. We'll be okay. Once they're in bed, I'll watch a movie on the iPad."

"You sure? Helen would understand if I send her a text."

"Go, babe. You've put a lot of effort into this. You should be there. It's a long time till the next Halloween. You don't want to miss out."

She bent over the chair, kissing her husband on his thinning brown curls. He smelt of Olbas Oil, she thought absently as she crossed the lounge to her two sons. "Are you two going to be alright with Daddy?"

"Yes, Mummy," Finn replied.

"Oscar. Time for a bath?"

The two-year-old boy looked at his mother and smiled. "Baff baff," he said, his eyes and nose red from the cold that had him its grip.

She bent down and kissed them both. Finn reached around her neck, pulling her into him. "Have fun, Mummy. Love you."

Tears peppered the woman's eyes at her son's heartfelt words. She squeezed him tightly, drinking in his scent. The toddler climbed up and joined the cuddle, giggling as he hugged them both with all his strength. "I love you both too. To the Moon and back."

"Come on boys," the man said. "Let's let Mummy go to the fete. She will come and give you both a kiss when she gets home."

She gently relieved herself from the cloying limbs, straightening her long brown skirt, before turning to her husband. "Thanks, babe," she said as she kissed him full on the lips. "I should be home just after ten. I hope."

"No rush. We'll all be asleep. Go. Have fun with the pumpkins." She smiled at his comment, knowing that there would be hundreds of the large orange vegetables lining the streets of the village where they lived.

. . .

Gemma stepped out of the kitchen door at the side of the house. She pulled her dark coat around her, feeling the first nip of winter as she walked down the garden path that led to the main footpath of the village of Belbroughton. The sleepy settlement lay south-west of Birmingham, nestled between the Clent Hills to the east and Kidderminster to the west. As soon as her dark boots hit the concrete slabs, Gemma could see pumpkins all around her. The village held a Halloween fete every year, with people travelling from the neighbouring villages to join in the fun and games as autumn gently wound its way towards winter. This year Gemma was helping, running one of the stalls. Her friend, Helen, was the principal organiser of the event, relying on her villagers to chip in with as much support as possible. She smiled as she walked around a bend in the road towards an old public house called The Talbot Inn. All of its windows were adorned with pumpkins. Devilish glowing smiles shone out through the glass into darkening skies. *This is going to be a memorable night,* she thought, as she removed the glasses from her face. She stopped for a moment, wiping them with a handkerchief that she'd pulled from her leather shoulder bag, before setting them back in place. She looked at herself in the pub window, pushing her hair behind her ear before nodding at her reflection. *Not too bad for thirty-two,* she thought before continuing on her way towards the large field on the outskirts of the village.

SEVEN

Two days previously, Kyra, Torben and Rex had been sitting in the confines of the cockpit, staring in awe as the ship settled after its descent through the wormhole. They had sat in silence for several minutes, staring out into the black void of space. Millions of miles ahead of them, a yellow sun cast its light across the solar system. It was Torben who had broken the spell, gently coaxing the ship forward until they were skipping through the unknown system. After a while, a large red planet with a scar running along its width had appeared before them. Torben and Kyra had left Rex to man the ship as they went about their business with renewed vigour. They had dined together, a warm familiarity settling over their fledgling relationship. No kisses were exchanged in the two days it took to reach the shimmering blue planet. However, budding feelings were starting to blossom in the hostile vacuum of space.

Torben and Rex sat in the cockpit, the craft stationary, gently moving with the planet's orbit. "There it is again. A signal coming from our starboard bow. Some kind of electrical pulse or signal. Drop the cloak over us, Rex."

The little hominid flicked a switch above his head, his eyes scanning space through the cockpit window. "There, Captain. Look!"

Torben looked past the pointing furry fingers, out through the glass into the black vacuum beyond. A large shape appeared above the blue planet below it. It was a concoction of white tubes, connected together in an unusual shape. "It looks like a station. If it's manned it's a good job we dropped the cloak. No one can see us here. If they got word of us to their kind, it may cause panic down there."

Rex looked at the planet Earth. He suddenly forgot about everything as his eyes focused on the beautiful white clouds that framed the planet. He could make out the oceans and the land. Strangely shaped landmasses stared back at him. *I'm going down there. I am actually going down there,* he thought. His captain's words bounced off his deaf ears. He shook himself free of his trance, Torben's words finally getting through. "Shall we start our descent, skipper?"

"Yes. Enter the co-ordinates, be ready to start our descent in ten minutes. Let the crew know that it's show time. The landing crew will need to move quickly. I just need to go and find Kyra. She should see this."

"I agree. She should," Rex said as he punched numbers into the heads-up display.

Torben knocked on Kyra's cabin door. The corridor gently pulsed at the floor and ceiling, a purple light bathing the white walls. The partition hissed open, showing Kyra standing in the gentle glow. "It's show time," Torben said, smiling.

"Come in," Kyra said, walking back into her cabin, her hair bobbing on her bare shoulders. She walked over to a chair, slipping a jacket over her grey vest top and sitting down. Kyra pulled on her brown leather boots, clipping a buckle in place on the back of each calf. She looked at Torben, who was stood fidgeting. "What's the plan when we get down there?"

"We observe, taking imaging profiles of the land. The language they speak is called English. I will upload that through our neural links before we make contact. Once we have sent the pulse back to Valkash, we can make our move."

"This is a historic day," she said embracing her captain. He returned the hold, drinking in her fragrance. To Torben, it smelt like flowers, mixed with anti-bacterial scrub. It mattered little to him. He was already starting to fall in love with her. As they pulled apart, Kyra kissed him, full on the lips. After the initial shock, Torben's eyes closed as he let himself be kissed. It felt good, warm and fuzzy as he pulled her into him. She broke the kiss, her eyes momentarily out of focus. "We should do that again, Captain. And soon."

He laughed, extending his hand towards her. "Yes, we should. Come. Let's go and make history."

"You should have stayed at home," Helen said, as she broke the hug with Gemma.

"I didn't want to let you down, hun. Besides, there is a decent turn out. How many do you think so far?"

"At least a hundred. More will arrive I'm sure, even though it looks like rain tonight. Right. I'll pop over to the village hall to grab the rest of the raffle tickets. Will you be okay here for five minutes?"

"Sure. I'll hold the fort. I'll make sure the pumpkins behave themselves."

"Gemma Andrews, you are a star," the older woman said as she walked off towards the lights of the village.

Gemma stood, watching people milling around the field, slowly making their way around the perimeter, where dark trees stood silently against the oncoming night. Most of the visitors were looking at stalls at the entrance, leaving her free to watch the comings and goings. A noise in the sky like distant thunder made her look up. *Thunder in October. That's not right,* she thought as she looked towards the horizon. It was then that she noticed a disturbance in the sky. Her eyes just about picked out a shimmer in the darkness. She stepped away from the stall, trying to focus on the area of sky where she'd seen movement. Nothing unusual presented itself to her. *Hmm. Strange. I swear there was something there,* she thought as she absently pulled at a pink elastic band on her wrist. She focused her attention on a young family, who were looking at the items on display at her stall. Gemma turned away from the sky, greeting the people with a warm smile. Behind her, hovering a few hundred feet above the trees, Shimmer050 sat silently. Taking it all in.

"Do you think she saw us?" Rex said as he manned the controls.

"Not sure. She certainly stared at us for long enough, but it looks like we're okay for now. How long until the imaging is complete?"

"Two minutes. The language upload is complete. We're almost ready to begin," Rex said expectantly. The trio sat there, observing the strange. alien landscape. They could see figures moving around the field, stopping at awnings, lit by orange globes. They sat in silence, completely in awe of the spectacle in front of them. A noise from the console broke their trances. "Imaging finished," Rex said.

"Okay. We'll send the pulse back through the void, once we have analysed our subjects." Rex gently coaxed the ship forwards, until it was a few hundred feet away from the field.

Underneath, a farmhouse sat quietly, smoke rising from its chimney. The animals were in their pens for the night. Cows, pigs, chickens, and a few horses, huddled together against the oncoming chill of autumn. Above the farmhouse, an invisible beam spread across the land, removing all traces of life. "Hold there, Rex," Torben said, the ship coming to a halt over the field. "Okay. Get ready with the teleport beam. It should not take long to round up the rest of them." Torben nodded to himself as the figures in the field dissipated into thin air, leaving the field devoid of life. Torben stood, leaving the cockpit with Kyra, heading aft in tandem. The ship gained altitude, Rex increasing their speed until they had broken orbit, away from the pull of the planet's gravity. He set his course for the strange red planet, a contented smile playing over his furry face.

Helen made her way back from the village hall, her arms full of things for the event. Her chestnut hair bounced off her coat collar as she hurried towards the fete. *I really must lay off the cakes,* she thought as she broke out into a sweat. Since having her two children in her late thirties, she had noticed a thickening of her waist. She'd tried all the weight loss plans. Zumba, along with a torturous activity, where she rolled around in a wet park, heading home afterwards, constantly shivering. Nothing seemed to stick, except for the cakes and savouries that she munched through on a daily basis. Helen would start afresh after the New Year, she told herself as she rounded the entrance to the Halloween fete. She stopped dead, only taking a few tentative steps after the initial surprise. The field was empty. The woman walked over to Gemma's stall, her boots digging into the soft earth. There was no sign of her, except for her leather bag that sat silently on the trestle table. *Where have they all gone?* she thought as she surveyed the field. She could make out a few children's buggies, along with a few toys that lay on the wet grass. *What the hell has happened?* Her next thought made icy fingers crawl across her skin. *Terrorists? Surely not. I'd have heard something,* she thought as she made her way back towards the village hall, her smartphone primed for action.

EIGHT

GEMMA'S EYES FLUTTERED OPEN. SHE LAY THERE FOR A moment, looking at the white ceiling. She could sense a gentle pulsing of colour somewhere, her head turning to its left. She saw white walls that changed their hue every few seconds. A large white door with a window set in the top stood at one end of the strange room. *Am I dreaming?* Her eyes moved further, taking in a long line of windows set in the white wall. *Am I in hospital?* She sat up, her head woozy. Sleeping forms lay all around her. She recognised a few people from the fete; the family that she was talking to lay close by. She climbed to her feet, feeling slightly shaky. *Where am I?* she thought as she headed over towards the door. Her progress was halted as she met an invisible field that fizzed when she touched it. She pushed again, her palms crackling gently. The force field was impenetrable. The woman walked over towards the line of windows, her feet sounding loud in the confines of the room. Other people were waking up around her, groggily wondering where they were like Gemma had seconds before.

"Hello," a woman called over to her. "Where are we?"

"I don't know," Gemma said, her throat feeling dry.

A child began crying. "Mummy. I want to go home. I'm scared." The boy's mother cradled the child, rocking him gently while her eyes played frantically around the room.

The double doors opened, two people entering. Gemma headed over to them, noting that they looked like something out of a sci-fi movie. "Where are we?" Gemma said, noticing how attractive the tall woman was.

The man looked dark and moody, his dark hair and brows giving him an imposing aura. "Hello. My name is Torben. This is Kyra. You are aboard my ship, heading for Valkash."

"What ship?" a man said as he approached, his voice unnaturally loud. "Where the hell are we?" More people were walking towards Torben and Kyra, the restless murmurings growing steadily louder.

"My ship," Torben said calmly. "Shimmer050. We have journeyed far to be here. You are travelling to your new home, a planet called Valkash, on the other side of the cosmos. There you will live out your lives in a replica of your homes, for the enjoyment of tourists from many different worlds."

Exclamations could be heard echoing off the walls as the news carried to everyone. "Is this some kind of fucking sick prank?" a large man said as he pushed himself to the front. He stood eyeball to eyeball with Torben, his hands pressed against the force field. "Take us back to Belbroughton. Now!"

Torben turned towards a control panel on the wall. He pressed a button before turning back to the humans. A mist descended on the captives, subduing them. "I know this is a lot to take in. But I have my orders. You will be at your new home soon. It won't be as bad as you think. You will have comfortable lives. Now, we must leave you to check on the rest of the cargo. Food and drinks will be sent through to you shortly. I will ask the crew to provide something more comfortable for you to rest on. I can see that you have children here. The crew will be along shortly. At the far end of the room,

there are facilities where you can wash and relieve yourselves."
The aliens left the room, leaving the villagers staring after
them. Unsure of what to say or do next.

———————

Sarah opened her eyes as if she was trying to awaken from a
long foggy sleep. She blinked a few times, trying to shift the
fug that hung over her. In front of her was a glass wall,
encasing her. The woman looked up, seeing a bright light
overhead, and thin red laser-like strobes moving up and down
her body. She looked to the floor, blinking rapidly, noticing
that her leather boots were still on. She placed her fingers on
the glass in front of her, noticing the slight vibration that the
glass gave off. *Where am I?* she thought, looking to her left. In a
larger glass bubble next to her, a cow stood, its head gently
rising and falling as more lasers scoured the animal's flank.
Past the cow, a sheep stood on nervous legs, turning around
inside the enclosed space. The last glass enclosure contained
various birds, all flapping around excitedly, bouncing off the
toughened walls, trying to escape. *This is a dream,* Sarah
thought, noticing the two strange figures close to a twin pair
of doors. They stood watching her, a holographic display in
front of them. She could see them conversing with each other,
with Sarah unable to hear the exchange through the glass
cocoon. Panic spread through her body, her fists bunching
before they started hammering on the glass prison. "Let me
out of here!" she shouted. "What the fuck do you think you're
doing?" She continued for a full minute, but the strange
beings stayed unmoved by her tirade. A faint hissing noise
invaded the chamber, and Sarah started looking up as a gentle
mist fell from above, drifting over her. She suddenly felt heavy,
her eyelids drooping as she slid down the glass walls to the
floor. Then, darkness.

"Your reports, Captain," a white-clad figure said to Torben as he entered the cockpit.

"Thank you," Torben replied, accepting the small device from the male, who turned and left without another word. He pressed a small button on the device, seeing a holographic figure appearing before him. He watched the display, looking at the blonde female in front of him. A soft female voice sounded across the cockpit, Rex seemingly oblivious to the information being imparted as he looked down at the strange planet below him, its oceans mesmerising the hominid.

"Ninety-nine percent of the human composition is made up from six elements. Oxygen, carbon, hydrogen, nitrogen, calcium and phosphorus. Most of the remaining percentage is composed of, potassium, sulfur, sodium, chlorine, and magnesium. Average life expectancy is between seventy-five and eighty-five Earth years. Humans are susceptible to the following conditions; cancers, organ deterioration, neural impairment and haemorrhage. This subject has no such conditions and would be considered of good health."

Torben listened, less intently, to the analysis of the indigenous animals that they had captured, his interest waning. "Rex, upload the information to the pulse."

"Okay, skipper." He waited a few seconds, nodding to himself. "Ready to deploy." A small black box, cylindrical in shape, shot out of the back of Shimmer050, a mini shockwave appearing as it gained altitude. Seconds later it was passing the International Space Station, heading for Mars. Millions of miles away, across the Solar System, the fabric of space started to contract. A dark bubble, a few feet across began rotating slowly, pulling the unseen box towards it. Three minutes later the box ploughed through the bubble at the speed of light, creating a ripple in space that fanned out in all directions. Moments after, the bubble vanished, returning the cosmos to its normal state.

Helen stood in the misty field, the blue light from the police cars cutting through the fog. Two officers had questioned her, telling Helen that they may need her to make a formal statement. *Where have they gone?* She thought. *They can't have just vanished on the wind.* Her thoughts were interrupted by a man's voice.

"Helen. Any news?" The man approached her, his unruly mass of dark hair almost covering his bleary eyes.

"Nothing, Hugh. I've spoken to them again a few minutes ago. I suppose they are doing what police do. Where are the boys?"

"Agatha from next door is sitting with them. They are already wondering where Gemma is, and it's only been twelve hours since she was last seen. I can't for the life of me believe that in the time it took you to walk to the village hall and back, over a hundred people vanished in the night. It's like something from a movie or the *X-Files.*"

"I keep thinking about it. There was hardly any traffic through the village. It was very quiet. The loudest noise was coming from The Talbot. And even that was not loud. If someone had driven in and snatched them, surely I'd have heard them approach. A coach or lorry would be needed. Unless they were all shepherded on foot."

"But you'd probably have heard people struggling or calling for help. From what you've said, it looks like they just vanished."

Hugh's voice cracked with emotion, his anxiety levels increasing with every minute that passed. Helen put her arm on his shoulder, squeezing it gently. "They'll find them. They can't have gone far, Hugh. Wherever they are, they'll be home soon."

Gemma woke once more, her head woozy. A few of the villagers were standing close to the doorway, talking quietly. Her neck was sore, her mauve coat not really suitable as a make-shift pillow. She stood up, her feet sliding over the smooth white floor as she made her way to the others. "More food?" she said, eyeing the two tables laden with provisions.

"Looks like it," a man said wearily. He turned to Gemma, a half smile trying to transform his coffee coloured face. "I'm Loz."

She looked at the man, liking his friendly face. He looked roughly her age, with closely cropped dark hair. The man towered over her modest height, although she could sense no threat from him. "Gemma. I've seen you around the village."

"Likewise. You have two little boys?"

"Yes. Finn and Oscar." A stabbing pain deep in her chest almost made her cry out in anguish. *What am I going to do?* Tears formed at the corners of her eyes, as the situation dawned on her all over again. She was trapped.

"I keep expecting a TV presenter to appear from a secret doorway, telling us all it's been an elaborate hoax."

"I really don't know what to make of this. It's just unbelievable."

Two male figures walked into the room, gently depositing a young blonde lady on the floor before walking back out of the enclosed space. Gemma looked over at her, wondering where she had come from. Other villagers were looking too as the woman curled up on the floor and closed her eyes, drifting off to sleep as the ship gently thrummed underneath her. People headed over to the table, the smell of food rousing them from their sleep. Gemma took a plate, filling it with strange looking fruit and biscuits, grabbing a bottle of pink liquid before heading back to her spot in the corner of the room. She absently nibbled on her food, watching families queue for the offering. Small children clung to their parents' clothing, shuffling behind them as the throng of villagers grabbed what food was on offer. She placed the plate on the floor, picking up the bottle. Unscrewing the lid, Gemma took a long pull on the liquid, liking the sweet fizzy taste that seemed to re-energise her slightly. An elderly woman headed over towards her, the plate in her hands shaking as she walked.

"Can I sit next to you while I eat?" she asked, her accent neutral and soft.

"Sure," Gemma replied as the woman slowly sat down heavily, leaning against the gently thrumming wall.

"You're Gemma, aren't you?"

"Yes. I'm sorry, but I don't think we have met."

"I'm Rose. Helen's aunt. I was at the fete with the others. I thought something wasn't right. I could see the sky shimmering above the field."

"I saw that too," Gemma replied. "It looked like something was hovering above us. Then we all woke up here."

Their heads turned as the doors at the far end of the room opened. Shouts and curses rang out from the villagers as a man and woman entered. They stood there, arms folded over their chests, becoming lost from sight as a throng of villagers crowded the invisible force field that separated them from the abductors. "I am going to remove the shield," the man said. "Do not try anything."

Gemma climbed to her feet as a crackle filled the room. She walked over, shouldering her way to the front of the group. "Why have you done this?" she uttered. "You have taken me away from my family. There are laws against that."

"Please, stand aside," Torben said softly. They did so, allowing the captain and Kyra into the long room that throbbed gently from the ship's engines. The duo stood next to the table, their expressions blank. "My name is Torben. This is Kyra," he said motioning to his left. "You have questions. Please proceed."

"Where are we?" Loz said as he cradled his plate in the crook of his elbow.

"You are on board Shimer050, an exploratory vessel, sent to your planet to take a sample of the species that live there. We are heading to another planet on the far side of the universe."

"Why?" Gemma shrieked.

Others joined in, advancing on the strangers, who stood next to the table. Kyra pulled a small device from her pocket, aiming it at a villager. "Step back," she commanded quietly.

"Fuck you," the large man shouted, meaty hands reaching for her. A flash from the device lit the room, and the man slumped to the floor lifelessly. Villagers exclaimed in unison, moving back a few steps. Loz looked down at the villager, dragging him along the smooth white floor with a meaty paw, away from the others.

"We have our orders," Torben said solemnly. "You need to get used to this. We will be at Valkash in a few days. Your home has been recreated. You will live out your days there. You will be provided for."

"We have families back at home," Gemma said, tears running down her face. "I have two boys, who need their Mummy."

Another woman stepped forward, her chestnut hair framing an attractive face. Dark glasses sat on her nose, tears forming at the corners of her eyes. "My Mother is sick. I left her at home. She needs me."

Her soft voice almost struck a chord with the ship's captain. He braced himself. "As I said, we have our orders. Eat some food. We will be back shortly. The villagers stood in silence as the duo left the room. The doors hissed shut, cocooning them in the low-slung room. The woman with the glasses turned to Gemma. "Come and sit down hun," she said softly, taking the younger woman by the arm. "We all need to get our heads around this. But we need to eat."

Sliding down the wall, Gemma absently nibbled at a brown piece of fruit, almost liking the grainy texture. She looked at the woman next to her, guessing that she was approaching forty. She instantly liked her friendly expression, a reassuring smile slowing her pulse somewhat. "I don't think I've seen you around the village," she said.

"Probably not hun. I live in Wales. I was visiting mum, as her health has taken a turn for the worse. I'm Caroline," she said extending her hand.

"The younger woman took it, squeezing it gently. "Gemma. Sorry to hear about your mum."

"It's okay. She's on her own now. Her health has been deteriorating of late, with trips to the doctors and the hospital. I was in the process of moving up to Belbroughton to spend some time with her. That now looks like it's gone to shit."

"Despite her predicament, Gemma smiled, liking the woman more and more. She absently flicked the pink band on her wrist, twirling her thumb around it.

Caroline looked down and smiled, holding her own wrist aloft. "Snap," she said, twanging the band against her own wrist. "Helps, doesn't it."

Gemma nodded. "Yes, it does. More than people might think. I hope they have some, wherever we are heading."

"Try not to worry. I am sure there is some way out of this."

"Do you remember anything?" Gemma asked as a memory floated back to her.

"No, nothing," the other woman replied.

"I've just had a flashback. Well, I think I have. Something about all of us walking towards a shimmering light. I could see three figures, standing motionless in the field."

"Really? Well, I don't remember anything," Caroline said as she removed her black framed glasses. She dabbed at her eyes with a tissue before placing the glasses back in place."

"Yes. I remember. I remember dragging my feet across the grass. As if something was pulling me towards it."

"Sounds a bit scary if you ask me," the other woman replied, an anxious knot forming in her stomach. Silence descended over the two women, thoughts of loved ones flooding their minds as they headed into outer space.

NINE

"ARE YOU OKAY?" KYRA ASKED AS TORBEN PACED HIS quarters.

"I was until we spoke to them. I never thought about their families. Are we doing the right thing, Kyra?"

"I'm not sure. But as you said, we have our orders. The Lomogs have provided for us when we needed it most. We need to remember that. Without them, we would be teetering on the brink."

"I know," Torben said, sitting on a white couch. "It still doesn't make me feel any better."

Kyra sat next to him, taking his strong hands in hers. She held them gently, kissing him lightly on the cheek. "It's all very raw at the moment. They are in shock. As a species, they are very unevolved, unlike us. Let's get them to Valkash. Let them settle in."

"Then what?"

"I don't know. We leave them there I suppose. I am sure that we will have other assignments."

"I haven't thought that far ahead," Torben said. This all came out of the blue. My friend Ark and I were just bumming around the galaxy, delivering supplies to outposts. When this came along, we both jumped at it."

"Where is your friend now?"

"He's out there somewhere. Several light years from here, rounding up his own group of species. Although, if I know Ark, he's probably trying to get some of them into his bunk."

"Oh right. Are all freighter pilots like that?"

"Some are. We travel across space, which can be a lonely place. I'm not like Ark though. I don't feel the need to have a girl in every outpost."

"Good to hear it, as you may have snared one on this journey." She moved closer, kissing him tenderly. Torben returned the kiss, pulling Kyra into his embrace. She came to him willingly, the first stirrings of warmth coursing through her body. Breaking the kiss, she looked into his eyes. "You're the first person that I have kissed in a long while."

"Likewise, Kyra. I am sorry if it brought up emotions and memories."

She kissed him again, her hands unbuttoning the front of his tunic. "I think it is time to make some new memories," Kyra said as she pushed him gently onto the couch.

Sometime later, Torben and Kyra sat down in the cockpit. Rex looked at them, trying to discern the expressions on their faces. He smiled, noting the warmth that seemed to be radiating from the humans. "Everything alright?"

"Yes," Torben said a little too quickly. "Although our passengers are not happy. And who can blame them? We've taken them from their families, to live out their days on an alien planet."

"I suppose so. Although, skipper, I've been watching their newsfeeds. It seems that the planet could be on the brink of all-out war. Many different factions are opposing each other. We may have spared these people."

"What kind of factions?" Kyra said, suddenly curious.

"They worship different deities. It seems that this has caused wars to rage for centuries. Millions have perished. And it looks like there are other factions that are developing nuclear weapons, to be used against others."

"Nuclear. They really are unevolved," Torben said.

"Yes. They have only made landfall on their closest satellite. Many years before. They have limited technology, which is nowhere near to what the Biflex had up until recently. I don't think they will be chasing us anytime soon."

"Good. How long until we reach the safe zone?"

"At this velocity, roughly fourteen hours, skipper."

"Can we pick up the pace? I want to get to Valkash as soon as possible. These people need to be settled into their new environment."

"I can increase throttle, which will save us some time."

"Good. Let's do that, Rex. Kyra, shall we take a walk?"

"Of course, Captain," she said readily. "Let's go."

Rex sat at the controls, increasing the power until the ship was almost at full velocity. He switched to autopilot, letting Shimmer050 guide them out towards the safe zone. On the screen in front of him, the co-pilot watched more information coming through from the world they had just visited. He sat watching intently as a large red planet appeared on the horizon. A deep scar running across its surface.

They lay in the bunk, a thin sheet covering their naked bodies. Kyra's head rested on Torben's chest, her fingers tracing lines across his toned stomach. The captain stared up at the gently pulsing ceiling, a serene expression on his face. During his lifetime, Torben had taken several lovers, but only one serious partner. The memory of her face was starting to fade. It had been several years since they had gone their separate ways, with Torben focusing on his work. Now, however, he lay in his bunk with another. Someone who he wanted to forge a partnership with. He knew that she was coming to terms with the loss of a loved one. Torben only hoped that she was ready. Because he was.

TEN

BELBROUGHTON

HUGH WALKED FROM THE KITCHEN, CHECKING ON HIS TWO sons. They sat there quietly, munching on biscuits as a children's program kept them mildly entertained. The man turned back to the kitchen as the kettle announced it had finished boiling. Shuffling across the quarry-tiled floor, Hugh prepared himself his fifth coffee of the day, noting that it was closing in on noon. A small television in the corner of the room projected itself silently across the kitchen. Hugh had turned the volume down as the story of abducted villagers continued as the main story of the day on the news channel. He sat heavily at the table, running a hand through his thinning brown hair. *Where the hell you babe?* he thought as he sipped at his milky drink. *You can't have gone far. It can't be terrorists. Can it?* His thoughts were interrupted by a knock at the front door. He grabbed his coffee, heading down the hallway towards the front of the house. Opening the door, Hugh was greeted by two men in long, dark coats.

"Mr Andrews?"

"Yes," Hugh replied tentatively.

"My name is Lewis," the taller man said. He looked a good ten years older than Hugh, with sandy blonde hair and wardrobe-like shoulders. "This is Mr Hendry," Lewis said with a nod towards the other man. He stood there, ram-rod straight. His dark features giving nothing away. "We're from *GCHQ.* Can we take a few moments of your time?"

"Sure," Hugh replied, noting the tension the men exuded on his doorstep. "Come in." He led them back to the kitchen, turning towards them. "Would you like a hot drink?"

"No thank you, Mr Andrews, we are both fine," Lewis countered smoothly. The man looked over at the television, his brow creasing. "I take it you have been watching the news this morning."

"All morning," Hugh replied.

"Have you heard of *GCHQ?*" Lewis asked as he surveyed the kitchen.

"Yes, I've heard of you. Government Communications Head Quarters. A bit like the NSA."

"Correct, although we're not quite like our American cousins. They are aware of the situation though." He paused. "One hundred and seventy-two people are missing, your wife being one of them. Can you walk us through the events of last night?"

"Sure," Hugh said sitting down at the table. He took a swig of the cooling coffee, his mind clear. "Gemma left about seven-ish. She was helping out at the fete in the village. We were all supposed to go with her, but our boys are not feeling too good. So, I stayed home with them. She said that she would be a few hours. That's the last I heard from her. The first I knew that something was wrong was early this morning. I was wiped out last night, as you can see," he said indicating his red nose and watery eyes. "Helen from the village had sent me a text around ten-ish, but my phone was on charge in the kitchen."

"We have spoken to Helen," Lewis said, his tone neutral.

"So, what the hell has happened to my wife?"

"Honest answer, we simply do not know at this point, Mr

Andrews. We've checked traffic cameras. There was little movement in or out of the village last night. It's not easy to move over a hundred people without someone knowing about it. Even if it was terror-related, it would be almost impossible to abduct so many people in only a few minutes, with no sound made." The mention of terror made Hugh's stomach start churning. "Although all lines of enquiry are being followed at this point."

"So, what do I do? Just sit here and wait?"

"You have no other option, Mr Andrews. Believe me, many agencies are on this. If your wife is out there, someone will find her and the others."

"What happens if you can't? I have two boys who are missing their Mummy."

"Try not to worry too much. We are doing all we can." A few minutes later, Hugh was sat at the kitchen table, twirling a small card in his hand. He absently looked at the name embossed on the front, wondering when Mr Lewis would be in touch.

———

"Are we set, Rex?" Torben asked as he sat down at the controls. Kyra sat just behind them, looking out at the expanse of space in front of them.

"We are, Captain. Coordinates are locked in place. Just say the word and we'll make the jump."

"Execute," Torben said. They sat there as the ship gently started to rotate in silence, a beautiful red planet coming into view on the horizon every few seconds. Flashes of lighting strobed around the cabin before they dropped through the void, coming to rest on the other side, Thirteen billion light years from Earth.

"We're here," Rex said in awe, looking towards the horizon. A large gas cloud filled their view, a few thousand miles from their position.

"Good job, Rex. How long until we reach Valkash?"

"If we put the throttle down, we can be there in a few hours."

"Good. Get us there. Let us unload our cargo and celebrate."

"Are you buying?" the little hominid said curiously, a mischievous expression playing out across his face.

"Yes, Rex. Drinks are on me. We just need to find a bar. I've never been to this planet before."

"None of us has," Kyra chirped from behind the two pilots.

"If our message arrived on time, their village will soon be finished. It will be like home from home, just without their loved ones." Torben instantly regretted his statement, a pang of guilt spreading through his chest. He looked at Kyra, who squeezed his hand, a knowing smile on her face.

They sat in silence as the ion drive propelled them forward briskly. After an hour, a small moon appeared on the horizon, its pock-marked surface staring back at them from its blue surface. "The moon is called Yarveld, the only moon of Valkash."

"Doesn't look too inviting, Torben said as he shifted in his seat.

"It looks like it might even be too sparse for you, Captain," Kyra joked, punching his shoulder playfully.

He turned to her, a smile transforming his features. "You just think I'm a real rough-neck."

"All adds to your charm, Captain," she said smiling. Rex sat there, smiling too. He had known Torben for a long time and was happy that he may have met himself a mate.

. . .

An hour later, their eyes were all collectively focused on Valkash. The planet hung in front of them, low clouds framing the blue orb. "Rex, take us down to our docking bay," Torben said, sipping at the graff that Kyra had brought from the ship's mess.

"Initiating descent. We should be there shortly," the Hominid stated as the ship broke the planet's orbit. Dropping swiftly, an amazing vista presented itself. Huge glass domes rose out of the land, almost touching the low clouds. The entire horizon was filled with the objects, save for a mountain range that ran across the globe like a fractured spine. "Wow, what a place! The Lomogs have been busy."

"Yes, they have," said Torben, his eyes taking in the strange planet below them. "They have terraformed each individual enclosure to match the atmosphere of its inhabitants. That is some feat of geological engineering. Biflex technology had started experimenting with Terraforming. But not on this scale. This is incredible."

"Indeed, it is," Kyra added as she absently twirled the lock of hair between her fingers.

The ship dropped lower until it was hovering a few hundred feet from the planet. "There she is," Rex said as he pointed towards a low hangar, nestled against a small wooden hillock. "I hope they have somewhere I can grab a drink."

"I'm sure there is somewhere, my friend. Let's get our passengers offloaded. Then we can get some refreshments."

"Aye-aye, Captain," the Hominid said, a jovial expression etched on his furry face.

The ship landed smoothly, its vertical thrusters placing it in the centre of the landing pad. Jets of smoke spewed from ports along the length of Shimmer050 as the rear doors opened silently. Torben and Kyra descended the ramp and saw a tall figure standing a few feet away, smiling warmly.

"Welcome to Valkash," the man said. They appraised him cautiously. He stood a full head over them, four arms hanging loosely by his sides. His head was black, with silvery tattoos adorning his skull. White eyes peered back at them above a nose that consisted of two small slits in his face. "I am 2104, Commander of the northern quadrants. But you can call me Ash. You must be Captain Fraken?"

"Yes," he replied. "But you can call me Torben. This is Officer Zakx, Kyra to her friends."

A long black arm, rippling with wiry muscle extended towards Kyra. "Welcome to Valkash. You must be in need of refreshments?"

"Our co-pilot is," Torben replied readily.

"Well, our landing party will take care of your cargo." 2104 turned, pointing towards a large door in the corner of the hangar. "If you head through there, we have something that we think can accommodate yourselves and your crew. Just say Ash sent you."

"Thank you, Ash," Kyra said, her stomach beginning to rumble. "That is very kind."

"Think nothing of it. After all, you have travelled far to get here. It is the least we can do for you."

Five minutes later, Torben, Kyra and Rex were walking through the door in the corner of the hangar. "Wow," Rex said as he looked at the collection of stalls and outlets in front of them. "That place has my name all over it," the hominid said, pointing to a small cantina with the name Rex emblazoned across the front in green blinking neon. They made their way to a small bar, with chrome stools lined up against the dark wooden counter. They seated themselves and watched as three drinks appeared from recesses in the bar. "Wow," Rex said, his green fingers encircling the tall glass in front of him. "How did it know what I wanted?"

"We are here to serve, Rex," a computerised voice echoed through the cantina.

"Woah," Rex said. "I could get used to this."

"Don't get too comfy, my friend," Torben said as he sipped at his drink, liking the cool tang it gave off. "We will be leaving soon, heading back to Biflux."

"I know, skipper. At least I can enjoy the moment."

"Yes, you can," Kyra added, wiping froth from her lips.

Torben looked at her, smiling as the woman blushed slightly. "My kind of woman. Who can sit at a bar and drink suds with the best of them."

"Well, when I was growing up, we had the largest brewery in Cantis at the edge of town. From an early age, I was sampling my Father's beer. Not that he knew that of course."

"Does your family still live in Cantis?" Torben asked inquisitively.

"Yes. My parents still live there. I have one brother, who lives nearby. He's an engineer at Halycon."

Torben knew of Halycon. It was where the Lomogs tested their new technology, in partnership with the Biflex people. "Sounds an interesting job. Especially now with all the advancements that are being made."

"It sure is. My brother, Max, will soon be heading off on assignment to a nearby star system."

"Sounds great," the Captain said, liking the fact that he was finding out more and more about the woman sat next to him. He looked at Rex, who was finishing his first glass. The counter slid back silently, another tall glass of beer appearing from below, along with three plates of local delicacies. They all looked, their mouths starting to salivate at the sight on display. Freshly cooked bread held dark meats, covered in a sticky paste. The aroma made the threesome forget about their drinks as they tucked in.

"Oh my," exclaimed Kyra, a dark smudge of sauce smeared across her cheek.

"Here," Torben said, offering her a napkin from the counter. "Watch those fingers."

She leaned over, playfully nudging him with her shoulder as she took another bite.

Rex reached for his own napkin, the sandwich all but devoured. "That was something else. skipper, can we not stay here forever?"

"Sure. I will have a word with Ash. He can put you on kitchen duty."

The hominid smiled as he reached for his beer. Thoughts of unhappy souls from the other end of the cosmos, forgotten. For now.

ELEVEN

THE DOORS HISSED OPEN TO REVEAL A TRIO OF STRANGERS walking into the room. Caroline and Gemma stood up stiffly, eyeing up the new arrivals. The leader stood in the centre. His black head almost touching the ceiling. His main set of arms lay crossed over his considerable chest. The other two limbs lay by his side, motionless. "Welcome to Valkash. I am 2104, your guide and commander from this moment onwards. You have questions. Please," he motioned with his smaller arms.

"Where are we?" Caroline said, walking towards the three strangers. She noted with trepidation that the smaller two figures in front of her were armed.

"As I said, you're on Valkash. A small planet close to a yellow star."

"What are we doing here?" Gemma asked, standing next to Caroline.

"The Lomogs have just come out of a long protracted war. This war has ravaged us. Valkash is a way to start recouping those losses. We have set up the planet as a giant attraction, where species from all around the cosmos can come and visit, bringing their wealth to our doors. You are to live here, showing the varying visitors what it is like on your own planet."

"That's outrageous," a man said stepping forward. "You have abducted us from our home. There are fucking laws against that."

"On your world yes," 2104 said. He peered down at the man, noting the steel in his eyes. He didn't seem intimidated by 2104's size and appearance, which made the giant wary. *He may be trouble*, the giant thought, his compatriots agreeing through their neural links. "However, we are not governed by your laws. Your planet is 13,000,000,000 light-years from here. Your species is primitive, almost animal-like compared to us. No one knows that you're here. And no one is coming to find you. You must get used to your new surroundings."

"And if we choose not to?" the man said defiantly.

2104 stepped forward, a black hand grabbing the man by the throat. He lifted him easily, holding the man aloft until his head bounced off the white ceiling. "Then you will be dealt with."

"Leave him alone," Caroline said. "Can't you see that we're all freaked out? You've kidnapped us, bringing us here away from our loved ones. How the fuck do you expect us to react?"

2104 lowered the man to the floor, allowing him to stumble backwards into the villagers. He stood there, massaging his neck, eyes burning into the giant in front of him. "The Lomogs have been good to the Alliance. They helped us when we needed them most. We are in their debt. That's why we had to do this. I appreciate that you are upset. Believe me, I do. However, nothing can be done about that now. You will be shown to your enclosure. The habitat will match your planet's, down to the last detail. I suggest that you all make yourselves at home. That will be all for now." 2104 walked out of the room as cries and shouts erupted from the villagers behind him. A minute later he was walking down the ship's ramp, his hearts unusually heavy as they throbbed in his chest.

Gemma walked into her house, closing the door slowly behind her. She slid to the floor, sobs wracking her body. The house was empty, artificial sunlight streaming in through the windows. *This is not happening*, she thought, her mind travelling to her loved ones. She stood up shakily, walking into the lounge. *Oh my God!* She thought. The scene in front of her was eerie. *It's just like home, without my family.* The furniture was exactly as it was back on Earth; even the television was the same brand as the one that Hugh had picked the previous Christmas. The woman walked over to a picture on the mantelpiece, gently lifting it from the wooden surface. "Oh Christ," she said. Gemma stood on rubbery legs, looking at a recreated photograph of her family. It had been taken a year before, at a family party. The photo she now held was slightly out of focus, not as crisp as the one that adorned her lounge back on Earth. "How did they do this?" she muttered, her voice hollow in the empty vessel that should have been her home. The picture was placed back in its place, Gemma taking a tour of her new surroundings. Each room of the small cottage was almost an exact replica of her home, 13,000,000,000 light years away. She exclaimed, almost smiled when the taps in the kitchen worked perfectly and the upstairs toilet flushed. It all seemed like a surreal dream, or nightmare in Gemma's case. She walked into her bedroom, tears rolling down her cheeks at the sight of it. The bed looked identical to her own; even the scatter cushions were the same design. She walked over to the curtains, drawing them deliberately, blocking out the artificial light. Climbing into bed, the last thoughts were of her two boys. *I will escape this place. Mummy is coming home soon.*

. . .

A few streets away, Caroline walked through her mother's detached bungalow, tears also falling freely. "This is so fucked up," she said as the woman stepped out of the front porch onto a gravel driveway. She leant against a red Nissan, her blue eyes scanning the recreated village. A thought occurred to her as she pushed herself from the car, her boots crunching the gravel underfoot. She navigated the tree-lined streets, heading out of the village on a country lane. Half a mile later, she pressed her hands against a solid glass wall. "We're in a giant fucking Goldfish bowl," she said, her eyes peering through the barrier. A steel walkway lay on the other side of the wall, with another similar glass structure only a few feet away. Caroline stood there, looking for any signs of life on the other side. Her wait was not a long one as a large animal appeared a few minutes later. "Holy fuck!" she exclaimed as a huge mammal with long red fur peered back at her. It reminded her of a bison, but larger. Much larger. It plodded forward, its six legs silently breaking through the forested undergrowth. It collided with the invisible wall, roaring in defiance. Caroline could not hear the roar. But the huge maw, filled with sharp teeth, was enough to startle her. "I hope you cannot get into our enclosure," she said, her heartbeat increasing. "Enclosure. Is that what we are in? Some kind of alien zoo?" She zipped up her fleece jacket, walking along the wall, away from the strange beast on the other side. After several minutes, Caroline came to a glass doorway, set in the wall. A small control panel at chest height beeped back at her. A green handprint pulsed on the pad, making the woman curious. She carefully placed her palm on the reader, and the pad turned red immediately.

"*Warning. Access denied, Caroline Dixon. Please step away.*"

"What the fuck," she exclaimed. "They know everything."

"Yes, they do," a female voice behind her replied softly.

Caroline spun around, her pulse ramping up. In front of her stood a woman, dressed in flowing skirts and a purple fleece jacket. "God! You gave me quite a fright."

"Sorry about that," the woman replied, walking over to the glass wall. She tapped it twice, the noise muted. "I feel like one of those hamsters at the pet shop."

Despite the situation, the younger woman smiled, liking the stranger's turn of phrase. "I'm Caroline."

"Katie. Pleased to meet you," the older woman replied steadily. Caroline appraised her, liking her friendly, attractive face. She seemed to sport a perpetual smile, her eyes creasing as her cheeks lifted ever so slightly.

"Are you from the village?"

"Not quite. I was visiting a friend. I am from the Netherlands. I was over in the UK for a week, in the hope of enjoying a relaxing vacation. It looks like I got more than I bargained for."

"Well, you're not wrong there. Can you really believe this is happening?"

"Oh yes, why of course?"

"Really?"

The older woman settled against a stone wall a few feet away. "I'm sure you've read of alien abductions over the years in the news?"

"Well yes," Caroline started. "But I never thought they were true. I always thought they were part of a hoax or something."

"But of course. We've all probably had the same thoughts. We've all heard of Dracula, but we discount it as fairy-tales. Yet, if he walked around the corner, we'd both probably think, jeez, it was all true."

"I suppose. I never really thought of it like that." She paused, unsure of what to say next. "So, what do we do?"

"I don't think we have much choice, my dear. No one is going to find us here. We have to make the best of things."

"You seem quite relaxed about the whole thing?"

"Believe me I'm not. I would rather be back on Earth, wandering around the English countryside, enjoying tea and cake. However, I am realistic. We are here, and we will stay here until either they decide otherwise, or we escape."

"Escape?"

"Why yes. A ship brought us here. What's to stop it taking us back? We are on the other side of the universe. I have read up on various things over the years. We can barely make it to the Moon. We're twenty years away from travelling to Mars. We have nothing that can even get us out of our solar system. Believe me, Earth cannot help us. Only we can."

Caroline's shoulders sagged, the enormity of the situation dawning on her. "Mum's sick. Very sick. I was moving to Belbroughton to live with her. Without me, she's gonna struggle y'know." A tear fell from her eye, landing on her hand.

The older woman could see she was teetering on the edge, walking over and embracing her. "Your mum will be okay. Let the system take over. Someone will be looking out for her. You, Caroline, need to concentrate on yourself, and the rest of us."

Caroline sniffed, gratefully accepting a tissue from the older woman. "Thank you. I'm glad you came along when you did."

"I was out exploring like you. I was wondering whether it might be worth traversing our borders, to see what is out there."

"Do you mind if I tag along?"

"By all means, dear. A travel companion is always a good thing." They headed off together, walking through the outskirts of the village. Following the glass wall that held them captive.

TWELVE

"Understood. I will see you back on Biflux." Torben relaxed in his chair, the communication ended. He looked over at Kyra and smiled. "Oh well. Looks like we'll be heading back home tomorrow."

"I know. Our crazy adventure is at an end. What will you do when you report back?"

The captain crossed his hands behind his head, his fingers weaving into his dark locks. "I guess I'll be given another assignment. Ark will be back too. He's the other pilot I told you about. We've worked together a lot over the last year or so. They may team us up once more. And you?"

Kyra looked out through the cockpit window, watching as throngs of busy workers attended to their duties. "I honestly don't know. I only took this assignment to put some distance between myself and the war. I'm sure that my people back on Biflux will have something for me to do. Maybe I will take some time off. Go and visit my family."

"Sounds like a good idea. Cantis will be beautiful at this time of year."

"You're not wrong there. The snows are due soon. It

becomes a magical place when the suns are at their farthest points."

"Hmm. I could do with a break myself. May I join you?" The words were out of his mouth before he'd realised what he'd said.

"Really?" Kyra's eyes were now locked on his, an almost incredulous expression spreading across her face.

"Sorry. Did I just jump the gun?"

"What makes you say that?" Kyra was teetering, her pulse quickening.

"We've only known each other for a short time. I do not want you to think I'm too keen." *Shit!*

"Are you not keen then?" Her eyes seemed to grow darker, almost engulfing the fidgeting captain.

"Yes. Well, you know?" He was becoming tongue-tied, unable to get his words out.

"You know?"

"Look. I really like you. Which is strange as I tend to be a bit of a loner. And you've just lost someone close. So yes, I am keen. But I don't want to rush you, Kyra."

She laced her fingers into his, pulling the man's hand into her lap. "I am ready, Torben. I did not expect to meet anyone so soon after losing my partner. Let's just see how it goes. I have no expectations of you. But I like being with you. Let's go and get some mountain air and see what happens."

"But what if we do that and we become closer, only to be separated by our upcoming assignments?"

"Let's worry about that when the time comes, Torben." She leant forward, kissing him gently. Rex, who was sat making preparations for the journey, turned around and smiled at the budding romance that was unfolding before him.

"Okay," Torben said as they broke the kiss. "Are you ready to show me the sights of Cantis?"

"Oh, I think I can keep you entertained, Captain," she said, a mirthful expression spreading across her face.

A few days later, Shimmer050 gently touched down inside bay 106. Rex set about shutting the ship's engines down whilst Torben walked down the main ramp into the vast hangar. He looked around as porters and workers set about his ship, heading up the ramp in teams, trolleys clattering behind them. "I need a drink," he said to himself as he exited the hangar, knowing that he was only a few minutes' walk away from the Sars club. Lomax Spaceport was a hive of activity, with throngs of pilots, travellers, and workers bustling past Torben as he made his way to the familiar canteen. His wrist vibrated slightly, telling him that a message was coming through. A face appeared on the display, making him smile. "Hello, Kyra."

"Hello, Torben. Have you made it to the club yet?"

"I'm almost there. Has your call finished?"

"Yes. A moment ago. I am to report to command seven days from now. If we leave soon, we can be in Cantis before nightfall." .

"Sounds good to me. I will order you a beer. How long will you be?"

"I'm not far behind you. Just had to sort out the deceased member of the crew."

Torben suddenly felt guilty. Here he was, looking forward to the next few days when a family who lived close by would be mourning the loss of a loved one. "Okay. I will see you shortly."

He clicked off the device, heading into the Sars club, his shoulders sagging slightly after the conversation. Torben started scanning the room as a voice rang out. "You're back," Ark exclaimed.

"Hey. When did you get back?"

"A few hours ago. I've been here ever since."

"Trust you to set about oiling your tubes as soon as you landed. Typical pilot."

"Let me get you a drink. Then we can compare adventures."

A few minutes later, they sat in a quiet booth in the corner of the club. The whitewashed walls barely lighting the sombre interior. Torben looked over at the opposite table, smiling an acknowledgement at the alien pilots who sat sipping their drinks. "Why did you get two drinks?" Ark asked. "Is someone else joining us?"

"Yes. One of the crew said she'd grab a drink with me before she heads home."

"She! Tell all, my old friend."

"Calm down. There is nothing to tell. It's just a crew member."

Before Ark could answer, a female voice made them both look up. "Starting without me?" Kyra stood there, smiling at the two pilots.

"I was just keeping yours safe until you got here," Torben replied, blushing slightly.

"So considerate," she replied, kissing him on the cheek before sliding next to him on the leather bench.

"So, this is the crew member that was joining us for a quick drink?" Ark said, his green eyes boring into Torben's.

The older man's shoulders slumped. "Kyra, this is Ark Ramkle. Ark, this is Kyra Zakx."

The younger pilot extended his hand, liking the cool firm touch that grasped it. "Pleased to meet you, Kyra. What's a good-looking woman doing with an old relic like this?"

"Likewise, Ark. Oh, I'm sure you can fill me in on what this old relic is like," she said playfully elbowing Torben in the ribs.

"Okay. The rat is out of the sack. Kyra and I are?" He paused, unsure of what to say next.

The woman decided to take charge, showing the bumbling

captain the way forward. "An item. Torben's coming home with me to Cantis. We're going to spend some time together before our next assignments."

"You old dog," Ark said, looking at Torben. How did you manage that? I have been on a ship full of droids and hominids. Even the planet we plundered was devoid of anything worth chasing. The females are odd, to say the least. Smelly too. They stink like the back of a swamp pig."

Torben laughed, glad he'd been reunited with his younger friend. "So, no intergalactic love then?"

"Nothing. Although, the tender has been looking over a few times since we sat down. So maybe I will be getting lucky later."

Kyra rolled her eyes. "Are all pilots like this? What about Torben here?" She made it sound playful and light. However, she was curious about the man who she'd only recently met.

"Nah. He's too old for chasing females. He'd rather sculpt some lame piece of rock, or look at a dumb painting. Is this what happens when you get old? If so, I'm going to get my fill while I still can."

They all smiled at each other, raising their drinks in unison. "So, tell me about your trip?" Torben said.

"It went smoothly enough, although we did lose six crew."

"Six! How did that happen?"

Four were killed by one of the hominids. I told you before we left, they are huge. We tried to take him down without a fight, but he had other plans. He literally pulled four of the crew members apart. It wasn't fun, scooping them up into gurneys off the forest floor. The other two were killed by a large cat. It sprang from the undergrowth. We managed to salvage one body. The other poor bastard is still there, probably in a pile of cat dung."

"How awful!" Kyra said, placing her drink down on the table-top. "Have you notified the families?"

"Yes. Well, my Medical Officer did. The bodies were

unloaded just after we'd landed. It is a shame. The six that died were all good men. Brave too. They faced up to the beast without hesitation. It was only when the second one went down that the others tried to flee. But it was too late."

"How did you round them up?" Torben asked.

"I managed to stun it. Due to the terrain, we couldn't land like others could on some planets. We literally had to round them up. We stunned a few indigenous animals, laying traps for the reptiles and cats. It seemed to work well. How about you? What adventures have you had? Apart from the obvious."

Torben shot him a stern glance, which only lasted for a moment. His friend's enthusiasm was infectious. "It went very smoothly. They were all rounded up with relative ease. It was only once we were travelling home that we had issues."

"What kind of issues?" the younger pilot asked quizzically.

"The humans were angry and scared. I suppose they have every right to be. After all, we snatched them from their homes and families, taking them across the universe to live out their days in a virtual prison."

"When you put it like that, I guess they have a point." Ark took a long pull on his drink, eyeing his friend as he did so. "So, what now?"

"We have a few drinks, then head to Cantis," Torben replied smoothly, liking the closeness that the women next to him gave off. Her smooth fingers gently rested on his arm, sending goosebumps across his lightly tanned skin. "How about you?"

"I'm gonna stick around here for a day or so. I could call in and see my family on the way to Command. I will see how it goes. If I get lucky, I may skip the family."

"Sounds like you've got it all mapped out," Kyra said smiling.

They all raised their glasses, clinking them lightly as the world passed them by.

THIRTEEN

VALKASH

THE VILLAGE HALL WAS CROWDED, ALMOST EVERY SEAT WAS taken as the crowd settled down. A few people stood at the front of the hallway, their eyes scanning the expectant faces of the abducted villagers. Caroline looked at the man stood next to her, not liking the air he gave off. She remembered him falling to the floor onboard the space ship as the abductors zapped him with their stun gun. "Someone needs to take charge. We need to elect a leader if we're going to get out of here. For those of you who don't know me, my name's Pete Haines." Caroline watched as he strutted across the floor, trying to generate some support from his fellow villagers. *Smug twat*, she thought, as she appraised him. He looked to be a few years older than her, with short dark hair and a rubbery face. She could see the first traces of red veins across his nose and cheeks. She had seen them before, on her father's face. A father that was all too keen to have any kind of drink in his meaty paw.

"Are you putting yourself forward?" a man shouted from the back of the building.

"Yes, I am. I'm used to managing people. It's what I do." A few disconcerted murmurs drifted across the hall.

"Well I'll put myself forward too," the man said, as he left his family sitting huddled together. As he stood next to the others, the man addressed the room. "My name's Martin Williams. My wife Kimberly is sat at the back with our two sons, Tristan and Lawrence." He looked towards the rear of the hall, catching a reassuring smile from his wife.

"So, we have two candidates?" Pete interjected before his rival could carry on. "Is there anyone else who would like to put themselves forward?"

"I will," Caroline said quickly, catching the disapproving expressions of the two men next to her. "

"And you are?" Pete said, hands placed on his expanding hips.

"Caroline."

"You're not from the village, are you?" Martin said, trying to push for an early advantage.

"No. I was visiting my mum when all this happened. I am in the process of moving to Belbroughton though."

"I really think that an elected leader needs to be a resident of the village," Pete said, his head moving up and down, making his jowls shake.

"I agree," Martin agreed. "Someone who knows the villagers. Someone who can come up with a plan to get us all back home."

"Back home?" Caroline said. "Has it sunk in yet as to where we are?"

"For all we know, Carol, we could still be on Earth, part of some elaborate hoax."

"Caroline."

"Huh?" Pete said.

"My name's Caroline."

"Whatever! My point is that someone needs to be in charge who will think outside the box."

What a prat, she thought. *Think outside the box. Did he get that from The Apprentice?* "Okay. If no-one else is to put themselves forward, I suggest we put it to a vote?"

"Agreed," Martin said impatiently.

"Okay," Pete began, trying to project his voice. "All villagers who think I should be in charge, please raise your hands?" Several hands went up, Pete trying to count them all.

Caroline looked at his attempt, smiling to herself. "I have an idea. I will move to the entrance of the hall. Martin, you move over to the window. Pete, you stay here. Everyone can move to the person that they choose as leader. Then, we tally up." Pete looked at her sourly, his skin reddening. "Just thinking outside the box," she said as she turned to walk towards the entrance.

"Okay, guys. Move to who you think should be the leader of the group." The villagers all stood up, shuffling and walking over to their preferred candidate. After a minute, the hall was split into three groups.

"Have we all decided?" Martin said. They all agreed in unison as the three potential leaders began counting. A few minutes later, Martin and Caroline walked back to where Pete stood.

"How many, Martin?" Pete said.

"Forty-two," he replied, pleased with his score.

Pete. How many did you get?" Caroline asked.

"Fifty-one. And you?"

"Fifty-seven," she replied neutrally. So, I guess that decides it." Pete looked over at the group at the entrance to the hall, seeing that most of Caroline's group were women. He let out an exasperated sigh, striding out of the hall, leaving the rest in silence.

"Okay, well, you're in charge," Martin said, trying his best to look indifferent.

"Right. I need a team of people to help me. A mini-committee. Who's interested?"

Several women stepped forward, Gemma at the front of the group. "Count me in."

"Me too," Katie added.

"If you need another, I am more than happy to help." Martin looked at his wife, his face reddening. "Sorry, love. I am on the school board. I am good at this kind of stuff."

"Whatever," her husband replied, following the other losing candidate out of the hall.

Kimberly looked over at her two sons, smiling thinly. "Can you go with Daddy please?" They left the room, playfully bumping shoulders with each other.

Caroline looked at the remaining villagers, the weight of her position becoming apparent. "We will meet again at the same time tomorrow. The four of us will stay here for a while and discuss a few things." The throng of people filed out, leaving the four women standing in the empty hall. "I think we should sit down and discuss things moving forward."

"I agree," Katie said as she looked over towards a kitchenette. "Do you think we could rustle up something to drink?"

"Let's take a look," Gemma said, heading over to the corner of the hall. She tentatively tried the cold-water tap, pleasantly surprised when a jet of cold liquid shot out into the steel sink. "At least we have water." She looked at the kettle, quickly picking it up, filling it halfway. She smiled when the red light flicked on, the boiling cycle working. "Not sure how they knew that we'd need this. But I am thankful." She opened the cupboards, amazed when she was presented with a series of steel canisters. The woman unscrewed the lid of the closest one, inhaling a heady aroma that reminded her of home. "Bloody hell! We have coffee."

"That's something I suppose," Kimberley said as she pulled the door of the fridge open. "We have milk too by the look of it," she said, unscrewing the cap of a clear plastic container. "Not sure what kind of animal produced this, but it smells like ordinary milk."

"If I have coffee, I can put my mind to anything," Caroline quipped, trying to brighten the mood. The other women smiled at her, liking the Welsh woman's logic. Five minutes later they were seated at a small square table next to a small stage. Steaming coffee enveloped the foursome, slightly lifting the dark clouds that threatened them. "So," Caroline started. "What kind of things do we need to talk about? I am thinking about laying some ground rules for the villagers."

"What kind of rules?" Kimberley said as she cupped her white mug in both hands.

"Oh, I don't know. Things like not letting the children wander off on their own."

"Sensible," Gemma said, noting a slight power struggle starting to occur. She looked at Kimberley, wondering if there would be trouble.

"I suppose that's a good place to start," Kimberley responded evenly. "After all, we don't really know what is out there. I took a walk towards the edge of the village earlier. Beyond the glass wall, I spotted a few huge creatures. I certainly would not want them getting into the village. Keeping the children away from them is a good idea."

"It's all very good setting rules for us all," Katie said. "But we also need to formulate another plan."

"Oh! What kind of plan?" Gemma asked, a curious edge to her voice.

"Why dear. A plan of escape of course."

"Escape!" Kimberley blurted. "How do we do that?"

"Well, I don't rightly know at the moment. But if you think I want to spend the rest of my life in a giant goldfish bowl, surrounded by alien beasts, you can think again. We came here in a ship. All we need to get home is another ship, with someone who knows how to fly it."

Kimberley was about to reply when the hall doors opened. The four women turned their heads as 2104 walked into the hall, his arms swinging loosely by the side. "I am afraid that escape is futile. I know that you will think about it. However, it is not possible."

"Why not?" Katie said defiantly. She walked towards him, gripping her mug tightly. "You are holding us against our will. Of course, we are thinking about a way home."

"And I cannot stop you from thinking such things. However, putting such things into practice will end badly for you. The ships that bought you all here have now left this planet. Only short-range freighter ships will be visiting, bringing supplies to all the inhabitants of Valkash."

"So, we're just supposed to live out our days in this fucking zoo?" Gemma spat. "I have a family at home. We all do. They will be worried about us."

"Please, sit. Let me explain exactly what is going on here," 2104 said calmly. The women complied, chair legs grating across the wooden floor. Ash walked past them, leaning easily against the stage, stretching his four arms out in a crucifix pose. "When I welcomed you all, I briefly explained about the war. A faction had waged war against the Lomogs, and anyone affiliated to them. Chaos raged across the systems, which all but crushed us. It was only by chance that their leader, Barajan, was captured. Once he was executed, the factions fell apart. The remaining rebels are scattered across the cosmos. Now peace can return."

"But why kidnap different species from across the universe?" Katie asked, her tone almost pleading."

"That was not our call. The Lomogs decided on such things. They have given us peace and wealth, along with technology that we never thought possible. Without that, the nearby systems would not have recovered from the war. We must do their bidding."

"But it's kidnapping!" Gemma spat, her face reddening.

"I know what it is. But we have our orders. My family are thousands of light-years away too. I have left them to come and work here. I too, wish to be with them again. And one day

I will. I have three little ones who will be missing their father. My partner, Artaq, is to care for them in my absence. It is a sacrifice that we have to make to ensure that peace remains, and mouths are fed. I understand that the four of you are now in charge. That is good. Rules need to be applied and obeyed. That is all I have to say. I trust that the refreshments are to your liking? There will be regular shipments of food to keep you all healthy. The eco-system is perfectly matched to your own planet. So, your plants will grow, and your animals will never go hungry. Now, I have to leave. There is so much to do." Before any of the women could reply, the large alien was striding out of the hall, leaving the door ajar. It creaked gently, just like it did in Belbroughton.

"Follow me," Caroline said, following 2104. The others complied, almost jogging after the departing leader. "There he goes," the Welsh woman said, pointing down the country lane towards the invisible barrier that kept them hemmed in. "Let's see where he's off to." The followed at a brisk pace, struggling to keep up with the giant's loping strides. After a minute he stopped at a glass doorway, placing his huge palm against the reader. The door opened silently, and 2104 stepped outside onto a steel gangway. As the women approached, the glass door closed with barely a rustle, closing off any hope of pursuit. They watched as the large alien walked away from them, becoming lost to sight as trees and hedgerows barred their view.

"Oh well. At least we know how to get through the door-way," Katie said.

"How?" Kimberley said, perplexed.

"He used his hand to gain access. All we need to do is chop it off and use it for ourselves."

"Hmm," Caroline murmured. "Have you seen the size of him? Cutting his hand off might not be as easy as you think. And it will probably piss him off too."

"Well. He has four of them. I'm sure he'd cope if he only

had three left."

FOURTEEN

BIFLUX

Torben stood motionless, watching the majesty of the Cantis glacier. A massif of rock and ice, twelve billion years in the making. His eyes flitted to where it met the crystal-like lake underneath it, slithers of blue ice calving into the deep waters. "Now that is something," he said, wrapping an arm around Kyra's waist.

"It sure is," she said, snuggling into the man next to her, trying to ward off the cold wind that blew from the jagged peaks above them.

"How far to your parents' home?"

"It's only a short ride," she said, tilting her head to her right. Next to the lake, a small town lay nestled into the side the mountain. "They live on the outskirts of Kiton. If you look over there, where the trees touch the waters, there are a few buildings. My parents live closest to the shore. There is a cabin on the water, where they have their crafts moored. That's where we'll be holed up. Not quite slumming it, but far from luxurious. Can you handle that, Torby?"

He loved the new pet-name that she had bestowed upon him. It made him feel warm inside, which was an unusual feeling in itself. Torben also loved how she snuggled in close to him, her long fingers kneading the muscles of his forearm under his thick jacket. "As long as there is a bunk, a beer and a fire, I will be just fine. Lead on."

They walked over to their transport, a silver land-glider with a glass-domed roof. As they approached the roof slid back, with two recessed doors sliding open to welcome the couple. "Strap yourself in. I will take us across the lake towards the cabin. We can unpack before I unleash my family on you." The craft rose into the air before heading down a grassy slope towards the water. It settled twenty feet over the glass-like surface, gently skipping over the water towards the town.

"What the hell is that?" Torben exclaimed as a dark grey shape broke the surface of the lake.

"It's a male Breekin. It's looking for a safe refuge for its pod. They come into the lake to calve every year. I'll increase our altitude. They are not dangerous, but they break the surface of the water and can reach some heights. They have been known to bring down low-flying craft."

"Fair enough," Torben said as the creature below them broke the surface once more. "Look at the size of that thing!"

"Impressive eh. Fully grown males can be almost a thousand feet in length. One washed up on the shores next to the town last year. It was taller than any structure in Kiton."

"How did you get rid of it?"

"We towed it back out to sea. This lake connects to the ocean. There are even larger predators out there that would be only too happy to have a feast like that."

"Remind me never to go swimming out at sea then," Torben said, grinning.

Kyra returned the smile, her face transforming. She reached across the cockpit, entwining her fingers into his, squeezing gently. "You'd freeze to death before any predators could take a chunk out of you. So, stay close to me. The cabin will be nice and warm, once we get the fire going."

"Sounds perfect," the captain replied, as Kiton started to fill his vista. A small collection of buildings that were sandwiched between the lake and the mountains, the town had a holiday feel to Torben. He'd stayed there a few times before, liking the laid-back atmosphere of the trading stalls and bars that dotted the main thoroughfare. As the craft scooted past, Kyra gunned the thrusters, turning left sharply away from the town. Torben smiled, liking the excitement as the small vessel flitted past trees on its right-hand side.

"And here we are," Kyra announced a few moments later, the craft settling into the water next to a wooden pontoon. A minute later they were dumping their packs on the freshly painted wooden planks as Kyra anchored the ship in place, letting it bob and drift on the gentle waters.

Torben looked up at the main house, nodding his appreciation. Kyra's family home sat nestled under evergreen trees, with a high apex roof that reminded him of a mountain lodge. Most of the façade was of blackened glass that shimmered when the sun's rays caught it. "Impressive."

"Not bad eh. My parents have lived here since I was a little girl. Father did most of the work himself, preferring to get his hands dirty, rather than let someone else take the credit."

"Makes sense to me. What do your parents do?"

"They are retired now. Mother was a teacher and Father was an engineer at Halycon. That's why Max has gone there, to follow in Father's footsteps. You will like them both."

"Let's hope they like me."

"I'm sure they will. They were very fond of Relkon and were very upset when he died. But they know that the universe moves on." They shouldered their packs, walking along the pontoon towards the cosy looking cabin that sat on the water's edge. "We can leave our things here and unpack later. I am sure Mother will want to make us something for dinner."

"Lead on. I could eat a baby Breekin."

"You're funny," she replied as she closed the cabin door, linking arms with her man as they made their way up to the impressive house, the trees around it swaying in the stiffening breeze.

"Kyra!" a female voice called as they rounded the front of the house.

"Mother," Kyra called, her pace quickening until she embraced the older woman who was skipping towards her. They came together, hugging and laughing as they regarded each other. "I like what you've done with your hair, Mother," Kyra said, gently touching the steely locks that were being buffeted by the wind.

"Do you really like it? Your father decided to treat me for my lifeday." She looked over her daughter's shoulder, eyeing the dark-haired stranger. "Hello," she said warmly.

"Hello," Torben replied evenly.

"Mother, this is Torben. Torben, this is my Mother."

The older woman released her daughter, walking over to the man who stood nervously. "I'm Elsor. Pleased to meet you, Torben," she said, lightly kissing his cheek.

"Nice to meet you too, Elsor," he replied as he appraised the woman in front of him. She was tall, almost reaching his own height. Her steely grey hair bounced around an attractive face and piercing green eyes which regarded the world warmly. Torben could clearly see the family resemblance. "You two look like sisters," he said, trying to break the ice.

"I like him already," Elsor said. "Such a way with words too. Come. I've just finished my chores. I'm sure you're both hungry." She led the way, linking arms with her daughter as Torben followed a few steps behind. A glass door opened silently, and the threesome walked into a brightly-lit hallway. Elsor leaned against a wooden staircase, deftly flicking off her pumps before running her tanned fingers down her black leggings to straighten them. "This way," she beckoned to Torben, walking from the hallway into a large kitchen.

"Wow. This is quite a place you have here, Elsor," he said, clearly impressed.

"Thank you," she said happily. "Trevik, my husband, is quite handy with his tools. He built this house from scratch, using the surrounding trees to erect the frame. We lived in the lakeside cabin for two years whilst he built it. This was before Kyra and Max came along."

"It's something else," he said, running his hand across a light wooden worktop. The floor was a dark tile that perfectly matched the black units and the island that was the centre-piece of the large room. Windows ran the length of the three walls that made up the room, the lake its vista. "I'm not much of a cook. But I could get used to trying if I had that view."

"Well, sit yourselves down and I will fix us some lunch. All that gardening has made me hungry. Torben, what would you like to drink? Juice? Graff?"

"I'll have a juice please, Lady Zakx," he used the official term that was customary, showing his respect to the lady of the house.

"Call me Elsor. Lady Zakx makes me sound terribly old."

"Juice for me too, Mother," Kyra said as she sat down on a tall stool next to the island. Torben followed suit, resting his arms on the wooden worktop.

Elsor opened a large cupboard door, pulling out a glass jug that was filled with a dark liquid. She closed the cooler, walking over to the young couple, placing the juice in front of them. A recess in the counter slid to Torben's left, two large glass tumblers rising out of the cupboard beneath him. Kyra poured two glasses, taking a hearty swig. "Thanks, Mother. Just what I needed."

"Yes, thank you, Elsor," Torben said before he lifted the glass to his lips, enjoying the tart taste that the juice gave off.

"My pleasure. I will fix you both something to eat. I'm sure your Father will want something too."

"Where is he?" Kyra asked.

"Upstairs. A call came through about an hour ago. One of the pipelines up in the Tundra has developed a fault. He needs to fly up there to take a look."

"Will he ever truly retire?"

"That's what I said, love. But you know Father. Committed to the cause." A few minutes later the threesome were sat at the island, munching their way through Elsor's flatbreads. Torben enthusiastically scooped a spoonful of dark spread onto the unleavened bread, savouring the heady taste.

"These are so good, Elsor."

"Thank you. That's my homemade Zicky. Everything in that comes from the garden."

"It's delicious," he responded, wiping his lips with a paper napkin.

"So. How did you two meet?" the older woman asked.

"On the mission, Mother. Torben is the ship's captain. We got chatting not long after we took off. It kinda went from there."

"Romance in the stars. I like the sound of that. Where did your mission take you?"

Torben placed his glass on the wooden top, clearing his throat. "A small planet called Earth. It's pretty much on the other side of the universe. Thirteen billion lights from here."

"Oh my. That is some journey. Did you complete the mission as expected?"

"Yes. We rounded up a collection of the species from the planet, depositing them on Valkash."

"Kyra told me about that planet. Sounds like a giant theme park."

"In essence, that's what it is."

"I don't really like the idea of it to tell you the truth."

"We are both in agreement. After all, what right do we have to kidnap another species? Especially a semi-intelligent one that has been taken away from their families."

"But the Lomogs have spoken," Elsor responded evenly. "We are in their debt. This is but a small price to pay I guess."

"I know, Mother. But it still feels wrong."

"Who are you?" a male voice boomed from behind them. Torben turned in his chair to see a large man with a grim expression on his face, staring straight at him. In his large hands, he held a long rifle. The captain's eyes opened wider as the other man levelled it at his chest, slowly advancing towards him.

FIFTEEN

A FORSAKEN ROCK NEXT TO A DYING STAR

THE CAVE SAT ATOP A LARGE OUTCROP, LIGHTS FROM THE nearby space-port barely visible as a sand storm moved in for the night. Inside the opening, three figures sat around a small fire. Two females and a male regarded each other over the flickering yellow flames. "Are we set?" the one woman asked.

"Yes," the man responded, eyeing his leader. She sat cross-legged on the reddened floor, her unkempt sandy hair hiding a long scar that ran the length of her weathered face. His stare flickered slightly as she regarded him with her one good eye. What remained of the other eye socket was obscured under her fringe. The man looked at the flames, stirring the embers with a stick.

"I am ready too," the other woman stated flatly. The man glanced up at her, smiling thinly. She returned the gesture, her silvery teeth sparkling in the firelight. The woman's long, dark hair was tied in a tail that ran down her back. Her long limbs were covered in raised tattoos of unusual designs and hues. The man realised he was staring and averted his gaze once more.

The leader rose stiffly, running her fingers through her sandy hair, her other hand dusting her clothing. "Ullar," she said, regarding the other woman. "How long until we are ready to strike?"

"Less than a moon's cycle, Hameda," she replied respectfully.

Hameda looked at the man below her, smiling evenly. "Ragyi," she cooed. "When can we make our move? This inactivity is frustrating."

He looked up at his leader, trying to keep his voice steady. "The same as Ullar, give or take a day or so. The Lomogs were not so clever, leaving undetonated warheads lying around. Warheads that are ancient, but still operational. No one uses nuclear technology anymore. But the damage will be no less severe. They have been primed. All we need is the delivery system, which Ullar has provided. I think we are all set to make a statement."

"Good. Very good," Hameda said before making her way to the cave's entrance. "Ullar. Is the ship down there?"

"Yes. In a disused hangar. Ragyi's people are on their way, bringing the warheads."

"You say less than a moon's cycle. Is that our travel time?"

"Yes, Hameda. From our position in this system to Biflux should take roughly fifteen days, give or take. From there, we will have enough warheads to strike at a few other strategic sites. Valkash being the main one."

"Then let us be about our business. Whoever took my beloved Barajan's head is about to pay a heavy price. Not only in lives, but in power. Power that I intend to wrest back from those tin-framed bastards."

An hour later, the trio stood in the confines of the neglected hangar that Ullar had described. In the centre of the low-slung space, a ship sat quietly. Tendrils of steam seeping from large vents on its hull. Hameda walked over, her gait clumsy and stilted. She ran a hand over the grey exterior, liking the look of the inconspicuous freighter. "How fast can she go?"

"She is fast enough. 0.05 of Light Speed. That is all we need, Hameda. We want to remain inconspicuous whilst we travel. She's not the prettiest ship, so we need to remain off anyone's radar."

"Okay. But Biflux lies in another system. How will we reach it in time? Valkash too. Is there something that I do not know because the numbers do not stack up."

Ullar smiled, resting her hand on the ship's hull. "Wormholes."

"Wormholes?"

"Yes. The Lomogs have secretly positioned them across many systems, allowing ships to pass through, cutting down their travel time. Many of the new ships do not need them, as they are fitted with their own Singularity Drives, which allow them to jump across the cosmos instantly. However, many of the freighters that deliver goods are not fitted with that kind of tech. So those metal bastards created wormholes instead."

"Very clever. I almost like them for doing that. But not quite. If it aids our cause, I will gladly use their offerings before we crush them. I also think we should test out a warhead before hitting our two main targets. One of the new orbitals."

"Good idea," the man said eagerly. "There is an orbital relatively nearby. That will send out a message."

Ullar's face looked pinched. "But it might alert them, making strikes against Biflux and Valkash more difficult."

"You may be right," Hameda added sagely. "However, if we do it right, it might just appear to be an accident. It would not be the first station that has exploded. You've all heard about Sygnus 1." They nodded, remembering the stories that had floated across the galaxy about the first super-station. The main reactor inside the vast ring had malfunctioned before going critical. Millions were killed.

Ragyi looked down at a small screen fitted to his wrist. "They are almost here. We're in for a busy day."

"I like busy," Hameda replied. "Busy gets results."

"Daddy. What are you doing?" Kyra asked as she eyed her father warily.

"Trevik?" Elsor said quietly. "Are you alright?"

Torben eyed the man across the kitchen, noting the steely resolve in his eyes. The captain slowly raised his hands, his mind frozen.

"Are your intentions towards my daughter honourable?"

"Of course," Torben replied readily.

"Good," said Trevik. He lowered the weapon, a large smile spreading across his face.

"Daddy," Kyra exclaimed, skipping across the kitchen into his embrace.

"Hello Princess," he said, lifting her easily off the smooth floor. Torben took a step backwards, leaning against the island unit in the centre of the room. He breathed out, his heart still hammering in his chest.

"That was not how you introduce yourself to guests," Elsor said, trying her best to sound stern.

"Sorry, Elsy," he replied, using the pet name that he had given her many years before. He walked over to Torben, extending his hand. "My apologies. I'm Trevik."

"Torben," the younger man replied, matching the older man's grip.

"Strong handshake. Says a lot about a man," Trevik said, clapping Torben on the shoulder. "Is there any lunch left for the old man of the house?"

"Yes, Trev," Elsor responded, sliding a plate towards her husband. They were all seated as the wind outside strengthened, trees next to the lake swaying in unison.

"Mum tells me that you have to fly up to the Tundra?"

"Yes," Trevik said between mouthfuls. "One of the pipelines that supply power to the northern stations has developed
a fault. Their regular engineer is on leave. Bad back. Kids."
He let the word hang in the air whilst he took a swig of juice.
"So, the call came through. It should be routine. I will be back
in a few hours."

Kyra looked at Torben, who was gazing out at the vista.
"Why don't you go with Father?"

"Really?" the younger man replied, glancing at Trevik.

"Why not," Trevik responded enthusiastically. "I could use
the company."

"Only if you're sure," Torben replied, a whiff of excitement coursing through his veins.

"Are you handy with a rifle?"

"Sure. Since I was a boy I have hunted, with various
weapons."

"Good. You can keep an eye out whilst I check out the
pipeline. I will ready the craft. I will be back in five minutes."
The older man left the room, his rifle slung over his shoulder,
leaving the others to finish their lunch.

"You'll have fun," Kyra said. Father is a sweetheart really.
He will take good care of you."

"I'm sure he will," Torben said. "It's not your father that I
am worried about. It's whatever else is out there. They too
might be expecting lunch."

SIXTEEN

EARTH

HUGH SAT AT HIS LAPTOP, THE HOUSE UNNATURALLY QUIET. The children were at school and nursery, giving the man some time to do some digging. And he had just unearthed something. When not playing daddy to his two boys and husband to Gemma, Hugh was part of an online community called Black Knight. A worldwide smattering of gamers, authors, book cover designers and the odd hacker here and there. He'd just received a message from someone called Ezekiel, from Florida. He knew of Ezekiel, not always agreeing with his paranoid conspiracy theories regarding shape-shifters, secret societies and the social media Armageddon countdown. The man from across the Atlantic was convinced that social media was put on Earth as an experiment that would bring about the end of mankind, through fake news and religious reprisals. However, today he had found something that was of interest to Hugh; a leaked story on the Internet regarding an unknown object spotted by numerous amateur astronomers across the globe. From Perth to Venezuela, people were talking about an unknown disturbance in the Earth's atmosphere a few days before. Normally Hugh would pay this little attention, focusing on other more important issues. However, today was different. Today his wife was missing, nobody knowing how or why she'd suddenly vanished into the ether, along with count-less others. He would normally discount random accounts of UFOs, knowing that they were ten-a-penny. What he was looking at now was a message sent from the International Space Station to Roscosmos in Kazakhstan, stating that an unidentified object had briefly been observed approaching Earth's orbit. The Russian text had been translated, albeit clunkily. The message had given Hugh goose-bumps. *We have to report an unidentified object, spotted at 18:27 on October 18th. Before we photograph, it vanished. But there was something there. Two Cosmonauts and one Astronaut saw it too.*

"Jesus!" he breathed. "I need more info." He set to work a few minutes later, a hot mug of coffee to his left. After an hour, his coffee replenished once more, Hugh leaned back in his chair. "This is insane," he said, pulling his phone out of his trouser pocket. He reached across the desk, picking up the business card he'd received a few days before. He opted for the mobile number at the bottom of the card, not wanting to get stuck on hold.

It rang for a few seconds before there was a crackle on the line. "Hello?"

"Mr Lewis?" Hugh asked, his mouth dry, his voice raspy.

"Speaking."

"Hi. It's Mr Andrews. Gemma's husband. Have you heard any news?"

"Not at this time, Mr Andrews, although we are currently heading up several lines of enquiry."

"I know this might sound outlandish, but I've been reading several accounts on the Internet regarding an unidentified object spotted above the Earth. I was wondering if you'd heard anything about this?"

There was a pause on the line for a few seconds, which was enough to tell Hugh that Mr Lewis had heard something. The pause ended quickly, the voice on the end of the line trying to remain unflustered and neutral. "We try not to get caught up in conspiracy theories, Mr Andrews. We try to deal in facts. We've not heard any accounts of unidentified objects in and around the Earth's atmosphere in the recent past, if at all. I would discount such information. We are doing all we can to trace all the inhabitants of your village and we will not rest until they are all returned safely home."

"Sorry if that sounded a bit out there. I'm just worried."

"It's understandable, Mr Andrews. Sometimes our imaginations can run away with us during times of heightened stress. As soon as I hear anything, I will be in touch. Good day."

"Goodbye," Hugh replied, the line already disconnected. *He is hiding something*, he thought. *He may appear super cool, but my question caught him off-guard. I will keep digging. Someone out there must know something.*

Before he left the house to pick up his boys, Hugh logged into his Twitter account on his laptop. The man had several thousand followers, such was the community that he'd immersed himself in. His friend Ezekiel from across the Atlantic had almost 50,000 people following his daily updates, retweeting and liking his leftfield posts and links. He copied the statement from the International Space Station, tagging the American in it. As he hit *tweet*, Hugh knew that word would hopefully spread, spanning the globe in a short space of time. He was hoping that it would reach the news channels, getting some kind of coverage. Anything was worth a try, he thought as he donned his thick jacket before heading out into the village. A village suddenly devoid of life.

Paul Lewis sat at his desk, pondering the exchange on the phone with Mr Andrews. He looked over at his coffee cup, not realizing that he'd not touched the now cold milky drink since he'd sat down an hour previously. Paul stiffly rose from his chair, looking out at the parking lot beyond the window. Lines of cars sat quietly under a leaden sky, the English autumn now in full swing. He set off down the corridor from his office, turning left towards a small kitchenette. After setting a fresh mug in place, he pressed the Cappuccino button on the freshly installed coffee machine, leaning against the counter as coffee beans were being ground next to him. *What could I say?* he thought as his brew gently steamed next to him. *Yes, Mr Andrews, we know about the unidentified object too. So does the NSA, and Mossad.* His superior had informed him that the Prime Minister was chairing an emergency **COBRA** meeting at Downing Street whilst he stood waiting for his coffee. He looped his index finger around the handle, gently sliding the mug away from the machine, sipping the frothy head from the cappuccino before he sauntered back to his office, his feet feeling unusually heavy. As he walked into his outer office, his Personal Assistant looked up from her computer screen, smiling at him. "Your wife called, Mr Lewis. She'd like you to call her back when you can."

"Thank you, Sylvia," he replied, a half-smile tugging at his lips.

"Is everything alright?" she asked, standing up from her desk, manicured fingers straightening her pencil skirt.

"Fine. I'm just a bit tired."

"You don't look quite yourself, Mr Lewis. Maybe you're coming down with something. It is that time of year you know, bugs and the like." She padded around the desk, walking over to Paul, her hips swaying gently. The man looked at her advancing towards him, taking in her ample cleavage and dark nylons. She was barefoot, and Paul noticed for the first time a small toe ring that glinted beneath the dark material of her stockings. He knew that she had just turned forty. He also knew that she was divorced, and rather flirty. He had had no problem with that until recently. Sylvia was very efficient, thinking on her feet rather than asking for constant help and direction. There had always been a measure of sexual chemistry between them, which he'd accepted as normal. He was in good shape for a man approaching fifty, Sylvia complimenting him often on his suits, trim figure and well-kept blonde hair. She touched his brow with the back of her fingers. Fingers that felt cool and smooth. "You feel a tad warm, Mr Lewis."

Probably because I'm thinking about bending you over my desk, he thought, his coffee cup trembling slightly. "I'm fine really, Sylvia. I will stop by the chemist on the way home and get some *Night Nurse*. That always helps when I've got a cold coming on."

"Well if you need anything. Anything at all, just let me know." She turned and walked back to her seat, her chestnut hair bouncing rhythmically as she moved. Paul watching her, almost in a trance until he excused himself, slightly red-faced.

"Thank you, Sylvia. You're very kind. Now I must get back to it," he said as he retreated into his office. *Fuck! I need a cold shower*, he thought as he sat at his desk. He picked up his phone, hitting number two on his speed dial.

"Hi, love," his wife said as she answered the call.

"Hi, hun. Is everything alright?"

"What time will you be home?"

"Not sure yet. Probably seven."

"Okay. Well, I'm going to Zumba with Marsha. I will leave your dinner in the oven. Can you also pick up my dry cleaning on the way home? I forgot to pick it up on the way back from Merry Hill this morning."

"Sure," Paul said, not really paying attention.

"Okay. Well, I gotta run. See you this evening."

"See you later, hun. Bye." The line was already dead. He glanced across of the picture of his family on his desk. His two sons, Michael and Richard, smiled back at him as they flanked their mother. They were tall and blonde like their father. His wife was also smiling back, her chestnut hair framing an attractive face. The photograph had been taken a year before, at their holiday retreat in Looe, Cornwall. A lot had happened since then, and not all of it good. His marriage had taken a wobble, his wife Claire sleeping with another man who was a member at the local gym in Gloucester. Every time that she mentioned a gym class, Paul had a sinking feeling in his stomach. It was all his fault of course. Long hours, coupled with the boys heading off to University, had pushed his wife into the arms of another man. It had ended quickly when Paul found out, his wife stating that it was just a fling and that the man had paid her attention. Something that Paul was accused of not doing anymore. The last few months had been hard on him, ramping up his already high blood pressure. However, a few green shoots of recovery could now be seen sprouting in their relationship. They were spending more time together. Claire was spending less time at the gym, and less time with her single fifty-something friends. The sense of unease still gripped the man from time to time though. Still never quite leaving him be. He'd been married for twenty-seven years, proud in the knowledge that he had never strayed. Marriage was a long road, with several bumps, he'd always thought. You don't take the easy route just because it looks less bumpy. He took a sip of his coffee, clicking back into his mountain of emails as the afternoon wore on. *Might be eight o' clock*, he thought, as the darkening sky darkened some more behind him.

SEVENTEEN

BIFLUX

"OH HELL!" TREVIK SAID AS HE CLIMBED OUT OF THE CRAFT.

"What's wrong?" Torben replied as he joined the man next to the huge white pipeline.

"Something's ripped the control panel off the terminal. Here," the older man said as he handed Torben the rifle. "I'll get my tools from the craft. Keep your eyes open for predators."

"Okay," was his short reply as he took in the landscape around him. The Tundra of Biflux was a barren, desolate place. No trees or plants grew this far north. On the horizon, a cluster of mountains shimmered in the distance as the collective rays from the two suns cast their glow across the planet. Torben looked to the south, the line of evergreen trees that they had recently burst from still visible to the naked eye.

The older man came back with a leather pack slung over one shoulder. "Hopefully, it's just a few broken contacts. If not, the engineers from Halycon will have to pay a visit. Not today though. The suns will set within the hour."

Torben scanned the horizon once more, wondering what came out to play after dark. "Well, let's hope you can fix it. Then we can head back to Kiton."

"Tell me about it. Elsor is grilling steaks tonight on the patio. I don't want to miss that." They lapsed into silence for several minutes, the older man muttering under his breath as he tried to splice snapped wires together with a rubber sheath. The younger man circled the craft, his eyes playing out over their surroundings. He thought he spotted movement a few hundred yards to the south, and started walking a few paces, shielding his eyes from the setting suns. *Hmm. Probably nothing*, he thought as he slowly walked backwards towards the pipeline.

"How far does the pipeline run?" Torben asked, suddenly curious.

"It covers the whole planet. From pole to pole, north to south. It's actually a giant loop. There are research laboratories at both poles; the pipeline provides them with water, power, and other services."

"Impressive. How long did it take to construct?"

"Years. I oversaw most of the construction, many moons ago. It works really well, except when it gets damaged."

"What do you think caused the damage?"

"Hard to tell. We have some prints close by, take a look."

Torben walked closer to the pipeline, noticing the large indentations in the crisp snow. "Shit," he said as he stood in the centre of a giant footprint. "I hope whatever came by is long gone."

"Me too. It looks like Barnebaka."

"Barnebaka?"

"A large carnivore, white in colour. They roam the wilderness, picking up scraps or hunting smaller creatures that cross their paths." Trevik paused for a moment. "Almost done. I just need to refit the control panel access door."

"Great," the younger man whispered, wondering just how big a Barnebaka was. He turned, focusing on the patch of horizon that he'd been previously been scanning for life. Something looked different. A small rise of snow a few hundred metres away had vanished. Strange, he thought as he took a few steps forward, his boots crunching into the snow.

"Torben! Look out!"

The younger man spun around as a large white shape leapt over the small craft, landing between the two men. "Oh my…"

"Don't try and stun it. Set the rifle to automatic," the older man commanded.

The captain looked down at the trigger, his mind trying to compute how to activate automatic mode. A roar in front of him made Torben look up, his legs freezing to the ground like two stalactites. "Is that a Barnebaka?"

"Yes! Kill it!"

The creature was over seven metres tall, Torben guessing that it weighed more than the craft they'd travelled in. Its distorted feline features and large canines oozed menace as it advanced on him slowly. Its bristling white fur, stained with dried blood seemed to add to the danger he was now facing. Without thinking, Torben depressed the trigger, several blue flashes emanating from the barrel of the rifle. They found their mark, hitting the beast a metre down from its gaping maw. It roared in defiance, shifting sideways unsteadily as the tracer fire raked its fur. The beast tried one last advance, the life draining from its legs as it landed in a heap a few metres from Torben's boots. Before he could react, Trevik was snatching the rifle from his grasp. "What?" he said in a dazed tone.

"They always hunt pairs," the older man replied as another behemoth came charging towards them. The older man took aim, the barrel of the rifle tracking the movement of the monster bearing down on him. His breathing slowed as he depressed the trigger, hitting the dead creature's hunting partner full in the face. Red mist sprayed from the back of its huge skull as the beast died on the spot, toppling sideways, painting the surrounding snow a crimson red. "Good shooting, Torben. We should be leaving, especially after discharging the rifle. Any predator close by will be on us very quickly. Come." The young pilot needed no further coaxing as he followed the older man to the craft. Seconds later, they were ten metres above the ground, the ship slowly rotating towards the south. "Look. Razorbacks."

Torben watched in fascination as a pack of large wolf-like creatures appeared from the tree-line. They trotted forward, ten abreast. "Glad we left when we did."

"Me too. They would have had us for dinner. At least they will not go hungry. There is enough meat there to last them a few weeks. If they are feeding here, they will not venture south. A lot of the northern settlements have real problems with them. Hundreds of people are killed every year. I will send a message to Halycon. They will probably send drones up to wipe them out. Now let's go. All I can think about is Elsor's steaks."

"He was quite the hero," Trevik said as he clinked glasses with the others. "He took the Barnebaka down easily. Most men would have messed their pants and run in the other direction. Not this guy though."

"You've impressed him," Kyra said as Trevik stood next to Elsor, as she added four large steaks to the outdoor grill. "Just don't put yourself in danger again," she added, the woman's face dropping slightly.

"Don't worry. I'm not going to get that close again."

"Good. Relkon came down not far from the pipeline. I cannot lose you too."

Torben led her away from the others, sitting her down on a wooden swing bench. They looked out at the vast lake underneath them, both catching the shooting star that streaked across the sky above. The trees rustled gently in the cool breeze, the surface of the water choppy, white crests visible under the moonlight. "I know that you are still feeling the loss of Relkon."

"I loved him. But life does move on. That's what he would say. I never thought that I would meet someone so soon after his death. But I have, and I have grown very close to you, Torben."

"Likewise, Kyra. I've not felt this way in a long time. Since Hella."

"Was she your last partner?"

"Yes." He composed himself, feeling at ease as Kyra laced her fingers into his. "I was with her for a few years. We talked of a union, of a family."

"If you don't mind my asking, what happened?"

"My parents died, together in a fire at their home."

"Oh, I'm so sorry."

"It's okay. Anyway, Hella was staying with them. I was due back from an assignment, so she arrived a day before to welcome me home. When my parents went to bed, Hella stayed up drinking and smoking. I knew that she smoked, but she rarely did around me. She fell asleep on the floor of the living quarters, her pipe still lit. It somehow caught fire, spreading quickly throughout the whole house. Hella managed to escape. My parents didn't. They were overcome by fumes, probably. By the time the emergency responders arrived, the house was engulfed."

"Oh no! I am truly sorry," she said, hugging him.

Torben hugged her back, burying his face in her neck. "There was nothing the crews could do. I arrived the next day, seeing Hella sat on the front lawn, the house in ruins. I never blamed her. It was an accident, Kyra. Anyone could have made the same mistake. But Hella never got over it. She was consumed by guilt and grief. We tried to carry on, but it was no use. We drifted apart. Eventually, she called the whole thing off, taking an assignment on a nearby Orbital station.

That was the last time I saw or heard from her. Since then, I have just focused on my work. Travelling helps blot out the pain and loss."

"We have both lost. Maybe that's why we gravitated towards each other so quickly."

"I don't think it was that, Kyra."

"Really. Why not?" She pulled away from Torben, looking into his dark eyes.

"I just thought you were so hot."

She lightly punched his shoulder. "Trust a man to think on a more basic level." Kyra leaned forward, kissing him hard on the mouth. Torben snaked his arms around her, pulling her into his embrace. Up at the house, the couple watched on as steaks sizzled on the grill. Elsor threaded her arm through her husband's. "It's nice to see our girl happy again."

"Yes, it is. He seems a worthy partner. I have no fears over this one."

"Nor do I," his wife replied. "Maybe this is just what she needed."

"I think it's what we all needed, my love."

The next morning Kyra and Torben headed out of the cabin as the sun was low in the red sky. They were dressed accordingly, both wearing trousers, boots and warm jackets. "We can follow the forest until it reaches the headland."

"I'll follow you," he said. "I could do with a good walk after all that home cooking."

She smiled, prodding his midriff. "There's no fat on you. Which is a surprise, for a captain who just sits in his cockpit, looking out at space."

"I'll have you know I do far more than that. I could outrun you any day."

"Really? Would you like to wager that statement?"

"Sure. What did you have in mind?"

Kyra looked across the forest, evergreen trees dotted in haphazard fashion. "There. At the top of that small rise. Do you see the rocky outcrop?"

"I see it."

"Last one there cooks dinner tonight. And not just any dinner. It needs to come from the sea."

"You're on," he replied, readying himself for a bit of competition.

"Okay. Go," Kyra said, shooting ahead of the static Torben. He took off after her, his long strides scattering bracken as he quickly gained on Kyra's weaving run.

"You are about to lose," Torben said as he drew level.

She looked to her left, a determined smile on her face. "We'll see," she countered as they headed towards two trees that were barely four feet apart with low hanging branches. As they passed the trees, Kyra pulled a branch down, ducking below it as Torben ran headlong into it.

"What the…" he said as foliage and twigs filled his vision, making Torben give ground. He swiped the branch away, noticing that Kyra now had an unassailable lead as her strides took her towards her goal.

"Come on, old man," she taunted as her feet landed on the rocky outcrop.

Jogging up the last of the hill, he smiled at her, knowing he'd been outsmarted. "So, that's how you win? Are all folk from Cantis so devious?"

"We do whatever it takes," she panted, her breath coming back under control.

"I'll remember that for next time. So, where do we go now?"

Kyra pointed off into the forest, the lock of red hair shimmering in the sunlight. "You see up there?" she motioned. "Where the trees thin out, there's a pathway. That leads all the way to the sea. It's probably a good hour walk."

"We didn't bring any drinks," Torben said, his mouth parched after his exertions.

"It's okay. There is a small-holding next to a dry dock on the shore. They sell food and drink. We may even be able to have lunch there."

"You think of everything." They walked a steady pace up the gradual incline, the trees thinning out. Small animals crossed their path, darting into the undergrowth when they saw the advancing couple. "What kind of creatures do you have out here?" Torben asked.

"Nothing to worry about. The little furry ones that we've just seen are called bootles. We also have dak daks and wild swarts. Father could tell you more. He walks these forests all the time; mother does too. The further north you go, the more the animals become a little more challenging. There are large carnivores, similar to what you encountered with Father. However, we're far enough away. The most dangerous predators around us are in the ocean. And I don't plan on taking a plunge today."

"Okay. Well, I'm staying close to you. If anything attacks us, you can swat them away with a branch. You're pretty handy at that."

"Still smarting about that are we?"

"I was kidding. You're very competitive, just like me." They fell silent for a while, enjoying the landscape unfold around them. Torben took it all in, enjoying the sound of the waves as they crashed onto the peninsular below him. He spotted several birds of prey above, floating on the thermals, looking for food. Kyra walked next to him, her carefree stride matching his own. After a while they began a steady descent, the path becoming rocky and uneven. Torben weaved around trees as the path fell away into the forest on either side, with Kyra following suit until they came out on a flat path next to the sea.

"Bolorex Ocean."

"It's beautiful. Where I'm from in Walvak, the coastline is far more industrial. This is unspoilt. It's breathtaking."

"It sure is," she replied, taking his hand in her own. "If we walk along the path for about a mile, there is the small-holding I told you about. They do excellent graff, and spiced muffins that bring travellers from far and wide."

"Sounds great." They headed off, the rocky shore a grey barrier between them and the sea. Birds of all sizes could be seen over land and sea, bringing life to the horizon. To the right, the forest rose gradually, the sun filtering through the swaying branches.

"Such a peaceful place," Kyra said quietly. "I came here a lot after the war. The sea air seemed to help."

Torben wrapped an arm around her shoulder, kissing the top of her head. "I'm sure it did," as a stone build building came into view, perched over the sea on a rocky ledge. Small craft were moored on a wooden jetty nearby, and Torben noticed a sea-breaker a few hundred yards across the water. "Does that keep the big stuff out?"

"You can relax. Nothing longer than my arm swims in this cove."

"Good to know," he replied, noticing more craft parked across from the building in a small clearing. Some were grounded, and a few were hovering a few feet from the floor, awaiting their owners.

"So, shall we grab a bite to eat?"

"Sounds good to me," he responded, following her inside the building. Above the door was an intricately carved sign. *Bethelba's Cabin*. "Nice name."

"Lovely isn't it. Wait till you meet her. She is a sweetheart."

They took a table next to the sea as spray gently fell against the windows. Torben could see movement underneath the surface, roiling tails swarming together just a few feet from their table. Gentle music drifted across the interior, string and wind instruments adding to the ambience. The décor was to his liking too, with skulls of sea creatures adorning the walls. The centrepiece of the room made him gape in amazement - a huge skull set into the stone walls and ceiling with a fire grate inside the gaping maw, still filled with razor-sharp teeth. "Wow. That's pretty impressive," he said.

"It's a breekin skull. Huge isn't it. We should come here at night. When the fire is crackling away, it's quite a sight to see."

"Hello, Kyra," a deep female voice said across the room. Torben looked over at the advancing woman, his eyes widening for a split-second.

"Hello, Bethelba, lovely to see you."

The woman bent down, enveloping Kyra in a hug. "Not seen you here for a while?"

"No, I've been away on an assignment. This is Torben."

He rose from his chair, dwarfed by the woman in front of him. Craning his neck, Torben looked up at her, smiling. "Pleased to meet you," he said warmly, liking the friendly face of the proprietor. Her blonde hair that almost touched the ceiling was set in twin side tails that ran almost down to her waist, leather thongs woven into the braids.

She extended her hand which Torben took readily, his own hand almost lost from sight in her embrace. "Nice to meet you too. I hope you're hungry. We've just started to roast some razor shells on the griddle."

"Sounds just what we need, thank you," he said sitting down at the table.

"What can I get you to drink?"

Kyra looked at Torben. "Graff?"

"Graff sounds good to me."

"Okay. I'll bring them over, along with two menus. Relax and enjoy the view." She walked off, her footsteps thumping on the stone floor.

"She seems nice," he said.

"Bethelba is lovely, although she is not one to cross. She can be pretty formidable."

"I bet she can. She must be three metres tall."

"Easily. She's lived here all her life. The place used to belong to her parents. They died a few years ago in a fishing accident out at sea."

"Oh dear, such sad news," he replied, not knowing what else to say.

"Yes, it was. But Bethelba is a force of nature. She threw herself into the place, putting her own stamp on it. Mother and Father come here quite a lot."

"I can see why. It's very impressive."

"Just wait until you sample the cooking. You'll be setting up camp outside."

"Or in your cabin."

She smiled, reaching across the table to take his hand. "I could quite happily stay in the cabin with you for the rest of my days."

Goosebumps appeared across his arms, his face flushing. "Thank you, Kyra. You really are a wonderful Cantisian."

"And you're a wonderful Walvaker. One of the nicest I've ever met."

"Only one of them?" he said, mock indignation framing his features.

"The day is young. I may move you to the top of the list after sundown," she said with a playful wink.

EIGHTEEN

VALKASH

GEMMA WOKE UP WITH A START. ARTIFICIAL LIGHT STREAMED in through the windows. She had lost track of how many days she had been living this nightmare. It seemed like a month had passed when in reality it had been a little over a week. She rolled off the bed, wondering what the time was, which was ridiculous. *Who cares what time it is? It's not like I have to be anywhere.* Which technically was not true. She needed to be at a meeting. An escape meeting. Gemma padded downstairs in clean clothing, not quite the right fit nor colour. But it would do. Call it prison clothing, she had thought to herself a few days before when she had opened the wardrobe in her bedroom, the doors not quite closing properly.

Twenty minutes later, she was striding towards the village hall, her boots slapping the moist pavement. *How does it rain here? Do they have a sprinkler system?* Her thoughts were interrupted by a waving woman from across the street. "Hiya," Caroline called.

"Hello," Gemma replied in a friendly manner. "You ready to chop off alien hands and make a dash for it?"

"If only it was that simple eh? I'm sure we'd be tasered or

blasted by ray guns within minutes," Caroline responded readily. "Like something out of *Star Trek*?"

"Probably," Gemma replied with a half-smirk. "I'm more
of a *Star Wars* fan. *Han Solo* and all that."

"I see where you're coming from. Knowing my luck, I'd
end up with *Chewbacca*."

Gemma chuckled. "That bad huh?"

"Oh, I don't know. I like them hairy." Both women
laughed as they made their way to the entrance of the hall. A
group of villagers had gathered in the main room, sitting on
chairs in a haphazard way. Martin and Pete were slouched
against the stage, exchanging words. They quickly ended the
conversation as Caroline, Katie and a few other women
headed towards them.

Pete straightened up, trying to appear taller. He'd attended
a management course a few years previously, his tutor telling
him that it gave an air of authority. The problem was Pete was
under six feet tall, only a few inches taller than some of the
females heading his way. His dander was up though, ready for
a fight. "What's the order of the meeting? Space-age
cookery?"

"Fuck off, Pete," Caroline answered. "You're clearly pissed
that you lost the vote to a woman. Has your male pride taken
a blow? Is that why you're standing tall, trying to intimidate
us?"

"I don't have to answer to the likes of you. You're not even
a villager!"

"No. I'm not. Yet your villagers voted for an outsider over
yourself. So, what does that say about you? I'd go and ponder
that whilst we have our meeting."

Pete strode by them, nudging Caroline's shoulder enough
to raise a few collective gasps from the hall. Martin followed,
hands pushed deep into his pockets. "Ignore him," Gemma
said quietly. Clearly, he's got an inferiority complex."

"Or a tiny cock," Katie added drily, making the women

howl with laughter. Seconds went by until they regained their composure, turning towards the rest of the attendees, slightly red-faced.

Caroline addressed them. "We're working on a few things, nothing really to report as of yet. Hopefully, by the end of the week, we'll have something more to update you on. As you have all seen, food has been delivered around the village." People nodded as they'd all been coming across the pallets of goods that were sporadically placed around the replica village. "The reason for the meeting is to ask if anyone has any burning issues, apart from the obvious?"

A man at the rear of the hall raised his hand. Caroline nodded towards him. "Many of the kids are playing too close to the perimeter. Have you seen the things that surround us? I would hate to think what could happen if one of those creatures somehow got out?"

"Yes, we have. Why are they not using the playground?"

"Playgrounds are boring," the man replied. "Kids are kids. If there is a giant reptile a few hundred yards away, they will go and look at that. Some of the kids have been throwing stones at the glass walls, which is not a good idea."

"I agree," Caroline replied. "I'm no expert on this kind of thing, but I am pretty sure that these glass walls could cope with stones and bricks hitting them. But our kids should not be doing it. Many of us have had a good explore of the surrounding village. The place is a giant fishbowl. Nothing is getting out, nothing is coming in. But we need a rule. All children must not stray away from the playground and village centre. We've not got anywhere that we need to be. No work or holidays to think about, so is it unreasonable to ask that parents accompany their children to the playground and other parts of the main village? Does anyone have any objections to that?" The villagers shook their collective heads in unison. "Okay. That's one thing sorted. Anything else?"

A young woman with a child on her lap raised her hand.

Caroline had not spoken to her before, nor really noticed her until now. She nodded at the woman. "I have a nut allergy and I only eat gluten-free products. Do you think we can request this?"

A few people snorted and laughed, an older man turning to the woman. "Is that all you're bloody worried about? Gluten-free? In my day you ate what was given. There was none of this new-age crap. Nut allergy? Lactose intolerance? It's all a bloody con."

The woman looked embarrassed, turning a deep pink. However, she held her ground. "And maybe that's why the older generation didn't live as long?"

"Why?" the old man countered. "I don't bloody remember reading about masses of people dying because their biscuits contained bloody peanuts and gluten."

"I think this is getting out of hand," Gemma called out. "We will speak to their people when they are next here. After all, they've built a planetary zoo. They may be able to come up with something suitable. I'm sure we may have vegetarians and vegans amongst us. They should also be catered for?" The old man stood up, clearly bristling. Before he could direct his tirade towards Gemma, she nipped the argument in the bud. "I'm also sure they could supply us with various types of beer. I'm guessing you're a real ale man?"

"I like my mild," he replied, his face gradually softening.

Gemma smiled. She had tasted mild, a slightly weaker version of ale. She could almost smell the aroma, sparked from distant memories. "That was my grandfather's favourite. I will make sure we ask for something that fits the bill for you. What's your name by the way? I don't believe we've met."

"Bill," he responded, the bristle ebbing out of his body.

"Okay, Bill. Leave it with us."

. . .

They stood outside after the rest of the villagers had filed away back to their homes. Katie sat down on a bench, rubbing her ankle. "Bloody thing is playing up again."

"Are you okay?" Caroline asked, mildly concerned.

"I'll be fine. Just old age creeping up on me."

"Something else we may need to ask for," Gemma added. "Medicine. That can be the top of the agenda at the next meeting. We may have diabetics, people with high blood pressure or asthmatics. I'm surprised no one has raised it yet?"

"Me neither come to think about it," Caroline said. I'm on statins back home. I never gave it a thought until now. My cholesterol is probably through the roof."

Kimberley headed towards the path, turning towards the other three women. "I'd better go. Martin does not approve of our little union. So I'd better get back and see that the kids are okay."

"That's fine, hun," Caroline replied. "If this is a problem, just let us know. We have enough to worry about without rifts behind closed doors."

"I'm sure it will be fine. He's just a bit of an old dinosaur sometimes. Women should be cooking whilst the men make the decisions."

"Believe me, he's not the only man who shares that viewpoint," Caroline said. "We'll see you tomorrow, lovely." They all bid her farewell as another woman approached the threesome. Gemma had spoken to her a few times in the school playground. She was roughly her own age, with a young son. However, that's where the similarities ended. The woman approaching had closely cropped blonde hair, longer and messier on top. She had more tattoos than Gemma could count, and her ears and nose pierced numerous times. She reminded Gemma of a pop singer, who'd died a few years before. However, now on the other side of the universe, the name escaped her. She wore a black leather jacket, with a

micro mini-skirt and ankle boots. Gemma was slightly intimidated by her brash look.

"Hello," she said politely, her voice soft. "I'm Sarah. I was
wondering if you could request something for me?"

"We can but try, hun," Caroline said warmly. "What do
you need?"

"Tights. This is my only pair and I laddered them this
morning."

The women looked down at the woman's shapely legs,
appraising them in their own way. Running up the left calf, a
ladder could be seen against the flesh coloured material. Caroline smiled. "Not a problem, hun. I could do with a few new
pairs of knickers too." They all stood there chatting,
conversing like women do in every village on Earth. And
beyond.

"Oh my," Lawrence said, as he peered through the impenetrable glass. The boys had taken a walk to the far side of the
village, away from the houses and village hall. They both
stood, hands planted against the solid glass structure, eyes
wide open.

"Is it a ghost? Tristan asked as a wraith-like figure floated
in front of them. Its mouth was a blackened maw, eyes
burning back at them, tinged with red.

"I really don't know," the elder brother replied quietly.
"Look at the trees!"

The younger brother did so, his eyes taking in everything
before him. The trees and vegetation inside the opposite
enclosure swayed and pulsed, green and blue flashes
appearing on leaves and branches. "It's scary."

"It is a bit," Lawrence replied as more wraiths appeared
through the eerie forest. Winged creatures floated passed,
almost in slow motion, as they began climbing towards the

thick canopy above. The air in the forest seemed to shift and move, tendrils of mist wrapping themselves around tree trunks and branches. "I wonder what planet this is supposed to be?"

"Maybe it's like *Avatar?*"

"Don't be silly. There is no such planet."

"I'm not silly," the younger brother admonished. "It looks like something from a movie."

"If it does, it's not the kind of movie you should be watching. You're only eight."

"I'm nearly nine."

"Well I'm nearly thirteen, and even I would not watch movies with those in," he said, pointing as the wraiths peered at them through the glass walls. "Come on," Lawrence said. "Let's see if we can see any other worlds next to ours."

They walked off, Tristan taking his older brother's hand. They skipped down the tarmac roadway, heading off on another adventure.

A while after leaving the village hall, Pete and Martin stood on the fringes of the village, looking through the glass wall that held them captive. "Fucking bitch!" Pete spat, clearly riled from his earlier encounter.

"Relax, mate. They are women. Do you think they will be able to run this ship? No chance. Give them a couple of weeks and they will come begging for our help. What do you do, back on Earth?" Martin thought his question sounded surreal.

"I'm a site manager for a drinks company. Davies Wilmott. We transport our products across Europe. And you?"

"I'm a health and safety manager for a logistics company."

Pete did the math in his head. *Site manager beats safety manager hands down. I manage people. He's just a nerd with a clipboard. He may be a useful ally though. I will reel him in.* "A noble job. I wanted to go into safety a few years ago."

"Why didn't you?" Martin countered.

"Timing. This job came up so I took it. We have a few safety managers where I work. They are always fighting the good fight."

"That's what we do. Do you think your family are okay back home?"

The question caught Pete off-guard. His wife and children had been at their caravan in Weston-super-Mare when he had been taken. He was only at the festival so he could buy a carved pumpkin for their home. A pumpkin that his two children, Tabatha and Rex, would have loved. His wife, Jenny, would have made cakes and treats for the local children as they turned up at their impressive detached bungalow. It would have been a typical family Halloween. Pete may even have ventured out of his study to participate. Or he would have observed from the lounge whilst watching the football on his new Ultra High-Definition television. He missed his family, which added to his usual prickly demeanour. *If only this had happened a day later. I would have been in Weston with the others,* he thought sadly. "Yes, I do", he replied after a few seconds of melancholy. "But I'm glad they are not caught up in all this. They are probably worried sick. Plus, they would have to have gotten a train home, as I was due to collect them the following day. Fuck! What a mess!"

"Don't worry, Pete. We will get out of this."

"How? You heard what these people said. We're on the other side of space. I don't claim to be an expert on this. But if it takes a satellite thirty or forty years to reach the edges of our solar system, how the hell do we get home?"

"When you put it like that, yes, it sounds bleak. But there must be something we can do. I for one do not want to spend the rest of my days in a fucking bowl, surrounded by things that look like they come from a Hollywood movie. I want to get home. And soon."

. . .

A few hundred yards away, Lawrence and Tristen were hunkered down next to the access door at the edge of the village. The next enclosure they found offered no excitement for the brothers, who decided to head back towards the centre of the village, darting through fields to remain out of sight. They sat there, obscured from sight by a low stone wall, which they had erected a makeshift shelter over. No one could see them. Not humans, nor aliens. They were completely hidden. Lawrence looked at his younger brother, knowing that he had to take Tristan on his adventures or risk the little shit telling their parents about what they were getting up to. So here they were, hiding out away from everyone else. Their mother had told them that throwing stones at the monsters was strictly not allowed. Something they reluctantly agreed with. But she never said that they could not look at them. "Just keep quiet Tris," Lawrence said. "We don't want anyone to find our secret base."

"Okay, Lawrence," his brother said sternly, his blue eyes set defiantly. Lawrence leaned forward, ruffling his brother's curly blonde hair as a noise to their right startled them. He placed a finger to his mouth, telling his brother to remain quiet. He did so as a large pair of legs strode past them. The elder brother peered around the side of the shelter, watching in awe as the giant with four arms headed towards the village. His vision shifted left, eyes widening as he saw that the access door still open. "Stay here," he said before silently padding over to the door.

"What are you doing?" Tristan asked quizzically.

"Just gonna take a quick look," his brother replied, ducking into the door before it closed.

Tristan scrambled out of their hideout, looking to his right at the giant alien, his long strides propelling him towards the village hall. The young boy turned left, smiling at his brother who was standing behind a glass door. "Come back out Lawrence. Mummy will be cross if you are caught."

His brother mouthed something, the sound sealed off by the door and glass walls. On the other side, Lawrence looked at a control panel next to the door. It was different to the one of the other side. Lawrence had watched many movies where a handprint took the hero through security doors on his journey towards a happy ending. On this side, only a glowing green button presented itself. He leaned forward, pressing the button with his index finger. The door hissed open, and Tristan skipped from the village onto the metal walkway. He banged his feet on the ground, a hollow reverberation echoing through the thin confines. "Shh!" Lawrence hissed. "We don't want anyone to hear us."

"Look," Tristan said in awe.

Lawrence looked past him, along the metal walkway. "It's huge," he said as he took a step forward. The gridded walkway disappeared into the distance on both sides as far as the eye could see. They walked a few hundred paces ahead, coming to a stop at a recess in the walkway. There a large, rounded plate sat gently glowing on the floor. "It looks like a lift," Lawrence said, noticing a virtual control panel shimmering on the glass wall. He pressed a button, and the platform dropped down several feet until they could see another walkway below. It was deathly quiet, except for the occasional beep of an unseen machine below. "We'd better not go too much further," Lawrence said. "We may get lost in here. Mum and Dad would flip-out."

"Okay. Shall we go back?"

"Yes, I think we should," the elder brother said readily. They were about to turn back when a loud thump to their left echoed through the thin passageway.

"Look at that!" Tristan said, pointing through the glass.

"Shit," Lawrence said. "What the hell is it?"

"Dinosaur," the younger sibling said matter-of-factly.

"It's not a dinosaur. They died out millions of years ago. This must be a creature from another planet." They both watched, feet frozen to the floor as a silent roar emanated from the mouth of the reptilian-like creature. The boys had to crane their necks to look at it, such was its height. "It's the size of a bus. How many legs does it have?"

"Six I think. Look at its teeth."

Lawrence looked into the yellow eyes of the creature staring back, noting the feral look the beast had. It advanced again, bouncing its huge skull against the glass. The thing shook its head from side to side, turning away from the boys as it plodded through thick vegetation. "Let's see where the big green monster is heading," he said, pulling Tristan after him. A minute later, they were stood by the door that led into the alien enclosure, trying to see where the massive creature had disappeared too. "It's probably camouflaged by the forest."

"What's calloflaged?"

"Camouflaged. It means hidden. It's probably looking for its dinner." They stood for a few minutes, watching the strange forest pulsate in front of them. Trees and large purple plants seemed to sway back and forth as rain splattered against the glass.

"Look," Tristan said. "It looks like a rabbit."

Lawrence followed his brother's pointed finger to a gap in the undergrowth. A small brown mammal appeared, seeming to sniff the air. It was no bigger than a house cat, its nose unusually long, set underneath large dish-sized ears. "He's cute, probably making sure the big lizard has walked off."

"Let's take a closer look," the younger brother said.

"No, Tristan. We'll be in trouble if we go in there. And we may get stuck on the other side. Do you want the monster to come back and eat you?"

"No. But he's gone now. Come on. Just a little look," he pleaded as he pressed the button next to the door.

Before Lawrence knew what was happening, Tristan darted through the open doorway. "NOOO!" he shouted. It was the last noise that his baby brother heard. The younger boy collapsed to the floor a few feet from the doorway. Lawrence watched in frozen horror as his prone brother snapped in half from his sitting position. "TRISTAN!" he screamed, watching as gravity bore-down on the eight-year-old, crushing his body as if he were in an invisible press. Without thinking, Lawrence ran to his brother's aid, not understanding what was happening. Not comprehending the physics involved. He fell next to him, the oxygen in his lungs being crushed down to a molecular level by the atmosphere around him. The last thing he saw before his skull imploded was a lumbering pair of reptilian feet crashing through the forest in front of him. Then, darkness.

NINETEEN

"That's impressive," Ragyi said as he peered through the window.

"It's like a mini star," Ullar added, taking in the giant orbital station that floated in the vacuum of space ahead of them. "So bright against the darkness."

"It will be even brighter soon. Ragyi, are you sure that your contact will come through for us?"

"He will give his life for the cause. Once I send the signal, he will lock onto our position. He will deactivate a small section of the shield for a few seconds, allowing us to pass through. It's standard procedure. Freighters come and go. But most freighters have clearance codes. We don't. That's where Fazit comes in. He will let us through before creating the diversion we talked about."

Hameda nodded, remembering the plan. Once on the other side of the shield, the martyr would start a fire in one of the hangars, creating a panic. They knew their window was short. Ten minutes at best. Ragyi had assured his leader that they would have enough time to fire the magnetic warhead at the underside of the orbital. Once it was in place, it would detonate two minutes later, releasing a payload of fifty kilotons, destroying the station. Once obliterated, the shield that would halt their escape would vanish with the station, along with the millions that now called it home. *For Barajan*, she thought as she gripped the arm-rests of her seat.

"We're 100 miles from the orbital," the pilot said.

"Sending the signal. Move to within one click of the shield," Ragyi replied, pressing a button on his palm pilot. A minute later, it beeped. "Shield down. Head for the underside of the structure as quick as you can."

"Heading up now. Preparing warhead. There will be a few patrolling craft, looking for threats. Let's hope this old freighter doesn't draw suspicion. If it does, we have no way out. They will be armed. Things could get a little bumpy."

A few minutes later, the freighter hovered fifty feet below the massive structure. They looked up through the cockpit window, in awe of the size of the object that they were about to destroy. "It's huge," Ullar stated flatly. Like a small satellite."

"Not for much longer," Hameda said. "Pilot, are you certain that you can make this work?"

"Yes. The device is highly magnetised. We don't really need much propulsion. Polarity will do our work for us. As soon as it's attached, I will get us the hell out of here before the patrols spot us. I'll head vertically away from the blast zone. Any crafts in the vicinity will be vaporised."

"Good," she cooed. "Whenever you're ready."

The pilot swiped a finger across the heads-up display, pressing virtual buttons in front of his swarthy face. "Warhead deployed." Then a few seconds later, "warhead secure. Let's move," he said, depressing the thruster with his right hand. The ungainly freighter ploughed through space, heading towards the other side of the orbital. Two minutes later, they felt the concussion from the blast. A ripple in space fanning out in front of the craft, buffeting them in their seats. "I hope the shield is deactivated," the pilot said nervously. "Or we're all dead." A few tense seconds flew past until he breathed out. "We're though. The shield was shut down when the explosion took hold. Initiating rear camera."

The three others watched the carnage unfold behind them. The orbital silently breaking up into many smaller parts, large explosions decimating the interior landscape. The detail on the screen was such that Hameda could almost see the countless thousands being sucked out into space as the station fell apart around them. She smiled, not in joy for the innocent victims, but in the success of what they were about to achieve. "Pilot. How far to the nearest wormhole?"

"Not far. We should reach it in twenty hours. Once through, Biflux is another two days travel. Once we've hit it, we will take another wormhole that leads to the system where Valkash lies. If things go smoothly, we should have obliterated the remaining two main targets in six days."

"Excellent. Head for the wormhole. I think this calls for a celebration. Ullar, inform the galley that we require dinner for four, including our pilot, Ragyi."

"Yes, Hameda," the man said expectantly.

"Go to my quarters. And de-robe."

Later, the three of them sat around a white table as plates were cleared away, drinks refreshed. The space was low and grey, similar tables dotted around the room. A small window offered a limited view of the outside void. A void that was flying past at 6,000,000 miles-per-hour, propelled by a twin ion drive. Hameda had a perpetual smile etched across her face, Ragyi also. It was only Ullar that seemed level and neutral. She knew what had just taken place in her leader's quarters. She was not jealous. She took men and women, regardless of race or colour, into her bunk. She decided to break the warm glow that emanated from her friends. "What happens after Valkash?"

Hameda looked at her and smiled. "The factions will come back together. The Lomogs think they are scattered, which in essence, they are. However, I have been in contact with them. They knew that I was loyal to Barajan. Once they see what we have achieved, they will form a solid union with us."

"Where will you base this union?" Ragyi asked.

"Lundell."

The others sat back, smiling at each other. They had both visited the small moon that was in orbit around Biflux. They knew that it had a large base there that the Lomogs had quickly inherited from the Biflex people. It shared the same atmosphere with its host planet, with rainfall and one significant ocean. It was perfect. "What about security?" Ragyi countered.

"Minimal. The Lomogs rely on Biflux for their security. Once hit, the Biflex people will be in a state of disarray for a while. By the time we have returned from their attraction, the factions will be in orbit around Lundell. I will save one warhead, which will accompany us as we seize their base. If things go badly, I will detonate it, taking all of us at once. Then, no one will rule. But I don't think it will come to that. We will have a dozen ships, with over a thousand loyal fighters. The tin-framed bastards won't know what's hit them."

TWENTY

2104 AMBLED TOWARDS THE VILLAGE HALL, HIS ARMS SWINGING gently in the artificial breeze. He'd passed two male humans who were stood chatting on the outskirts of the village. He'd greeted them politely before heading further into the village, to find the leaders. A minute later, his lumbering gait brought him to the village hall, spotting four females standing outside. "Greetings," he said respectfully.

"Hello," Caroline replied, dwarfed by his bulk. "What have we done now?"

"I don't believe you have done anything? I was merely paying you a visit."

"Good. Because we have a request."

"I am listening," 2104 replied readily.

"Some of the villagers need medicines. Others can only eat certain foods too. If we're to stay here, we need the things that were available on Earth. Like alcohol, underwear and medication to start with. Does that sound okay?"

2104 keyed a command into his wrist pilot. "The order has been sent through"

"Thank you," Caroline replied, feeling a little easier. "Is there anything else that you need to talk to us about?"

"I am here to let you know that you can expect your first visitors very soon. Look up at the dome."

The four women did so, wondering exactly what it was they should be looking at. "And?" Katie said, slightly confused.

"Over there is a doorway," he said, pointing into the distance. "When the craft approaches, the door will open, placing the visitors into an ante-chamber. Once pressurised, the door will open, letting the visitors observe your village from the safety of the pods. They…" 2104 stopped talking as his wrist started vibrating. He looked down at the device strapped to his beefy forearm, his brow knitting in concern. "That cannot be possible?"

"What's wrong?" Gemma asked, slightly concerned.

"The perimeter door has been breached. The alarm is sounding. Someone from the village must have somehow gained access."

"But how?" Gemma asked, her concern growing.

"I do not know. But if they are inside the walkway, then they have." His voice died in his throat as he took off away from the women, sprinting at full-pelt towards the invisible walls that held them all captive.

"I don't like the sound of this," Gemma said, following the alien away from the village hall. The other three women gave chase, Katie lagging behind because of her sore ankle.

A minute later, 2104 reached the doorway, panting slightly. He looked left and right across the walkway beyond the glass, checking for signs of life. Ahead, a large green reptilian creature had its snout in the undergrowth, oblivious to the sets of eyes that were watching it. "Well?" Caroline said, trying to regain her breath as she came to a halt next to him.

"I can see nothing wrong from here," he said as the others came to a stop next to them. "The door into the control area is closed. And I can see no signs of intruders." He was about to speak again when he noticed something in the next enclosure that stalled his words. "Oh no!"

"What?" Sarah said. They all followed 2104's pointed finger, watching in horror as the creature in the next enclosure lifted its head, a pair of blood-soaked jeans hanging from its jaws.

"Fuck! Is that what I think it is?" Gemma said, her stomach turning to lead.

"Looks like clothing," Katie responded, the colour draining from her face.

"Stay here all of you," the alien commanded. "I will take a closer look." He left them, his feet dragging across the ground as he plodded towards the doorway. 2104 placed a hand on the pulsing control panel, the glass door sliding open silently. He stepped onto the metal walkway, his feet clanking, shattering the silence within. The four women edged forward until they were only a few feet behind him. On the other side of the glass, the creature pulled a lump of distorted flesh from the undergrowth, raising its head as it quickly gulped it down greedily.

"OH MY GOD!" Caroline screamed, just able to make out the shape of a ruined head with blonde hair before it was consumed by the reptilian creature in front of them. The women clung to each other as 2104 spoke into the device strapped to his wrist in a language they did not understand, or notice, as the horrific scene played out in front of them.

"Go back to the village," the alien said. "Gather everyone and see who is missing."

"What do you think happened?" Katie said, tears streaking her face.

"It's possible that someone from the village gained access to the walkway, although I cannot comprehend how they did it. Once inside, they must have accessed the next enclosure. If they did that, the atmosphere would have crushed them instantly."

"Oh god!" Caroline said, clinging to Sarah who was swaying in her arms.

"Go, now. I will be along shortly. The maintenance and rescue crews are heading our way. You do not want to see what they discover. Go to the village and perform a headcount."

The women headed off, their strides unsteady as the realisation of what may have happened suddenly sunk in. A minute later they came across Pete and Martin, who were chatting next to a stone wall. Both men instantly saw the expressions heading towards them. "What's wrong?" Pete said.

"Come back to the village with us. We need to round everyone up immediately. Someone may have gained access to the enclosure next to us."

"What? Are you serious?" Martin said, his voice edged with concern.

"Deadly serious. Come on. We need to do a roll-call."

Kimberley folded to the floor, Martin barely able to catch her as the woman's head bounced off the wooden tiles. A few shocked exclamations rang out across the room as the man held his limp wife in his arms, tears falling from his face. 2104 stood over him before turning to the villagers. "Everyone must proceed to their homes immediately."

"You bastard. You've kidnapped us, and now two little boys are dead!" a man spat from the rear of the hall.

Others joined in. "Murderer!" a young woman hollered.

"Bastards!"

"Monsters!"

"Please. Go to your homes," the alien persisted. "Our teams will find out what happened. No one is to leave their homes until I say so." Reluctantly, the villagers filed out, curses echoing through the emptying hall. 2104 looked at the four women in front of him, trying not to look at the man sat below him. "We will take a look at the imagery. We will find out what happened."

"What happened is that two boys have been killed!" Gemma replied, her voice edged with fury. "Two little boys who you've snatched from their homes. Now they are dead. Their blood is on your hands."

Martin looked up, his face streaked with tears, his eyes red-rimmed. "I'm going to fucking kill you. You've killed my sons." The alien tried to respond, realising quickly that his words were futile. He walked away, head bowed.

"We need to get out of here," Caroline said. "This situation is fucked up beyond belief. I am so sorry, Martin. Really I am."

"Get out!" he hissed. "All of you. Leave us."

The four women complied without argument, leaving the grieving man cradling his wife's head as more tears fell. Outside, the women stood in their own collective silence. Caroline walked off towards the outskirts of the village. "Where are you going?" Gemma asked.

"I don't know. I don't know anything anymore. I just feel numb." The others stood awhile, not knowing what to do. After a few minutes, they said their goodbyes, heading towards their respective homes, utterly broken.

"It has been confirmed by the footage. The humans entered the walkway as you exited. They must have been hiding close by."

2104 looked at the floor, his arms swaying gently. "How do we stop this happening again?"

"We? There is no we, 2104. You have been relieved of

your post," the figure said in front of him. Ash looked up at his superior, blanching at the look of fury on his dark face. He stood there, under a bright light that shone down from the ceiling, making the meeting all the more intimidating for Ash. He thought of his family, wishing that he was with them. Safe with them. Happy with them. "You will be sent back to your station. From there, your superiors will decide on your next assignment. Believe me, it will not be a good one. Now, leave. You have already created a huge mess. A mess that I have to clean up." Ash turned and walked towards the door, a feeling of utter dejection washing over him. As the doors opened, he turned left towards his quarters, wondering where he would be banished to, more thoughts of his loved ones bringing tears to his eyes.

TWENTY-ONE

BIFLUX

"DESTROYED? HOW?" KYRA ASKED, RUBBING THE LAST vestiges of sleep from her eyes.

"They do not know yet. They are not ruling anything out though. I really hope it is not the stirrings of another crazed faction." Trevik looked at his daughter, a feeling of unease settling over him. Outside the wind was stiffening, the trees swaying and protesting against the coming storm. White-caps could be seen by the shore, the waters becoming choppy and angry.

"I must tell Torben."

"Okay. I have a few things to take care of. Elsor will be down shortly."

"I will come back in a bit, Father." She walked forward, embracing him. Trevik closed his eyes, enjoying the moment. Moments that were too scant for his liking.

Kyra walked down the pathway to the cabin, steam from the mugs of graff lost on the breeze. A minute later she was battling the wooden door, finally latching it shut as the gale pummelled the rough planks. Torben lay on the bunk, his upper body exposed. Kyra looked at the man in front of her, a look of sadness on her face. "What's wrong? Your wrist pilot has been buzzing."

"An orbital has been destroyed," Kyra replied as she walked over to the bunk. She placed both mugs on a small wooden table, clicking her device onto her arm.

"Oh no, where?"

"Between here and Valkash. Completely destroyed. No survivors."

"Do they know how it happened?"

"Not yet. Orbitals have been known to malfunction, their reactors going critical. I don't know, it just seems a bit too much of a coincidence that it was destroyed just after the war has ended."

"I know what you mean. I feel truly sorry for the loss of life, but I am hoping that it was a malfunction, not an act of aggression."

"Me too," she said as she landed next to him, grabbing her wrist pilot. She cuddled next to him as an image appeared before their eyes. A holographic image of a man appeared, his bald head and dark glasses floating in front of Kyra.

"Medical Officer Zakx. You are to report to command immediately. We have a medical emergency on Valkash. Two human children have been killed. Also, the humans need medical supplies for certain conditions and ailments that they have. The file is attached to this message. When you report to your station, please visit my lab. Most of the items listed we are synthesizing as I speak. You must go to Valkash, administer the medication and find out the causes of the fatalities. Chief Medical Officer Bromax, out."

The image fizzled out, the wind outside the only sound they could hear. After a moment, Torben turned to Kyra. "Looks like our time together is coming to an end."

"I know. And I do not like it. I wish I could get out of this, Torby. But you know I can't."

He kissed her, wrapping an arm around her body, pulling

the woman into him. "I know. And I know that I will soon be given a new assignment. It just seems like time is against us."

"When will I see you again?"

"Soon, hopefully. I've just found you. I do not want you to vanish into the cosmos."

"That is not going to happen. I have grown very close to you, Torben, in a very short space of time. My feelings are growing stronger, which surprises me."

"Mine too, Kyra. I think I'm falling in love with you."

She hugged him, burying her face into his dark hair. "I thought I would be the one to say it first. I love you too, Torby. And as soon as I am back from Valkash, we can continue what we have started."

He kissed Kyra, rolling on top of her, her legs opening to accommodate him. "Tell me again."

"I love you."

The graff started cooling on the cupboard next to the bunk, the wind howled outside as they shut out the universe around them. Capturing every last moment of their time together.

As the sun climbed higher into the turquoise sky, Kyra and Torben entered the kitchen. Elsor looked up from her tablet, smiling a tired smile. "Hello."

"Hello, Mother. I take it you've heard the news?"

"Yes. It's truly awful. All those poor souls lost in the void of space.

"It is very troubling news," Torben added as he sat down at the island.

"I've received new orders, Mother. I am to leave immediately. There is a medical emergency on Valkash. I am to fly back to Lundell, where I will be transported back to Valkash."

"How long will you be gone?"

Kyra looked at Torben, a glint of steel in her expression.

"Not long, Mother. I have something to keep me on Biflux now."

Torben smiled, his face lighting up, despite the troubling new situation that had befallen their time together. "Sounds good to me. I've also received a new order. I will accompany Kyra back to Lundell, where I await further instructions."

"You young people, flying here and there. I know it must be exciting. I've never really strayed too far from my home. Which in a way, I like. But one day, just one day, I will ask Trevik to take me on a journey across the stars."

"You will, Mother," Kyra added, walking over and embracing the older woman. "But not just yet. I plan to be back soon. I miss you and Father. I want to spend some quality time with you. The snows are due soon. I want to be here as the year passes."

"Will you both be here?"

They looked at each other, smiling in unison. "I'm sure we will be, Mother."

Torben looked at Elsor. "I will make sure I am. I promise."

The craft levelled out, heading back to Walvak. Kyra deftly handled the controls, the ship barely making a ripple as it scooted along. "My Mother really likes you."

"Really?" How do you know?"

"A woman knows such things. I can just tell by the way she talks to you and looks at you. She thinks you are a good man, who makes her daughter happy."

"I think she is really nice too. Your Father also, although at first I thought I was a dead man."

"Father is lovely. But all fathers are protective of their daughters. I am sure it's the same all over the universe."

They lapsed into silence, happy to take in the view around them. The lake on their right gave way to a large forest that stretched all the way to the ocean on the horizon. To the left, craggy snow-capped peaks dominated the northern landscape, a few settlements clinging to their slopes. Kyra dipped the controls, the craft dropping through low-slung clouds as they neared the spaceport. "Requesting permission to land," she said as the port grew ever closer.

"Craft 91045, you are cleared for landing in bay forty-six."

"Thank you," she replied, following the outside edge of the huge terminal. Other small craft were hovering about their respective docking bays, a large freighter rising out of the bay next to theirs. As the ships came to a stop, the twin ion drives of the freighter kicked in, bathing them in a white glow as the hulk powered its way into orbit.

"I still love to see that," he said, pointing. "I will never grow tired of watching spacecraft take off," Torben said, watching the freighter disappear into the blue sky, its wake shimmering in the sunlight.

"Boys and their toys eh," she replied, nudging him gently as the ship dropped vertically into the confines of the docking bay. They unclipped their harnesses, walking out of the cockpit, down a metal ramp and into the hangar with their respective bags slung over their shoulders.

"Shall I walk you to where you need to be?"

"I'd like that," she replied, linking his arm with hers. The bay was largely empty, save for a few crates stacked neatly against the grey walls. The terminal was a hive of activity. Species of all shapes, colours and sizes made their way to their destinations. Many were sat outside the various cantinas that littered Lomax Spaceport.

Torben looked over at his beloved Sars Club as they ambled past, wondering if his red-headed friend was propping up the bar. "I could murder a cold one. But I can wait a while longer," he said, feeling the dryness in his throat.

"We can meet there when we both get back. I could help you knock a few back." He smiled, mentally adding that to his 'to do' list. A few minutes later they came to a large glass doorway, the whiteness inside the laboratory in stark contrast to the spaceport.

"I guess this is where we part," Torben said, already feeling a sadness washing over him.

"Promise me you will take care, wherever you're heading."

"I promise. And you take care too." They dropped their bags, embracing fiercely. The noise around them seemed to shrink away as they kissed, longingly yet tenderly. As they broke away, Torben saw tears in the woman's eyes. They seemed to sparkle against the light, the red lock of her hair shimmering as she nervously brushed it behind her ear.

"I love you, Kyra. Remember that always."

"I love you too, Torben. I will be telling you that again. Very soon." They came together again, almost feeling physical pain when they broke the embrace. "Bye for now," she said, blowing him a kiss.

"Take care," was all he could summon, his voice breaking slightly as he watched her head through the glass doors and out of sight. Torben stood for a few moments before hoisting his pack over his shoulder. He made his way to his command post, walking into the main office.

"Captain Fraken," a voice said, as a large male walked over to Torben.

"Commander Spelk," he replied. "What news?"

"Not good I'm afraid. One of the enclosures on Valkash developed a fault. A release of gas from the cooling systems killed all of the inhabitants. We need a fresh batch. Your ship is being readied in bay six. Rex is already on board, making preparations. You are to leave at once."

"Where am I heading?"

"I'll send you the details as you make your way over to bay six. It's a relatively short hop, within our own galaxy. If you make good time, you should be back in six days or so."

"Thank you, Commander. I will update you once we are underway."

"Safe travels, Fraken," he said in a clipped tone, turning on his heels before walking further into his command post. As Torben headed over to bay six, his thoughts returned to Kyra. *I miss you already. Hopefully, you will be back before me. Then we can return to Kiton and continue what we've started.*

TWENTY-TWO

LUNDELL

"BE BACK AT THE SHIP IN THIRTY MINUTES, KYRA," THE captain said in a friendly tone.

"Okay, Telion. I just have to grab a few things from the lab. I take it all supplies are on board?"

"They sure are," he responded positively. "We just need you on board too." She smiled evenly at him. Kyra had travelled with Telion before, liking his friendly manner. He was not so much a captain, rather one of the crew, such was his way. She thought of Torben. *I hope you are safe my love. I'll be back with you very soon*, Kyra thought, as she headed out of the docking bay towards the laboratory.

Thirty minutes later, Plateau126 broke the atmosphere of Lundell, heading into the inky blackness of space. Kyra lay on her bunk as the ion drives ramped up a notch, propelling the ship towards the safe zone at a speed that she could barely comprehend. She clicked on her wrist pilot, reading the accounts from Valkash. *How awful*, she thought, her eyes fixed on the words in front of her, describing the painful and instant deaths the humans had endured. She read on, a cold feeling settling over her as images of broken remains filled her vision. Scrolling down, Kyra looked at the medicine that was required. She had her supplies on the ship, knowing with a degree of certainty that replicas could be easily constructed in the labs next to the enclosures. Once her work was done, the laboratory crews on Valkash would be able to keep the inhabitants of the enclosure fully-stocked with medication for the rest of their somber lives. She sat up, rotating her legs off the bunk before standing up. Stretching her back, she padded over to the window, which was a rarity on most craft that ventured into deep space. "So beautiful," she said as she peered into the vacuum of space. She could make out distant stars, almost making out the shape of the galaxy around her. Far off, the galactic core was clearly visible, dotted with millions of tiny pin-pricks of light. How many stars are out there? she thought as the ship sped along effortlessly. Closer to the ship, a large asteroid ambled past slowly, rotating. Smaller asteroids and space debris were being pulled along by it, locked in an eternal dance by their host. Her eyes moved back to the galactic core, revelling in the sight it gave off. Light poured out from the nebulas, the super-massive hole spinning at impossible speeds, its beacon shooting out into space like a lone sentinel. She tore her eyes away from the vista, peeling her clothes off as she headed for the bathroom. A minute later, warm water pulsed against her torso, with Kyra welcoming the bombardment. She suddenly felt tired, the rigours of the past few days catching up with her. Her white towel was hung carefully a few minutes later as she headed for the bunk, its soft sheets helping to send her into the welcoming oblivion of sleep.

"How long until we reach the safe zone?" Torben asked, slightly impatiently as they headed away from Biflux.

"Twelve hours, skipper," Rex replied from the controls. His hands hovered over the virtual controls, coaxing the ship gently, altering the pitch slightly. Rex almost looked like he was handling an infant, such was his tenderness with the control panel of Shimmer050.

"Okay. I'm going to my quarters, Rex. I'm so tired. I will check on the crew when I wake up. Are you okay to handle things this end?"

"Of course. The crew are all taken care of. I checked in on them whilst you were receiving your orders."

"What would I do without you, Rex?" he said as he patted the hominid on the shoulder.

"You miss her, don't you? I can tell."

"Yes, I do, Rex. A lot," he replied as he headed out of the cockpit. Like Kyra, Torben took a brief shower, letting the pulsing amber under-lights soothe his aching body and mind. He welcomed sleep too, not thinking of his destination in a far-off solar system. He only thought of his woman and the lock of red hair that shimmered as she moved.

"Prepare the warhead," Hameda commanded as they neared the planet.

"*Preparing warhead,*" a distorted voice replied through the control panel.

"Pilot. How long until we reach Lomax Spaceport?"

The pilot, whose name was Zowie, looked up from his control panel. "On this heading at this velocity, we will break orbit in nine hours."

"Excellent. As you were. You two, come with me," she said to Ragyi and Ullar as she strode into the corridor beyond the cockpit. They entered Hameda's quarters, watching expectantly as their leader sank onto her bunk. "We are ready. The warhead will be primed by the time we are inside the planet's atmosphere. Once primed, we will drop down to within a few feet of the docking bays. As the pilot stated before, the bomb will stick to the roof of the port, giving us a few minutes to get out of harm's way. By the time it goes off, we'll be heading for Valkash."

"What damage will it cause?" Ragyi said, almost reverently.

"Catastrophic. The blast zone will be extensive. There are mountains to the north. The heat blast from the detonation will melt the glaciers, swamping all in their path. The engineering plant of Halycon will either be vapourised, or submerged. No one will survive."

"I think, this calls for a celebration," Ullar said smiling.

"Yes, it does. Go to the galley and bring back some refreshments. Ragyi." The man looked up at the woman on the bunk as she patted the space next to her thighs. "Come here." Ullar smiled as she headed out of the room, hoping that there would be some left for her when she returned.

A while later, the threesome lay on top of the sheets, spent and slick with sweat. Ragyi reached over, hefting a large tankard of cold beer. He handed it to his leader, smiling as it spilled over her naked breasts. "Ullar. Are you thirsty?"

"Yes Hameda," she said, taking her cue as she moved over her leader. Hameda lay back, enjoying the closeness of their tryst. A moment later, they lay entwined, limbs crisscrossed as the under-lighters began to fade.

"We should get some rest. We have just over seven hours until we are ready to go into battle." She looked over at the man, smiling warmly at the sight of his sleeping form. Hameda slowly drifted off to sleep as she played with Ullar's hair. The lights dipping even further until the threesome lay sleeping in the darkened quarters.

The ship dropped through the Stratosphere, heading towards the low cloud that blanketed the landscape. Hameda sat next to the pilot, her fingers tap-tapping on her armrest. "Not long now."

"No, Hameda. We should be in position in a few minutes. The cloud cover is a welcome bonus. Once we lift off, we will be hidden from any ground patrols. Lomax command will be able to see us, but we'll be out of harm's way by the time the warhead detonates."

"Good," she purred as they dropped down further towards the grey sprawl that was Lomax Spaceport.

A voice broke the silence, the pilot flinching. *"Unidentified craft. State your purpose?"*

"We've run into difficulties on our voyage. Request authorisation to land. Our ion drive is malfunctioning." The pilot moved the yoke from left to right, altering the pitch of the ship to make it look unsteady and floundering.

"Authorisation denied. Please find an alternative port."

"Negative," the pilot stated flatly. "We will not make another port. We're only minutes from a potential crash."

"Then crash somewhere else. If you do not alter course, you will be fired upon."

"How far away are we?" Hameda asked, her knuckles whitening as she gripped the armrests.

"We're at 10,000 feet. If I take evasive action, we can be above the port in less than a minute."

"Then do it. Hold tight everyone." Ragyi and Ullar strapped themselves into their seats, their expressions tight and nervous. The freighter moved sharply downwards, veering left and right between the clouds.

"Unauthorised craft. I repeat. Leave this zone or you will be fired upon."

"Hang on. This is going to get very bumpy," the pilot said.

"Shields up." A blue flickering light fizzed past the cockpit window, missing the craft by a few feet. "They're using proton cannons. The shield will only withstand a few direct hits."

"Get us down there," Hameda shouted as the ship rocked violently, the controls in the cockpit blinking out for a split-second.

"Three thousand feet," the pilot said as they dropped out of the covering clouds. "Target locked." He pressed a button on the control panel. "Ready the warhead. We only have one shot at this. Don't fail." Ragyi reached over, taking Ullar's hand. He squeezed, closing his eyes, hoping that he would open them again.

"Warhead ready. Timer is set at sixty seconds."

"That's cutting it fine," Hameda said, her usual confidence evaporating quickly.

"We will head off north at low altitude," the pilot said as the ship rocked once more. "The lower we are, the less chance that they can hit us. Right. We're here." The ship hung a few feet from the drab grey exterior of the spaceport's roof. The firing had stopped, an almost calm descending over the space-port. "Deploy warhead," the pilot said.

"Warhead deployed."

"Get us out of here," Hameda said as the ship lurched forward, almost skimming the structure underneath it.

"Unidentified ship. The port authority has been notified. They are locked onto your wake."

"Great," the pilot said. "Forty seconds to detonation. They're onto us," he said, noticing three green blips on his radar, closing in on their position.

"How far away are they?" the woman said.

"Five thousand feet. They are heavily armed, but they cannot match our speed," he said as he pushed the throttle to maximum. "Hold on." The freighter pulled away from the advancing craft, skimming trees before it broke out across a huge salt flat, heading north towards the tundra. Blue light shot past them, fizzling out into the salt pan as the freighter sped ever northwards. "Okay. Brace yourselves," the pilot said. They did so, even Hameda's eyes closing. *Please let us live another day.* A blinding flash echoed across the landscape, the pilot shielding his eyes as he passed a small settlement next to a large lake. "Detonation confirmed."

"Are we far enough away?" Ragyi said nervously.

"Yes. The craft following us looks to have crashed a few miles behind us. Hold on. The heatwave is about to hit," he said as the freighter began to climb. "Come on baby. Let's get through this."

Hameda looked at the rear display camera, an icy chill enveloping her as she saw the landscape turn red. In the distance, a huge mushroom cloud roiled into the sky, taking up the whole screen. A red wave of fire grew ever nearer as the ship ploughed upwards. "Will we escape the heatwave?"

"We should do. We're over a hundred miles from the blast zone. The heatwave will warm our hides, but the ship will get us through it. There is a landing zone at the pole. We can give the ship a quick once over before we head to Valkash. It will have to be very quick though, as they may be following us."

"Can we not just go straight to Valkash?"

"We could. But we've taken a few direct hits on our hull. The shield should have done its job. But I just want to be sure. The last thing we need is a hull breach in outer space."

"Very well," Hameda said as the ride became smoother. "It looks like we won through. Well done, pilot."

"Thank you. And please, call me Zowie," he said smiling.

"Thank you, Zowie. You have done well. Your place in history is almost complete. I have plans for you."

"Really? What kind of plans?" the man said.

"We can discuss them later. In my quarters," Hameda said, as she placed a weathered hand on his.

Elsor walked towards a large metal receptacle as a stiff warm breeze blew in from the water. Flocks of birds scooted past her, making the woman crane her neck towards the sky before depositing a handful of weeds into the recycling furnace. She walked back to the flower bed, assuming the position that she'd been in for the past few hours. She hummed to herself as weeds were placed on the clipped grass next to her knees. More birds flew past, their calls seeming more high-pitched than normal. Elsor stood up, flexing her back as she rose from the flowerbed. She looked towards the water, smiling as saw her husband striding towards her, tools hanging from a leather belt. "Do you fancy an early lunch?" she called.

"Sounds like a wonderful." Trevik's voice stopped abruptly as a blinding flash scorched his eyes.

"Trevik!" Elsor shouted as she fell to the ground.

The man rubbed his eyelids, stumbling across the grass towards the fallen woman. Shapes floated in his vision as he grabbed hold of his wife. "Elsor. Are you okay?"

"Yes. What's happening?"

"I don't know," he said, his vision clearing enough to see a large mushroom cloud start its ascent into the sky. "Oh no!"

"What?"

"It's an explosion. Towards Lomax. We need to get underground."

"Underground? Why?"

"Because it looks like a fission bomb has gone off."

Elsor knew enough to understand what kind of devastation was wrought from such an explosion. "The cellar."

"Yes. Let's move. Quickly." They scrambled to their feet, heading up the slope towards the house.

"Head around to the side doors. It will save us a few valuable seconds." Elsor obeyed, tracking left across the lawn. Trevik went down heavily, winding himself. He grunted in pain, rolling over on his back as his wife came to his aid.

"Come on, love. I've got you," she said urgently.

"Elsor. Look at me." She did, staring into his eyes, noticing the tears that were beginning to well up. "I love you. And I always will."

"I love you too, Trevik. Come on. We can make it." She tried to heave the man to his feet, failing as she fell next to him on the grass. He wrapped her in his embrace, closing his eyes. "I love you, Kyra," he uttered as the heat blast swept over them. Trevik felt a moment of exquisite pain before he was reduced to ash as the maelstrom covered the land. Their home was blown away on the wind, the evergreen trees surrounding it flattening like fallen wheat as the heat wave consumed everything in its path.

TWENTY-THREE

"WHAT KIND OF EXPLOSION?" TORBEN ASKED.

"The bad kind. Possibly nuclear. Lomax Spaceport and the surrounding areas have been totally wiped off the map." Rex replied gravely.

"Oh my god!" the captain said, collapsing into his seat. "Kyra. I must make contact."

"Okay. She will be almost at Valkash by now, skipper. I am sure she is safe."

"Me too," Torben said as he exited the bridge. He activated his wrist pilot, swiping through the holographic menus until her name appeared. He hit the virtual green icon below her name as he entered his quarters.

"Torben?"

"Thank god you're safe."

"Why? What's wrong?"

"There has been an explosion at Lomax. We think it's a nuclear detonation."

"What?" the scratchy voice exclaimed. "My parents. They…"

"Try and contact them, Kyra. Although it will prove difficult. The blast may have destroyed all communications in the surrounding area. They live quite far away. They may have made it to safety." He could hear muffled sobs on the other end of the connection, his heart constricting in pain.

"Where are you?"

"We've just come out on the other side of the wormhole. Our orders are to head to the planet and extract some more of its indigenous population. Where are you?"

"Heading towards Valkash. I must go to the captain, to see if they know anything. Torby. I hope they are safe. I cannot lose them. Not after losing so much already."

"Try not to think the worst my love. Find out what the captain knows. I will call you back soon. I love you."

"I love you too," Kyra said, her voice faltering.

Torben made his way back to the cockpit, activating the communication system. "Shimmer050 to command. Come in, over." Nothing but static reverberated around the cockpit. He switched channels. "Shimmer050 to Lundell Spaceport. Come in, over."

"This is Lundell Spaceport, over."

"We've just heard about Lomax. What has happened, over?"

"We don't have all the details, Captain Fraken. Lomax has been levelled, along with the surrounding areas. We are taking steps to ensure Lundell is protected, over."

"Shit. Okay, I will call back later. Over and out."

"What shall we do?" Rex said, his tone sombre.

Torben was momentarily torn. Should he carry on the mission, or head back through the wormhole. "Keep going. I will wait for communications from Kyra and Lundell before we take any further action. How far to our planet?"

"Not far. Just over nine hours, skipper."

"Okay, Rex. I will be back in a bit," Torben said as he headed out of the cockpit, his legs feeling leaden, his throat dry.

Kyra sat in the cockpit, her head in her hands. Tears ran freely from her eyes as she looked up at the captain. "Why?" she uttered.

"I'm so sorry Kyra," Telion said quietly. "Let us hope your family made it below-ground." He placed his hand over hers, squeezing gently.

She tried a half-hearted attempt at a reassuring smile, wiping the tears from her eyes. "I am going to my quarters. I will keep trying to contact them, Captain."

"As you wish. I will be here. If I hear any news, I will contact you."

"Thank you," she replied, shuffling out of the cockpit towards her quarters. People headed past her, the news apparently spreading throughout the ship. Crew members were crying, being consoled by others as Kyra tried to blot out the visions in front of her. Reaching her quarters, she hurried over to the desk, activating the screen. It shimmered into life in front of her, framed by a blue outline. Her finger swiped across the screen, the latest news coming from Lundell. "Oh no," she said, her tone desolate. On the screen in front of her was an aerial view of Lomax, taken by surveillance drones. She could see the devastation, the landscape burning, the once huge spaceport levelled. She swiped left, more images filling the screen. It was then that her resolve completely shattered. She could see the remains of Kiton and the surrounding forest. There was nothing left, except for a few burning trees that swayed in the stiffening breeze. "Mother, Father. Why? Who has done this?" She fell backwards into the chair, her whole body shaking as she sobbed uncontrollably. Kyra stumbled over to her bunk, collapsing heavily on top of it as she continued to cry. She felt her wrist pilot vibrate, turning over onto a pillow to see who was trying to contact her.

"Kyra," Torben said. "Can you hear me?"

She looked at the holographic image of the captain, her resolve crumbling once more. "Mother and Father are dead, Torben. I have seen the footage. The entire area has been destroyed."

"I'm so sorry, Kyra. Let us hope that they somehow managed to get to safety."

"There is no hope. Even if they had made it below ground, the fallout would soon hit them. They would stand no chance."

Torben knew enough about nuclear winters to know that she was right. He tried to vanquish the thoughts of family and loved ones that lived in neighbouring Cantis, his focus solely on Kyra. "I am aborting my mission. I am coming to get you, Kyra. I will tell Rex to set a new course for Valkash. We should be there in a few days."

"Please hurry, Torby. I have an awful feeling that the war is about to reignite, and that all will be lost."

Kyra traced her fingers across Torben's shoulders as he slowly came out of a deep, trouble-free sleep. "Morning," he said lazily.

"Morning, lover. I was watching you sleep."

He moved towards her, kissing her gently. "I like this bed."

"So do I. Especially when you're on top of it," she purred, trailing her hands across his flat stomach towards the white sheet that covered his bottom half. A clanking noise from outside made her turn towards the door.

"What is that?" Torben asked, feeling an ache inside that she was no longer touching his body.

"Breakfast. I set the net this morning. Looks like something has ventured inside. I will cook you grilled lemmots for breakfast."

"Lemmots?"

"The tastiest fish you'll ever have. They come in from the ocean, looking for calmer waters. We are in luck. You are in for a treat."

"I thought I was already in for a treat when I woke up," he said, testing the waters.

"That can be your dessert," she said, striding over to the wooden door.

A flash of light lit the cabin, blinding both of them. "What the?" Kyra said, shielding her eyes from the blistering whiteness.

Torben staggered out of bed, his sheet wrapped around his waist. He made it to the door, prising it open as a warm breeze flooded the wooden cabin. "Oh no!"

"What," she asked nervously.

"Look," he pointed at the horizon. A mushroom cloud was rising in the distance, turbulently heading towards the clouds. "Inside!" he commanded, slamming the door and barring it with a small cupboard. "Help me with the bed," Torben said, Kyra obeying dumbly. They dragged it over to the window, covering the glass panes with the wooden frame.

"What's happening, Torben?"

"That blast was nuclear. We only have a minute until the shockwave hits us. Is there a cellar?"

Kyra was about to respond as the bed exploded across the room, showering them in snapped timber and glass. Before they could speak, the cabin was enveloped in searing flames, consuming everything in its path. He managed to get one last look at his beloved Kyra as her hair ignited. He closed his searing eyelids as the world around him turned red. Then black.

Torben sat up in bed, the sheet damp with sweat. He sat there for a moment, panting and disorientated. After a few minutes, he pressed the intercom next to his bunk, his fingers shaking slightly. "Rex, how far are we from the safe zone?"

"About two hours, skipper. Are you okay?"

"Fine. I was just sleeping. I will take a shower and join you shortly."

"Okay. I'll have some graff ready for you."

"Thank you, Rex. I don't know what I'd do without you." Torben activated his pilot, Kyra's voice crackling across the cosmos.

"Torby, where are you?"

"We're not far from the safe zone. Once through, it's a relatively short ride to Valkash. Are you there?"

"Yes. We landed not long ago. I am in the lab, working on synthesizing medication for the Earthlings."

"Okay. Keep doing what you're doing. Once I arrive I will come and find you."

"Please hurry. I have a really bad feeling that another war is about to erupt."

"Try not to think too much about that. As I said, keep busy, that will take your mind off other things." He instantly felt guilty. The woman he loved had just lost her parents, a few short months after losing her partner. He needed to get to Kyra, not only because of the chance of impending danger, but also to keep her sane.

"I will carry on. I must pay a visit to the humans in a short while, so I can understand all their requirements."

"You do that. I will call you back shortly. I love you."

"Love you too, Torby. Please hurry." He ended the call, his whole body feeling empty as he headed for the shower cubicle. He stood there, hands planted against the walls of the enclosure, as steaming water pummelled his body. His mind, a whirling galaxy of thoughts.

TWENTY-FOUR

VALKASH

THE VILLAGE WAS QUIET, SAVE FOR THE OCCASIONAL SOUNDS of the birds inhabiting the trees next to the Talbot Inn. Streets around the pub were deserted, save for the four women that walked towards the glass dome that held them captive. "What do you think will happen next?" Caroline said to no one in particular.

"Who knows," replied Gemma, her eyes scanning the surrounding countryside.

"Maybe they will send us all home?" Sarah added hopefully, her leather jacket slung over one shoulder as her boots scuffed the tarmac.

"We can hope," Katie said dryly. "However, I am pretty sure we are here for the long haul." The ambled onwards until the dome came into view.

"Look," Caroline exclaimed. "Someone's there."

They all looked expectantly as the glass doorway hissed open, a tall woman that they all recognised striding towards them purposefully. "Hello," Kyra said evenly, switching her language to suit theirs. "I understand that you have requested medical supplies. My name is Officer Zakx, but you can call me Kyra."

"We have, Kyra" Gemma said coolly. We also asked for other things too. Food and drink, along with clothing."

The woman smiled. "I am aware of your request. Someone back at command is populating an inventory for you."

"Do you have any other news?" Sarah asked, noticing the backpack that the alien woman wore.

"I've not heard anything regarding your new guardian. I have been back at home, visiting my parents." Her voice faltered, tears stinging her eyes as her resolve crumbled.

"What's wrong?" Caroline asked as the strange woman bowed her head.

"My parents. They have been killed."

"Oh no," Caroline replied, leading the other woman towards a stone wall at the side of the road. The others followed, feeling a degree of empathy. They were women, after all, seeing the pain that the alien felt.

"What happened?" Gemma asked.

"I am not sure that I should share the information with you."

"Rubbish," Katie said. "Who are we going to tell? We are prisoners here. The least you could do is fill us in."

Kyra wiped her eyes, the red lock of her hair shimmering in the artificial daylight. "Okay. When we left you, I headed back to my home planet. The captain of the ship and I have become very close. Torben is his name."

"I remember him," Gemma said. "Dark hair, kinda serious looking."

"Yes. However, he is a good man. He only took the mission to bring you here because he was following orders. Anyway, we spent some time at my parents' home before being called back on duty. We're not sure how it all happened, but an orbital station was destroyed, followed by a nuclear blast near to my home. My parents," she paused. "They did not survive."

"We are very sorry for your loss," Caroline said, putting an arm around Kyra's shoulder. "We have all lost loved ones. Both here and back at home."

"Thank you," Kyra said, her tears receding, her composure regained.

"Who did it?" Katie asked.

"We do not know," Kyra replied. "Before you came here, a war was raging. The Lomogs won through in the end, scattering the resistance. I have a bad feeling that this resistance is making a play to reignite the war."

"Are we safe here?" Gemma asked, a sinking feeling settling over her.

"I hope so," Kyra replied. "We are a long way from the two explosions. I am sure that things are being done to ensure Valkash is protected. Now, I have medication for you. Shall we walk back to the settlement and allocate it to your friends?"

The women looked at Kyra, their defences melting slightly at the sight of the woman in front of them. *She's just a kid,* Caroline thought. *This whole mess is not her fault.* "Good idea," the Welsh woman replied. "We can go to the village hall. I will put the kettle on and make us all a cup of tea. Would you like that, Kyra?"

"I would. Thank you, that is most kind of you all."

"Nonsense," Katie said. "It's the least we can offer. You'd be surprised what a cup of tea and a good chat can do to sort out the universe's problems." They all smiled; Kyra too before heading back towards the village.

Inside the confines of the hall, Katie walked over to the kitchenette, filling the kettle with water before busying herself with the drinks. Kyra walked over to the stage, placing her pack on the polished wooden boards. A minute later, she had laid out a host of tablets in white plastic bottles. Each bottle was labelled in English, to Caroline's surprise. "High blood pressure tablets. My mum takes these back home."

"There is an inventory here that should tell you which medicines treat which conditions. You humans have a different genetic makeup to us. However, we do suffer from similar ailments. Synthesising these medicines was relatively easy."

"Well, that's something. I don't suppose you could synthesise me a pot of Ben & Jerry's Rocky Road?" Gemma chuckled, the joke lost on Kyra.

"What is that?"

"It's ice cream, hun. It's to die for. Maybe one day we can share a pot?"

"Okay. I may hold you to that," Kyra said warmly.

The clinking of crockery signalled the arrival of the drinks. Katie laid the steel tray next to the medicines, pouring each woman a cup of strong tea. "There is milk and sugar, help yourselves ladies."

They all stood there, sipping their drinks, each of them lost in thought. Caroline looked at Kyra over the rim of her cup, the steam from the tea clouding her glasses. "Is there a way out of here, Kyra?"

"I'm afraid not. Not unless the Lomogs decree it. I'm afraid that you're stuck here."

"But what about the explosions? Surely you can see that something bad is happening."

"I know. I'm waiting for Torben to arrive. He will take me with him."

"Then take us too," Gemma piped-up. "We have families back home. Families that need us."

"It is not my decision to make," Kyra said, setting her cup back on the tray. "Believe me, you have my sympathy. But I am not authorised to make such a call. That is for the Lomogs to decide." She moved away from the stage. "I must leave you now. I have work to do back at the laboratory. Do you have enough food?"

"Yes," Caroline said. "It gets dropped from the sky every few days or so. We are well-stocked."

"Good. Keep strong. Together you will all be okay, just don't think too much about trying to escape. You saw what happened to the children."

The women stared at Kyra as she left the village hall, digesting the subtle warning. "She seems nice," Sarah said. "She's just obeying her orders."

"I know," Caroline replied. "I just have a bad feeling that something is going to happen."

"So do I," Katie said solemnly. "It looks like we're caught in the middle of something. Like something from a tacky sci-fi movie. I don't want to die out here. I want to go home."

———

Kyra sat down heavily at her workstation, feeling the pain of the women she'd just spoken to. *This is not right. They should be with their families*, she thought as her wrist started to vibrate. "Torben, where are you?"

"We're on our way to you. We've not long come through the void. Rex promises to be there within a day. He's ramped up the ion drives. We are making good time."

"Good. That's a relief."

"Are you okay?"

"Not really. My parents are dead. I've just come from the village, where we left the inhabitants. Two children are dead. They managed to enter the enclosure next to theirs. The gravity flattened both of them. Plus, I've just spoken to some of the humans there. They want to go home, Torby. And I agree with them. What we have done is wrong. So very wrong."

"But we were under orders. I know what you mean. But I

can see no way to change what has been done. It looks like something is brewing. I can feel skirmishes ahead, maybe more so. I just hope all-out war is not on the horizon."

"Nor me. I have lost too much already. I cannot lose more."

"Try not to think about that. Just concentrate on the task at hand, my love."

"I will try. Just hurry up and get here. I really need you."

"I promise, Kyra. I will be there as soon as I can." A few minutes later, Kyra was walking through the corridors that connected the enclosures. Another lab was situated a ten-minute walk from her own. She needed to stretch her legs and think about anything that wasn't lost loved ones and impending wars.

"Valkash," Hameda stated as the small gathering peered at a holographic image of a planet that floated before them. "Forty percent ocean, sixty percent land. Most of the oceans lie in the southern hemisphere. The attraction that the Lomogs have built lies mainly further north. Over half of the planet's surface has been terraformed to match the inhabitants that live in the enclosures."

"So, what is your plan of attack?" Ragyi asked expectantly.

Hameda swiped her hand vertically across the planet, its northern pole coming into view. "There. Can you see the hole?" They nodded as one. "The Lomogs drilled a shaft in the planet's crust, which I am reliably informed drops right down to its core. That is where we will strike. However, after the recent explosions, they will be on high alert. We cannot just fly down there and drop off the bomb. Their shields will be up, blocking our path."

"So, what do we do?" Ullar asked.

"We can land close by. I have a contact on the ground who will allow us to land at a disused hanger, close to the pole. Weather will be a problem, as we can expect sub-zero temperatures and storms. Our pilot tells me that we have clothing for this environment. He has also shown me a small craft in the cargo hold. It is big enough for one passenger, along with the bomb. That is how we will hit them. The craft will drop into the shaft, detonating the warhead when it hits the planet's core."

"Will the bomb explode on its own when it hits the target?" Ullar asked.

"No. Someone will have to pilot the craft. They will need to detonate the bomb inside the shaft."

A silence fell over the group, the realisation of the task becoming apparent. "Who do you have in mind, Hameda?" Ragyi asked, his palms beginning to feel clammy.

"Either you or Ullar. It will be an honour for one of you to give your life for the cause."

Ullar and Ragyi stared at their leader, then each other. "Can no one else pilot the craft?" Ullar asked, her legs trembling beneath her.

"No. I only trust you two. You must decide and decide quickly, as we'll be landing soon."

"I will do it," Ragyi said, his voice almost faltering. "I would not expect Ullar to give her life just yet. I am ready for this task, Hameda."

Ullar walked over to him, embracing the man. "Are you sure?"

"Yes. My life has been meaningless until recently. I want to be remembered as the man who helped wrestle control back from our enemies."

"You are very brave, Ragyi, and noble too. Your sacrifice will not be in vain, I promise you that."

"I need to go to my quarters. I have loved ones that I need

to leave messages with. I will set a delay on them, so they only transmit once I have completed my mission."

"Very well. Come to my quarters when you are finished, Ragyi. We can discuss our strategy, along with a few other details."

"Do you need me to come?" Ullar asked.

"Not this time. Just the two of us."

"As you wish, Hameda," Ullar said, slightly deflated.

TWENTY-FIVE

EARTH

HUGH'S PHONE STARTED RINGING AS HE SAT AT HIS LAPTOP. HE swiped the screen, swinging his legs onto the corner of his desk. "Hi, Mum. How are you?"

"I'm fine," his mother replied in her soft Scottish brogue. "How are you bearing up? Any news? Are the boys okay?"

"No news, Mum. I'm okay. The boys miss Gemma. They've been sleeping in our bed every night since she disappeared. I dropped them at school and nursery earlier. The school is half empty, Mum. Many of the children who attend are also missing."

"Poor little mites. Be strong for them, son. They need your resolve to get through this ordeal."

"I'm trying, Mum. But it's hard. She's been gone for nearly three weeks now. No-one is contacting me. It's like she's just been forgotten about."

"I'm sure the authorities are doing everything they can, son. Try not to lose heart. I am sure that you will hear something soon enough." They chatted for a few more minutes, Hugh's mother telling the young man all the goings on up north, along with his father's knee replacement, which had happened the week before.

"Give Dad my love, Mum."

"I will. He sends his love too. To all of you. I'll give you a ring in a couple of days. Bye for now, son. Love you."

"Love you too. Speak soon." Hugh ended the call, looking at his laptop. A webpage detailing various alien abductions looked back at him. "People will think I'm crazy," he muttered to the screen. "But I know something out of the ordinary has happened to you. This was no terrorist abduction. Someone, somewhere knows what went down." He grabbed his jacket, heading out of the house towards the Talbot Inn. As he walked through the village, Hugh felt the onset of winter approaching, zipping his jacket up further to ward off the stiffening breeze. He turned right at the pub, noticing the newsagent across the road. It was closed, a notice adorning the front of the shop. *God, this place is a ghost town*, he thought as he plodded on towards the field where his wife was last seen. Ducking under the police tape, he made his way slowly around the field, not really sure what he was looking for. *What happened here? Where did you all go?* He skirted the field, tall hedgerows framing the large space on one side that gave way to the back gardens on the other side. As he walked on, something caught his eye that stopped him in his tracks. A gap in the expanse of greenery that drew Hugh towards the borders of the gardens. He moved closer to the hedge, disappearing from view as he pushed his way into the foliage. "Bingo," he said as he looked across the neatly trimmed lawn towards the cottage. He took his smartphone out, snapping a few pictures of the building before ploughing back through the hedgerow into the field. Hugh set off, his stride more purposeful that it had been in a while as he made his way out of the field towards the village. A few left turns later, he was looking at the same cottage but from the front. He smiled as something else caught his eye, and he started walking up the cobblestoned driveway towards the front door. After pressing the bell, he waited impatiently as the first drops of rain started to fall from the leaden skies above. The inner door opened, an old lady stepping into the porch slowly. She opened the door, a gust of wind blowing past her into the cosy cottage.

"Yes? Can I help you?"

"Good morning. My name's Hugh. I live in the village a few streets away. I take it you know all about the people that have gone missing?"

"Yes. My daughter, Caroline was one of them."

"I'm so sorry to hear that. My wife is also missing. It's been three weeks and I've heard nothing."

"Same here. The police have been around, asking questions. But since then, nothing. I am so worried about her."

"I bet you are," he replied solemnly.

"She was thinking of moving to the village, relocating from Wales to look after me. My health is not so good just lately, and I've had a couple of break-ins over the last year or so."

"That's the reason why I am here. May I come in?" Hugh asked as the rain started falling heavier, flattening his thinning brown hair.

The elderly woman hesitated for a few seconds before stepping aside in the small porch, allowing the man to enter the cottage. He removed his shoes, mentally cursing as he noticed a large hole in his hiking sock. "Go on through," the woman said. "I'll put the kettle on."

"That's very kind of you," he paused, unsure how to address her.

"Margaret," she said, smiling.

"That's very kind of you, Margaret," Hugh replied warmly as the elderly woman closed the front door and shuffled down the hall to a small country kitchen.

"Sit yourself down while I brew the tea."

"Thanks." He pulled up a chair, resting his elbows on the

wooden top of a small pine table, noticing the garden beyond. He then looked at the woman, thinking that she reminded him of his own mother. She was dressed simply. A black pair of slacks, dark slippers and a purple fleece jacket. Her hair was steely grey, tightly curled and neat, like the kitchen in which she stood.

"Now then," she said as she placed two mugs on the table along with milk and sugar. "Why don't you tell me why you're here."

"Sure," Hugh replied as he heaped two spoonsful of sugar into his mug along with a good glug of milk. "I've just been walking around the field at the back of your property. Not sure why. I guess I just wanted to try and see if the police had missed anything. And it looks like they have. Did they ask you about your CCTV cameras?"

She considered the question as steam from her mug fogged her glasses. "No. I don't think they did. Why?"

"Because they may have asked to see the footage from the cameras. What kind of system is it? Does it record?"

"Yes, it does. My son, David, installed it a few months ago. I was broken into last Christmas, and also earlier on this year when I was on holiday. I went to Bournemouth with a few of the ladies from the village. We try and get away a few times a year. I do enjoy my outings. Not much else going on really."

Hugh nodded, liking the woman's take on things. "I don't suppose you've checked the CCTV for the night of the disappearance?"

"No, why would I?"

"Because the camera at the rear of your house points directly into the field beyond. I know it's a long shot, but there may be something of interest on your system. How do you view the images?"

"On my computer. Something else that David installed. I know I'm an old duffer, but I quite enjoy using it. I like looking at family photos on Facebook. And I also do my grocery shopping online. I've never driven, so when my Robert died a few years ago, David installed the computer, so I could stay connected to the world. Buses around here are not the best y'see. Getting anywhere is a struggle."

"I'm sure it is, Margaret. Would you mind if I took a look at the CCTV footage?"

"Do you think it will show anything?"

"I honestly don't know. But I am climbing the walls at home. No one is speaking to me. I am at my wit's end."

"I bet you are. Do you have children?"

"Yes, two boys, Oscar and Finn."

"How old are they?"

"Six and two. They miss their Gemma terribly. It's been really hard on them."

"Poor little mites," she said, which made Hugh smile. *She has more in common with Mum than I thought.* "Well, once we've finished our tea, I will let you take a look for yourself."

"That's great. I really appreciate this, Margaret. I know it will probably show nothing, but it's worth a try."

A few minutes later, Hugh sat at the elderly woman's computer, double-clicking on the CCTV icon on her home screen. A window appeared, which Hugh expanded so that it filled the screen. "I will leave you to it for a few minutes. I need to put a wash on."

"Okay, Margaret. I am sure I can work out how to rewind the footage." She nodded, leaving Hugh hunched over the screen as he figured out how to travel back in time. "October 14th," he said, smiling tightly as clear images from the rear camera filled the screen. He stopped the cursor at 19:00hrs, mentally playing the timeline over in his head. From the camera's vantage point, Hugh caught the occasional glimpse of activity as heads passed by the gap in the hedge in sporadic fashion. He sat there, watching closely as the minutes played out in front of him.

"Anything?" Margaret asked as she walked back into the spare bedroom.

"Nothing of interest yet. The images are very clear though. Your son must have spent a fortune on this system. It's very good."

"Well he's doing rather well for himself down in London. I never asked him how much it cost."

Something caught Hugh's eye on the screen. "There," he said, noticing the time at the bottom right-hand corner. "Elven minutes past seven," he said as a bright flash lit the screen. "Did you see that?"

"I missed it. Can you go back?" the elderly woman said.

"Hang on," Hugh replied, winding the clock back a few seconds. A bright flash lit the screen, followed by blue lightning that echoed across the footage. "Oh my god!" Hugh said as a large shadow appeared on the other side of the hedge. It seemed to hover there for about a minute, before fading to nothing before their eyes. More flashes of lightning lit the screen before the footage returned to normal.

"What do you think it is?"

Wanting to sound guarded, Hugh offered a bland answer. "Not sure. Some kind of storm, which makes no sense to me, Margaret. What do you think?"

"I have no idea. It certainly looks strange. Like those old *Frankenstein* movies in the '50s." The phone in the hallway started to ring, disturbing the quiet cottage. "Hang on a tick," she said, making her way out of the spare bedroom.

Hugh pulled out his smartphone, selecting video before winding the clock back to the start of the unknown phenomena. He held the phone steady, videoing the CCTV footage, his mouth hanging open in amazement. *This is unbelievable*, he thought as Margaret's voice filtered down the hallway towards him. *This was no terrorist abduction. This was something else. Some-*

thing otherworldly. Aliens. His thoughts were interrupted as he heard the old lady hanging up the phone. Quickly he stowed his own phone in his jacket pocket, trying to look nonchalant as she peered around the doorway. "Would you like another cup of tea?"

"Erm, no thanks, Margaret. I have taken up enough of your time."

"It's no trouble. What do you think happened to them?"

Feeling guilty, Hugh came clean. "I honestly don't know. I have recorded the footage, Margaret. I hope you don't mind?"

"Why would I mind. I would not have thought to check it myself. What are you going to do with what you've found?"

"Honestly, I am thinking of going to the papers. I won't mention where I got the footage from. Our secret is safe, I hope."

"It's okay. If the police want to snoop through my system, they can. I have nothing to hide."

"Just do me a favour please, Margaret?"

"Of course."

"Don't mention this until I have looked into this further. Can you do that for me?"

"But of course. And thank you for coming to see me. At least I know that there are people in the village that are going through the same thing as me. I do hope they find Caroline. And the others too. Such a mystery. Like *Tales of The Unexpected*. Do you remember that?"

"Can't say that I do? When was that out?"

"Oh, I can't really remember. Many moons ago Hugh. Probably before you were born come to think of it."

"Well, it certainly looks like something from the *X-Files*."

"Yes. I have watched a few of them. Mouldy and Sully isn't it?"

Suppressing a laugh, Hugh nodded cheerfully. "Yes. Something like that. Anyway. I will be in touch, Margaret. Many thanks for your help. I really appreciate it."

"Oh, it's not trouble, dear. It's nice to have the company. I hope to hear from you soon."

A few minutes later Hugh was hot-footing it back home, his smartphone grasped tightly in his palm. *No one knows anything? Bollocks. It's a fucking cover up. Well, it's time everyone saw the truth. Maybe then, something will be done.*

TWENTY-SIX

PAUL LEWIS' PHONE STARTED TO VIBRATE ON HIS DESK AS HE typed out an email. His eyes darted to the phone, a sinking feeling settling over him when he saw Hugh Andrews' name flash in front of him. He let it ring, not wanting to speak to the man from Belbroughton. *What can I tell him? We know nothing, apart from unconfirmed sightings of an unidentified object.* The phone fell silent, Lewis breathing a sigh of relief as silence descended over the office. It was short-lived; the black gadget beeping twice, signalling an answerphone message. Fearing the worst, Paul dialled the number to retrieve the message, hitting the speakerphone icon on the glass screen.

"*Mr Lewis. It's Mr Andrews. I've just discovered something very interesting. I really hope you've not been lying to me, and the rest of the village. I will give you thirty minutes to call me back. If not, I will go public. I don't want to do this, but I am a desperate man.*" The automated voice that followed gave Paul a list of options of what to do. He ended the call, his mouth dry, palms clammy. He was about to pick up the phone to call him back when it began ringing again.

"Hi, hun," he said, his voice edgy.

"Hi. What time are you home tonight?"

"Erm, not sure, why?"

"I've got a class at seven. I won't be home until nine."

"Okay," he said tentatively, his stomach beginning to churn. "I will probably be home before you leave."

"Don't rush. I know you're busy Paul. I will see you when I get back. Bye for now."

He opened his mouth to reply, the line already dead. Paul sat there his insides in turmoil. *Could it be happening again?* he thought. Try as he might, he could not shake the feeling that all was not well in his marriage once again. He stared out of the window for minutes, not really seeing anything as his fingers drummed on the white desk. An idea came to him. One that he tried to push back into the recesses of his mind. *It's snooping. I should just trust her,* he thought. *Shit, okay, just a quick look, just to make sure,* he decided as he clicked on his internet browser. He opened Facebook, entering his wife's username and password. Details that she thought were safe. But Paul was one step ahead as he punched enter. Her page appeared, a few notifications highlighted at the top of the screen. He decided against clicking on them, which may raise suspicion at his wife's end. Instead, he clicked on the messenger icon, a drop-down box appearing on the screen before him. At the top was a message sent ten minutes previously from Steve, making Paul's heart beat faster until he could practically hear it. He opened the message, scrolling up before he had a chance to read any of the content. After a few clicks of his mouse, the message came to its start, dated two days before. His eyes floated across the screen, looking at the small round icons that indicated the sender. Eventually, his eyes locked onto the start of the conversation. A conversation that would change everything.

Hey.

Hello. How are you?

I'm okay, Steve. How are you?

So so. Busy at the new gym.

What's it like?

Not as nice as the old one. The scenery there was much better....

Lol. You shouldn't be looking at the scenery. You're there to work!

I know. It's fine. It pays the mortgage. Claire – I miss you. X

Paul felt a sickening feeling at the sight of the first kiss of the conversation. He loosened his tie, planting his elbows on the desk as his heart started thumping in his chest.

We're not allowed to miss each other x

I know that. But I can't help it, babe. I can't stop thinking about you x

I know. I think about you all the time too. Even though I shouldn't. x

How are things at home? X

The same. Things are boring. Paul's never here. I'm like the forgotten wife x

That's bad. You are gorgeous, Claire. Any man would want you. I want you. X

Really? What about Jenna? X

We've broken up. After what happened between us, we never recovered. I decided to call it quits. x

Oh. I'm sorry to hear that. Are you okay? X

I think so. The last few months has made me realise what I want out of life. X

And what's that?"

YOU, BABE x

But we can't. I'm married. I have to think of the boys. X

Claire. They're grown up. It's time you started thinking about yourself for a change. X

But the house? The mortgage. It would be such a mess. X

Is that all that's keeping you with him? A mortgage? X

No. But it would be such an upheaval. Paul would not go nicely. He would make it difficult. X

Wanker! He treats you like shit but would fight you all the way if you left him. Tosser! X

Lol. I take it you're not a fan? X

No. He's a prick. You're a princess. You deserve to be happy. You deserve a man who treats you like you're the only woman on Earth. Someone who takes you to bed, not to watch tele and read books. You need an alpha who gives you everything you need. Xx

Tears fell from Paul's face as he read the texts. He knew there and then that his marriage was over. He could see the way the conversation was heading.

Well, you certainly knew how to deliver in the bedroom, Steve. That's one memory that no one can take from me. X

Nor me. The sight of you riding on top of me. How you pushed my head between your legs, craving my caress. I will always remember that babe. X

Stop it. You're making me wet. Xx

Are you alone? X

Yes, why? X

I am too. At home. On my bed, stroking myself, thinking of you. X

Oh god! X

Where are you? X

On the sofa at home. X

A picture appeared on the screen that made bile rise in Paul's throat. It was Steve's erect cock, proudly protruding from his boxers, taunting him.

This needs to be in your mouth, babe. Then, your tight pussy. X

Oh god. I'm so wet, Steve. I know I shouldn't, but I can't help it. X

Show me. X

Another picture appeared on the screen, making Paul gasp in pain. It was a selfie of his wife's most intimate place. A place that only he should see. Looking at it now, a deep anger flared inside him. He read the last few lines, seeing the plans that his adulterous wife and her lover had made for tonight.

He felt sick, his heart hammering in his chest. His thoughts drifted to his boys. Young and innocent in all this, who would undoubtedly suffer as a result of this. He cursed aloud, slamming his open palm onto the desk as the door opened.

"I've brought you a cup of coffee, Mr Lewis." She stopped in her tracks, seeing the look of desolation on her boss's face. "Shall I come back later? Are you okay, Paul?"

Paul Lewis was a proud man. He was not overly emotional, nor did he show his feelings, except in certain circumstances. However, his resolve was crumbling, as was the life around him. "No, Sylvia. I'm not. My wife. She's," he paused, trying to steady his shaky voice. "She's started up the affair she'd had a few months ago. I have just found proof." He lowered his head as the woman padded across the office towards him, placing the mug on the dark coaster in front of him.

"Oh, Paul. I am so sorry to hear that," she said as she perched herself on the desk next to him. The woman reached across, squeezing his hand, noticing the messages on the screen. She turned her head away, not wanting to pry as she walked over to the window. Sylvia turned, wondering what to say for the best. "I know how you feel, Paul. My ex did pretty much the same to me last year. I thought I was going crazy, until I found him out, pretty much the same way that you have. I was made to feel like this was all my fault. That I was to blame. I really am sorry. For what it's worth, she must have rocks in her head. You're a lovely man, good looking too. Why would any woman not think that was enough?"

Paul blew out a breath, half smiling as he reached for his coffee. He took a sip, letting the hot liquid burn his throat. The pain felt good. It felt real, because the rest of his body felt numb. "Thank you, Sylvia. I really don't know what to do. I know where they're going to be. Should I confront them?"

"Best not to, Paul. It will only make matters worse, believe me, I know."

"You're probably right. Plus, he's a lot younger than me. I may end up in hospital."

"Just let her do whatever she's going to do. You cannot change it. Even if you confront her today, she will do the same in the future. I think you need to accept what is about to happen, Paul. As hard as that sounds."

"Maybe I should do the same. Get myself a mistress. That way we can continue to live-out our sham of a fucking marriage."

"I know you're hurting. And I understand why you would want to get some sort of revenge. But revenge never ends well, Paul. It might feel good at the time, but it will do more damage. You're a great looking guy, and you're still young. Your boys are grown up. You can start again. There would be a queue of women waiting to date you, believe me."

He smiled again. "Thank you, Sylvia. Talking about it really helps." He regarded the woman in front of him. "How about you? Have you started over?"

"No. I was with my ex for nearly twenty years, and I did rather well with the divorce settlement. We lived a comfortable life, which helps now that I am on my own. Our daughter is at University too, so it was a clean break. I am enjoying my life. I have a few close friends. We go dancing on Saturday nights in Cheltenham and have had a few girly weekends over the past few months. I wouldn't go back to my old life, Paul. I'm enjoying the new me far too much."

"Good for you, Sylvia. I'm sure the men will be queueing up for you too. You're a very attractive woman."

She smiled, blushing slightly. "Thank you. I'm not used to compliments, Paul. But that was nice to hear." She walked over and kissed him on the cheek, wrapping her arms around him. "I'm here if you need me. Day or night. If you need to unload, or just want a coffee, just say the word."

Paul was momentarily lost in the woman's embrace. He drank in her perfume, liking the closeness of her body next to his. They stood there, for what seemed like minutes until Sylvia finally broke the embrace. "I don't what I would have done, had you not come in. Probably would have ended up making a fool of myself later. Thank you, Sylvia. I may take you up on the coffee one day. When I am less of a wreck."

"You do that, Mr Lewis," she replied. "Day or night." The words hung in the air as the woman headed out of the office, smiling at him as she closed the door behind her.

Hugh walked back from the kitchen, sitting down on the sofa with his steaming cappuccino. He checked his phone, disappointed that there was no missed call from Mr Lewis. He checked the time, *Thirty-six minutes, he's not calling back.* He logged into Twitter, pasting the tweet that he had earlier composed, armed with hashtags to enable his message to reach the largest audience possible. He had also tagged several of his friends, along with many government agencies across the world. Before he hit *tweet*, Hugh uploaded the video clip taken from Margaret's CCTV footage. He sat there, sipping his coffee as the video uploaded. *Let's see what happens now?* he thought as he posted his message, hoping that it would go viral. He didn't have to wait long for a response. His coffee was still warm as his phone started pinging repeatedly. He checked the time, noting that he needed to pick the boys up from school and nursery. Grabbing his coffee, he headed out into the kitchen, leaving his phone on the sofa. *I'll check out what's happening when I get back*, he thought, as he discarded the empty mug in the sink before heading out of the house.

"Paul, have you seen this?" John Hendry said as he bustled into Lewis' office.

"What is it?" Paul asked indifferently as other things clouded his mind.

"Take a look," Hendry replied, handing Paul a piece of paper.

His eyes scanned the page, his pulse quickening as he read the tweet. "Shit. How the hell did he obtain this information?"

"No idea. I have looked at the video on Twitter. It appears genuine, Paul. Somehow, Mr Andrews has figured this out. And now it's out there."

Paul's mobile phone started vibrating, a sinking feeling washing over him as he saw his superior's name flash up on the screen. "Hi, Karen. Yes, I've just read it," he said as the woman on the other end of the line issued orders. "Understood. We're heading up there now. I'll update you when I have more information." He ended the call, standing up from his desk. "You fancy a trip?"

"Belbroughton?"

"Yes. Karen will handle things at this end. We need to speak to Mr Andrews. And quickly."

Forty minutes later, the black BMW pulled up outside the row of houses, the onset of winter evident as the two men stepped out of the car. Leaves blew past Lewis as he stepped from the pavement to the path that led to the house. Two short raps on the door signalled their arrival. Both men could hear children playing within as the front door was opened by Hugh. "I wondered how long it would take for someone to bang on my door. I suppose you'd better come in." He led them into the kitchen, flicking the kettle on. "Would you like a drink?"

"I'll have a coffee please, Mr Andrews. White with two," Paul replied evenly.

"Same for me please," Hendry added as he leant against the kitchen worktop.

"I take it you saw my tweet? I left you a voicemail message,

Mr Lewis. I gave you ample time to respond."

Hendry looked at Lewis, who looked away, almost sheepishly, turning his attention back to Hugh. "You've created a real shit-storm, Mr Andrews."

"That was my intention. I take it by you being here that government agencies are in a bit of a flap?"

"You could say that. Where did you get the CCTV footage?"

"As they say in the movies, I am not at liberty to say. I am not being difficult, I am just desperate. My wife is missing, along with half of the village. That CCTV footage shows that this was no simple abduction. You can clearly see a shape moving across the field, with lighting then a bright light. I'm no expert on UFOs, but it very much looks like the kind of thing you see at the movies. What do you know?"

The question was simple in its delivery, leaving both men momentarily at a loss as to how to respond. Paul sighed, his shoulders relaxing. He was guessing that the man's admission about leaving him a voicemail message would come back to haunt him in due course. He knew that Karen would want his head on a spike for that lapse. His marriage was collapsing, along with his career. He was at a crossroads. "Honest answer, we simply do not know. That footage is the first time we have seen anything that could determine how they were abducted. There has been plenty of chatter across the wires. Various agencies across the world spotted an anomaly a few weeks ago, but no concrete evidence of extra-terrestrial activity has been found. Until today. Unfortunately for you, Mr Andrews, our own agencies have been alerted. I should imagine that your door will be knocked on again very soon."

"By who? The police?"

"Not the police, Mr Andrews," Paul said as he took a sip of his coffee. "I would imagine that *MI-5* will be en-route to speak to you."

"Well, that's fine. I have nothing to hide and I have done

nothing wrong."

"No, you haven't," Hendry replied. "But they will be crawling all over the village by the end of the day. The *CIA*, along with other intelligence agencies, will be asking very searching questions, Mr Andrews. This could get messy."

"I'm not concerned about that. I am only concerned about Gemma. My boys miss their mummy. Surely you can see the situation I am in?"

"We can," Paul replied. But your actions could spark panic, depending on just how viral your tweet becomes. Newspapers will be contacting us, along with other agencies. And not just in the UK. It could create a ripple effect across the globe."

"And is that a bad thing?"

Paul considered the question before replying. "Are you a religious man, Mr Andrews?"

"No. Not at all. My parents raised me Catholic. But once I grew up, I could see just what a sham it all was."

"Daddy," a voice said from the doorway. "I want *Peppa Pig*," the toddler exclaimed from the other side of the kitchen.

"Hang on a minute," Hugh said, heading into the lounge for a minute. He returned, settling himself down at the table once more.

"So, you're not religious?"

"No. Why?"

"Because, Mr Andrews, half the population of the world is. You only have to switch on the news channels to see how religion dominates our society. People live their lives by the word of many books, many of them with an unwavering certainty that a God does exist. Can you imagine what will happen if all that is suddenly called into question? There could be mass hysteria. Looting. Civil wars. The world as we know it could change forever."

"All because we discover that there is life out there?"

"Yes. I'm not religious either. Far from it. I am a bit of a science nerd, truth be told. I am fascinated by the idea that we are not alone. The idea that someone is out there. Although, snatching our citizens is not quite the way that I would have liked to have had that confirmed."

"So, what now?"

"We don't know. Yes, the footage you have is hard to discount. I'm sure that someone at *MI-5* is checking the video, to see that it hasn't been modified, which I am sure it hasn't. What happens after this moment is anyone's guess."

"But Gemma is still out there. If she was taken by some alien race, how do we find her?"

"Let's just say that she was taken by an extra-terrestrial race. Why, is unclear. We've all read about alien abductions over the years. It's usually some guy in Montana, who leaves a bar in the middle of nowhere, turning up days later, rambling on about being experimented on. Nothing like this has ever happened before. To snatch a village and disappear into the ether is quite something. And if that is true, Gemma may be a long way away. We've barely made it to the moon. Travelling to Mars is still years off. Did you know that to reach our nearest star with conventional rockets would take many thousands of years? If your wife is out there, we've got no technology even close enough to ever find her, or the others."

Hugh let out a sigh, slumping in his seat. "So, she may be lost forever?"

"Try not to think the worst just yet, Mr Andrews. We're still doing all we can. However, after your little social media stunt today, it's going to be magnified and discussed by pretty much everyone on the planet."

"I never did this to cause trouble. I did it to raise awareness that something out of the ordinary may have happened."

"We know. And for what it's worth, many other people would probably do the same thing. Just expect a lot of activity in the village. And expect many questions over the next few hours and days."

TWENTY-SEVEN

THE SHIP LANDED IN THE DISUSED HANGAR, JETS OF STEAM expelling themselves from vents on the underside of the hull. A minute later a ramp opened, slowly settling itself on the grey concrete floor of the large space. Hameda strode out purposefully, followed by Ragyi and Ullar. A small huddle of people on the far side of the hangar walked over slowly, the biting temperatures making movement difficult. "Hameda", one man said. "Welcome to Valkash."

"Thank you, Jaka. Are we set?"

"Yes," the man replied readily. "Security is very tight across the planet. However, up here, not many patrols have been seen."

"Ragyi, Ullar. Show the men the craft in the cargo hold. We need to move quickly if this is going to work." They did as their leader asked, heading off towards the ship, leaving Hameda and Jaka alone.

"Who will pilot the craft?"

"Ragyi. He is ready to give his life."

"Does he know that the bomb will probably not destroy the planet?"

"No. I have not divulged that information."

"Probably wise."

"How much damage will the bomb cause?"

"To be honest, I can only speculate. The chances that the planet will be destroyed are slim. The temperature down at the core is several thousand degrees. Your man will have to set the timer and just hope for the best. Chances are, he will be dead before the bomb has even gone off. The ship may break up to, such are the temperatures and gravitational forces down there. However, I do think that a successful detonation will upset the terraforming that has been done. All of the enclosures are surrounded by armoured glass. I've assessed the depth of the hole, along with the topography of Valkash. I am sure that if your man hits the mark, it will cause earthquakes due to the concussion the blast will have on the tectonic plates under the planet's surface. Best case scenario, most of the enclosures will be destroyed, along with all their inhabitants and staff."

"I will happily settle for that. Mass carnage is almost as appealing as a collapsing planet," Hameda replied smoothly.

"Once your man is in position to move, we all need to get the hell out of here. From this hangar, it will take him two minutes to reach the shaft and another three to four minutes until the bomb detonates. Not a huge window."

"Then we will be ready to take off as soon as you give the word, Jaka."

A loud, whirring sound echoed across the hangar as the cargo bay doors opened. A small ship was lowered from the ship, hanging a few feet from the ground as Ragyi and Ullar walked down the main ramp with the bomb. Hameda and Jaka headed over. Jaka spoke first. "You'll need to set the timer for no more than eight minutes."

Ragyi nodded, priming the timer. "Then what?"

"My men will type the coordinates into the ship's navi computer. Once you leave the hangar, the ship will guide you to the pole. It is hard to miss. The shaft is in the middle of an extinct volcano. Take the ship out of autopilot and fly straight into the hole. There will be workers there, but they won't be able to stop you once you pass into the shaft. Just keep heading down until the bomb goes off. I wish you luck, my friend. For the cause."

"For the cause," Ragyi replied, his features grim, yet resolute.

"We will ready our ship, then give you the signal."

The five men headed off towards a small craft in the corner of the hangar, heads hunkered down against the howling winds that battered the building. Hameda turned, embracing Ragyi. "This will not be in vain. Your bravery will turn the tide in our favour. In generations to come, people will speak your name across the systems. Systems that have been returned to their rightful order. I love you, Ragyi."

"I love you too, Hameda. I do this for all our sakes. I am not afraid."

Ullar hugged him. "Go in peace, dear friend."

He returned the embrace, tears streaming down his face. "And you, Ullar. We have lived our lives close together. I will take many happy memories with me. You need to see this through with Hameda."

"And we will," Hameda replied, tears falling freely. "Are you ready?"

"Yes," he said, climbing into the snug cockpit. "You had better get going. I will wait for the signal before I begin my mission."

"As you wish. Take care," Hameda said softly, squeezing his weathered hand. Ullar simply nodded, not able to speak as she walked towards the ship.

A bright light emanated across the hangar, the signal that Ragyi was waiting for. He watched as the small craft lifted off, its twin Ion drives propelling the ship out into the harsh polar environment and off into orbit. The larger ship followed suit, disappearing into the sky, leaving him alone. "Right. Let's move," he said, as he pulled back on the controls. The ship rose steadily until it was above the hangar, battered by the polar storms. "Engaging autopilot," Ragyi said to himself as the craft began its journey towards the volcano on the horizon. "Activating timer." He kept his vision straight ahead as the clock began its descent, beeping every second as he sped on. The beeping seemed to slow his pulse, relaxing Ragyi as the mountain rose up before him. "Deactivating autopilot," he said as he crested the barren summit, his eyes taking in the splendour in front of him. The extinct volcano spread out in front of him, the jagged rim looking as sharp as a predator's teeth. "Now isn't that something," he said, as the scene unfolded. His eyes caught the hole in the surface, a black crude circle in the bottom of the crater, surrounded by small grey buildings. He propelled himself downwards, seeing figures waving at him, jumping up and down. A loud warning sound erupted across the crater, the figures scattering as Ragyi shot into the entrance of the dark expanse. He flicked on a switch on the console, activating the external lights, allowing him a minimal vista. Ahead he could see a yellow glow, which seemed to increase with each beep of the bomb sat next to him. He checked the clock; less than two minutes showing on the red timer. "Better increase speed," he said, shoving the throttle to its limits. The front of the craft began to glow, small rocks bouncing off the fuselage and cockpit. One large boulder cracked the glass above Ragyi's head, and a hissing sound started bombarding his senses as he fought to keep the ship on course. Sweat dripped into his eyes, his clamped hands slick with sweat as they gripped the controls. The outside environment was changing in front of him, the hull of the ship beginning to break apart as he dropped towards the core. The splinter in the glass above him grew like a spider's web, splaying out across the domed enclosure. "FOR THE RESIS-

TANCE!" the man screamed as the glass imploded, shredding his upper body before it was reduced to ash by the fiery core around him. His charred hands relinquished control of the ship, the hull battering into the molten rock at the shaft's perimeter. The gamely craft finally lost its fight, breaking up and becoming scattered and singed as the bomb ticked down its final few seconds. A white flash lit the confines, sending a shockwave in all directions. The buildings on the surface were consumed by white heat, the workers vapourised as deep tremors rocked the planet, sending shockwaves towards the fragile surface. And to its core.

Hundreds of miles above, Hameda looked at the pole, her expression sad. "Thank you Ragyi," she uttered, turning towards the pilot. "What do you think?"

"Hard to say. But he was down there for a good four minutes before the bomb went off. Even if the planet does not collapse, I'd expect massive earthquakes, followed by a succession of aftershocks. You have dealt the Lomogs a severe blow."

"Let us hope so," she replied solemnly. "I do pity the innocent lives that have been lost and will continue to be lost. But this is for the greater good. This is for peace."

Ullar watched on silently, her grief hidden well below the surface. *Goodbye Ragyi. I truly loved you. And I always will.*

"What was that?" Kyra said as her workstation started to vibrate.

"It sounds like an earthquake," one of the laboratory technicians said, peering at her over his glasses.

"Has one happened before?" The shelves on the wall next

to her started to vibrate, glassware and utensils toppling off, smashing and clattering on the lab floor.

"Not that I know of. We'd better see what's going on."

"You stay here. I will go and find out." As she left the lab, a red warning light in the corridor began to flash, a loud alarm accompanying it.

"*Alert, alert. All personnel to proceed to their quarters. Security breach. All personnel to report to their quarters,*" the robotic warning rang out.

Kyra turned back to the lab, informing the workers to head to their quarters. They did so, hurrying out of the lab, a worried look on each of their faces. A man strode down the corridor towards her, his uniform telling Kyra that he was a member of the security force. "What's happened?" she asked as he tried to bustle past her.

"To your quarters please, we have a security breach."

"What kind of breach?" Kyra asked as she followed the man towards her quarters.

"A bomb has gone off at the pole. Please, to your quarters."

Kyra obeyed, heading to her room, her pulse racing. Once inside, she tried to call Torben, frustrated that there was no answer. She chose another option, calling Telion. "Kyra. Are you okay?"

"Not sure. We've just been informed that a bomb has gone off at the pole. Have you heard anything?"

"We've just heard too. There is a deep shaft at the Pole that runs to the planet's core. If a bomb was detonated inside the core, it may unsettle the planet's axis and topography."

"Oh no. Where are you?"

"Heading back to Biflux. We've just come out of the wormhole, ordered back to base by command."

"I'm scared, Telion. Too many bad things are happening."

"Try to stay calm, Kyra." I am sure that you'll be okay.

Just let the security forces deal with it. I am sure they will keep you all updated."

"Hope so. I will call you back Telion, should I hear anything else."

"Okay. Take care, Kyra. Over and out."

She walked over to the bunk, lying down heavily. "Hurry Torben. Please," she said as a single tear fell from her eye.

TWENTY-EIGHT

"A BOMB?" TORBEN SAID, HIS LEGS BEGINNING TO SHAKE.

"Yes, skipper. That's what's coming through on the wires. Could be nuclear. At the pole."

"What's at the pole?"

"A deep shaft that drops into the planet's crust."

"Fuck. That could de-stabilise the planet."

"Yes…yes it could."

"How long until we reach Valkash?"

"Just over an hour."

"Make it faster. I have a bad feeling about this."

"Okay, Captain. Increasing power to one hundred percent."

"How long will that take off our time?"

"Thirty minutes maximum."

"Okay. I will try to contact Kyra. Let me know when we're nearing the planet." Rex simply nodded, a grave expression on his face. Torben turned and walked out of the cockpit, heading for his quarters. He swiped his wrist pilot, calling Kyra.

"Torben. I've been trying to reach you."

"Kyra. Sorry. It may have been interference due to the explosion. Are you okay?"

"I'm scared, Torby. It's happened again. This is not going to stop, is it?"

"I don't know Kyra. We are less than two hours from Valkash. Be ready, I'm coming to get you off that rock. I will land in the docking bay close to your lab. Meet me there."

"Okay. Hurry, please."

"I love you."

"I love you too, Torben Fraken." She ended the call as a large tremor ran through the structure, the wall next to her bunk shifting until a large crack appeared. She cried out, falling back onto the floor as debris and dust started falling from the suspended ceiling. *I've got to get out of here?* she thought, as more tremors rippled through the building. Grabbing her jacket, Kyra raced back out into the corridor and saw a few people peeking their heads out from their quarters. She made her way down to the docking bay, a few command staff milling about around her, unsure of what was going on or what to do. "Back to your quarters," she said hurriedly."

"Our quarters are not in this quadrant. They are on the next level down. What is happening?"

"An earthquake," she replied, not wanting to alarm them any more than was necessary. She heard a noise like crunching ice on the far side of the docking bay. "The doors. Look!"

The man she'd spoken to turned, heading over to the large glass doors that sealed them inside from the harsh environment beyond. He was about to speak when the doors shattered inwards, obliterating him. Kyra ducked behind a large crate as the docking bay became a maelstrom of glass and noise. She looked to her left, crying out at the sight of two dead females a few feet away. Dark blood spread from their prone forms, edging its way over to her. The wind outside the docking bay roared across the low-slung space, sending glass particles in all directions, the noise deafening. She stayed motionless for a few minutes, listening for danger. Carefully, Kyra peeked her head over the crate, slowly rising before walking over to the lip of the docking bay. Her dark hair was buffeted by the outside storms, and she grabbed hold of a rail close the edge. She looked out at the expanse in front of her, a giddy sensation overwhelming her as she looked down. Lights dotted the far walls of the structure, flashing in intermittent reds and greens. She peered over the lip, looking in awe as the lights fell away into the darkness below. On the horizon, lightning crackled, lighting up the forbidding landscape that sent wind and rain towards her. Kyra lowered herself to the floor, leaning out into the black expanse. She could make out another docking bay, a hundred metres below her. The doors were intact, for now. She made a quick decision, sprinting back out of the bay into the corridor beyond as stronger tremors rocked the planet. Kyra swiped her wrist pilot, the signal connecting. "Torben. The whole place is about to collapse."

"Where are you?" he replied, his voice an octave higher than normal.

"Just outside the docking bay where we'd landed before. It's in pretty bad shape. The doors blew in and the ceiling looks like it might collapse at any moment."

"You need to find another bay. They are all below you. Can you use the sky car?"

Kyra ran to her left, noting with dread that the sky cars were shut down. "No. They must have been deactivated because of the emergency."

"There must be another way to the lower levels?"

"Hang on," she said. "There is. Through the enclosures."

"Okay. Take another route. Keep the line open and tell me where you end up. Be safe."

"Okay. I am heading towards the enclosures now." She raced along the corridor, stumbling and hitting the side walls as the whole structure began to shift. After a few hundred yards, she came to a small glass doorway. Kyra pressed her hand to the panel, pleased that it was still working. The door hissed open, her loud footsteps clanging along the walkway towards the ladders that led below. She was about to descend when something caught her eye. *The villagers.* They were six of them near to the doorway, peering in. Kyra ran over, opening the door that led into the recreated village.

"What the fuck is going on?" Caroline said as the stone walls that ran along the road started to shift on their foundations.

"There has been an explosion. We're not sure what kind of explosion, or how it happened. But the whole place is falling apart."

"Oh no," Gemma said, clutching her neck. "What are we going to do?"

Kyra could see more villagers a few hundred yards away, standing in the middle of the road. "Round them all up. Tell them to come with us. We're getting out of here. And fast."

Sarah took off, heading towards the villagers on wobbly legs; the women watched her fall, landing on all fours in the middle of the road. Unsteadily she rose to her feet, continuing on to the gathering throng of humanity. Some ran off into the village, others headed their way. A giant sky cart fell from the roof, shattering into thousands of pieces at it landed on an old barn. Shrieks and cries rang out from the advancing villagers, children screaming, women trying to comfort them as their men herded them urgently. "What the hell is going on?" Pete said as he reached the doorway.

"There has been an explosion. The planet is unstable," Kyra said, matter-of-factly. "You all need to come with me. We have no time. We must get out of here."

Pete turned, cupping his hands to his mouth. "Everyone follow us. We're getting out of here."

Countless villagers came around the corner, old and young, trying their hardest to navigate the shifting country lane as it buckled and writhed. A crack opened up in the tarmac, Loz falling into it face first. Others came to his aid, lifting the young man to his feet, shepherding him towards the waiting group. Distressed animals ran for shelter in the neighbouring field, their calls drifting over to Caroline and the others. "What about the livestock?" Gemma said.

"We'll have to leave them, hun. They can't come with us."

Tears formed at the corner of Gemma's eyes, the injustice of their situation starting to boil over. "They will die?"

"So will we if we do not leave immediately," Kyra said. I'm not sure how long all this will hold for," she said, motioning with her hands. "It may already be too late. We must leave, now."

Caroline looked over the villagers. "Is anyone left behind?"

Mutters and hushed conversations erupted amongst the villagers, heads shaking and shoulders shrugging as a few more came jogging along the lane. "Hard to say. The call went out."

A large crack reverberated behind them, the walls of the enclosure beginning to splinter. "Right. We go. Now!" Kyra shouted, heading through the doorway onto the walkway beyond.

"You lead them," Caroline said to Gemma and Katie. "I will take up the rear."

"I'll stay with you," Sarah said, a nasty welt appearing on her forehead from her earlier tumble.

"Right. Follow me," Gemma called, heading through the doorway after the retreating Kyra. Villagers filed in, some becoming squashed as they fought to get into the tight confines of the steel walkway. On the other side of the glass, a huge reptilian beast headbutted the glass, clearly spooked by the shaking of the earth around it. Villagers screamed and hollered as they barged past each other, heading towards the metal ladder that led to the level below. After a few minutes, the last of the villagers were inside the walkway, queuing like they were waiting for a bus. Gradually, the numbers dropped until only a few remained.

Caroline stood at the doorway with Pete and Martin, as a far-off droning noise carried to their ears from the village. They all turned, their mouths falling open at the sight in front of them. Black wraith-like figures floated towards them, their forms shifting in the artificial light. "What the fuck are those?" Pete said, gripping the doorway in fear.

"No idea," Martin replied, his throat feeling dry. A knot forming in his gut.

"Whatever they are, we're not hanging around to get to know them," Caroline said urgently as the three shapes came within a hundred yards of them, red eyes seeking them out from their black silhouettes. The woman headed onto the walkway a few paces behind Martin, towards the familiar blonde figure who was stood waiting. Caroline ushered Sarah towards the ladder hurriedly as Martin dropped to the level below. Pete was twenty feet behind them, his gaze still fixed on the advancing ghost-like creatures. He stumbled on the metal grating, tearing his gaze away when the glass enclosure next to him shattered, showering the thin corridor in glass. The beast ploughed headlong into the opposite wall, splintering the glass.

"FUCK! GO!" Caroline screamed as the beast advanced on them. Sarah fell from the ladder, landing heavily on the walkway below. Pete landed on his chest, looking up at Caroline as the atmosphere from the enclosure pinned him to the ground. He tried to call out, his arm barely lifting from the ground as gravity bore down on him. Caroline felt it too, struggling to edge backwards towards the ladder behind her. They locked eyes, the world around them freezing momentarily. Pete was about to mouth something when a large pair of jaws and teeth clamped onto his leg, pulling him backwards. Caroline screamed, pushing herself backwards in a futile attempt at escape. Then, she was falling, landing awkwardly on top of Sarah and a few other villagers who were lying prone on the ground. Strong hands hoisted her to her feet.

"Where's Pete?" Martin said, breathlessly.

"Gone. That thing got him."

"We need to move," Sarah shouted. "We're losing ground on them."

"They all looked along the walkway, watching as the small glass door that led to the main building beyond started to warp.

"Run," Caroline shouted, limping towards the doorway as quickly as she could. Martin was next to her, holding her under the arm to speed up their exit. A minute later they were all standing in a low corridor, the grey walls moaning under the weight of the structure above them. "That way," Caroline said, spotting the fleeing villagers as they disappeared inside another doorway.

They all came to rest inside the docking bay, Kyra standing next to the glass doors. "No," she cried.

"What is it?" Caroline asked nervously.

"We've lost power to the doors. They won't open." She swiped her pilot, a small holographic image appearing before Caroline's eyes. "Torben. We are in docking bay VK208. The doors have no power. What do we do?"

Caroline tried to listen in on the conversation, the noise around them growing louder as thuds and crashes echoed through the massive structure. "What did he say?" she asked as Kyra strode towards her.

"He is almost here. We need to head back into the corridor. He's going to blow the doors. Get everybody out. Now."

Minutes later, Kyra was standing next to the doors, Caroline next to her, watching expectantly as Shimmer050 approached. A bright light came from the front of the ship, the ship's speed decreasing until it hovered a few hundred yards in front of them. Below the ship, darkness fell away into the bowels of the planet, debris falling from the surrounding structure into the inky blackness. "Kyra. Can you hear me?"

"We're here. What are you going to do?"

"Rex is going to bring us in real close, then rotate the ship so the ion drives are facing the bay. That's how we'll blow the doors. You need to retreat to the corridor. Stay on the line."

"Okay. We're moving out of the bay." She took the Welsh woman's hand, guiding her across the low-slung space towards the door the led to the villagers. Slamming the door shut, Kyra looked at the mass of people. "Brace yourselves. He's going to blow the doors." The villagers complied, many moving further along the corridor, hushed tones carrying in all directions as they pulled loved ones to safety, children being cradled protectively against the coming onslaught.

"Are you ready Kyra?"

"Yes, Torben," was her brief reply as she huddled next to Caroline and Gemma. From underneath the door, a blinding light engulfed the corridor before a blast shook the villagers, who cried out in anguish. The door blew outwards, shattering against the stark concrete of the corridor's wall. Dust and debris blew across the area, covering the cowering villagers as Kyra and Caroline gingerly stepped into the hangar. Shimmer050 gently touched down, ejecting steam from its hull as the ramp dropped steadily.

"Kyra," Torben shouted, running from the ship towards her. She came to him, her boots crunching into shards of glass as they came together, embracing fiercely as villagers piled into the docking bay.

"Oh, thank god you're here, Torby. I thought I'd lost you." She kissed him, welcoming his arms as they embraced her.

"Everyone inside," Rex shouted, changing his dialect smoothly so the villagers understood his command. Villagers filed past him, being directed to the same holding room that they'd travelled in to this distant point.

"Torben, this is Caroline, Gemma and Sarah," Kyra said breathlessly.

"Hi," the captain replied. "We need to get moving. I have a feeling the whole place is about to collapse." A noise by the doors made them all turn as three dark shapes entered the hangar. The whirling forms hissed at them, their eyes turning from red to green in the shrouds of their shifting heads. "I've seen them before," Torben said. "They are from a nearby system."

"What are they?" Caroline asked, edging backwards.

"Svargens. And they are not friendly. Let's get out of here before they ruin our day." They needed no further coaxing as the roof above them started to buckle. Less than a minute later, the ship backed out of the hangar, Rex propelling them away from the stricken attraction. He increased altitude until Shimmer050 hung motionless a few miles above the planet. They sat there for minutes, watching as glass domes across the landscape imploded in succession. "Let's get away from the planet's orbit, Rex. If the worst happens, we could either be dragged into the planet's core or vapourised."

"Okay, skipper," the hominid said, turning the ship away from the devastation that was unfolding below them. They headed through the ionosphere, the cockpit window becoming dark as they headed into the black expanse of space.

"Head towards the wormhole. I will brief the passengers. Keep an eye out, Rex. Whoever dropped that bomb may be close by, looking for trouble." Rex nodded, taking a sip of graff as he deftly piloted the ship away from Valkash. Torben headed away from the cockpit, walking into a white rectangular room that was filled with frightened humans.

"Where are we heading?" Kyra asked expectantly.

"For the wormhole. I will contact Commander Spelk to get an update. I'm sure he won't be pleased that I disobeyed his orders. But looking at it now, it was the right thing to do. Valkash is gone. The Lomogs are under attack."

"From who?"

"The Resistance. Barajan may be dead, but his factions appear to have realigned."

"What do we do, Torby?"

"We wait. We're a few days travel from Biflux and Lundell. If things go bad, we can use the singularity drive to make the jump to another part of the cosmos." He walked amongst the villagers, suddenly feeling weary. "Listen up. You've met me before. My name is Torben. I brought you here. And for that, I am sorry. This was a bad idea, but I was only obeying my orders."

"What is happening?" Gemma asked.

"The war that we thought was over, looks to have restarted. Countless millions have perished. I will contact my command post on the moon of Lundell and await further instructions. In the meantime, the crew are preparing you something to eat and drink."

"Can't you just take us home?" Gemma asked, her voice pleading.

"That's not my call. Let's see what is happening in the Biflux system first. Please, get comfortable and take some food. Our destination is two days travel from here."

On cue, a crew member walked into the room, pushing a chrome trolley laden with provisions. Another crewmember followed, a tall reptilian being with bad breath and horizontally slitted eyes that made the children shy away, hiding behind wary parents. Torben took Kyra's hand, leading her out of the room towards his quarters. Once inside, they embraced, tears falling freely as recent events caught up with them. "I can't believe what's happening, Torby!"

"It's hard to take in. We were all foolish enough to accept that peace had returned to the systems. Now it looks like chaos will reign. I'm so sorry about your parents, Kyra. They were good people."

Hearing the mention of her family made Kyra buckle in

Torben's arms. He led her over to his bunk, lying her down gently. Slipping off his boots, he snuggled in behind her, enfolding the woman into his embrace. They lay there as the ship propelled them away from Valkash, the ion drives gently thrumming. After a few minutes, Kyra spoke. "Have you heard from Ark?"

She felt his body stiffen for a split second before he let out a long sigh. "Nothing. He was at Lomax when the bomb went off. There is not much hope that he'd survive. Such a waste. He had his whole life ahead of him." He sat up, wiping tears from his eyes before activating his pilot. "Commander Spelk."

"Fraken. Where are you?" the digitised voice replied.

"On our way back from Valkash?"

"Valkash? But I thought-?"

"Change of plan, Commander. Kyra Zakx called me from Valkash a few days ago. It seems that I was just in time. We barely made it out of there before the whole place went up."

There was a pause on the line. "Very well. After all, with no Valkash, your mission would have been pointless."

"What news from Biflux?"

"Not good. Over a hundred enemy ships are in orbit above Lundell. We're pretty sure that it's Barajan's woman, Hameda. She is leading the Resistance."

"Oh no. What will you do?"

"We are mobilising craft as we speak, monitoring the skies. If they decide to attack, we will be ready for them. Torben."

"Yes, Commander."

"Do not come back here. You're a civilian ship. You'd not last five minutes if the enemy decided to attack. Stay in touch. I will keep you updated."

"Okay, Commander. You take care."

"Over and out," was the clipped reply before the line went dead.

"What shall we do?" Kyra said as she sat up next to her captain.

"Let's continue to the wormhole. I will inform Rex about the danger. If anyone tries to attack, we'll make the jump, wherever we are."

"To where?"

"We have a group of humans that need to get home. Whatever happens, the least we can do is return them to their loved ones."

TWENTY-NINE

"The chatter on the wires is that the attraction was completely destroyed," Zowie said from his chair.

"That's good," Hameda replied. "Our ships are in formation above Lundell. Once we're through the wormhole, we will be joining them for the final assault."

"Okay. We're not far from the wormhole. In a few hours, we'll be in position above the moon. We're flying at full velocity. I don't see much point in concealing our identity. All of the military craft in the area are heading for the Biflux system. At this speed, our travel time will be cut considerably."

"Very good, Zowie," she said, placing a hand on his shoulder. "Very soon, this will all be over. The metal bastards will be wiped out. Only then can we begin rebuilding." She walked out of the cockpit, heading towards her quarters, limping slightly. *Damn leg,* she thought. *The years are creeping up on me.* Minutes later, Hameda was standing naked in the shower, lukewarm water cascading over her. Her hands slathered a rich blue gel over her body, sliding over the numerous purple scars that she had collected over a lifetime of toil and fighting. Towelling off, she padded across to her bunk, collapsing on the soft mattress. The gentle thrum of the ion drives quickly took her, sending Hameda into a deep, fitful sleep.

―――

"Captain Fraken. Come in, over."

"Commander Spelk. I hear you."

"What is your position?"

Torben relayed their coordinates, the line crackling for a few seconds as his superior digested the information. "Standby."

"Okay."

"We've received information from a reliable source. The craft carrying the perpetrators of the attacks are not far from your position. They are heading for the wormhole. Be careful."

"Is it a military craft?"

"Negative. It's a freighter. It's heading towards the wormhole, moving quickly."

"What do you want me to do, Commander?"

"Track it. Keep us informed of its position. If Hameda is on board, we want to take her out before she reaches Lundell. If she manages to make it to onto the moon it will be hard to displace her, let alone kill her. We think that the gathering ships are waiting for her to arrive."

"Do you have their signature? I can ask Rex to lock onto their position and keep close behind them."

Commander Spelk relayed the data, Rex punching it into the ship's computer. "I have them, skipper. Off to our starboard side, 10,000 miles ahead. They are travelling at 0.05 of light speed."

"Match their speed, Rex. How far to the wormhole?"

"Five hours."

"Okay. Keep on their wake, Commander Spelk. We are

following them, hanging back far enough so that they do not detect us."

"Good. I will contact you in a few hours, Captain. Good work. Over and out."

"Rex," Torben said. "Anything strange happens, contact me immediately. I'm going to see Kyra and the humans."

"Okay, skipper. I won't lose them."

Torben walked along the corridor, his mind a tumult of thoughts. He knocked on Kyra's door, waiting as a few crew members walked past, greeting him warmly. "Torben. What news?"

He moved past her, sitting down on the bunk. She joined him, holding his hand. "The craft containing the rebels is 10,000 miles in front of us, heading towards Lundell. Commander Spelk wants us to follow them. Hameda, their leader, may well be on board. It looks like they're going to hit Lundell, possibly using it as a command post."

"Can they do that?"

"Anything is possible. Commander Spelk is getting his ships ready to intercept her. It won't be easy. She has allies in position above Lundell, waiting for her to arrive. It could get ugly."

"Hameda. Is that Barajan's woman?"

"Yes. She has taken over the resistance."

"She killed my parents. Your friend too, along with millions of innocents."

"Yes. And I am sure that she will pay the price."

"I hope so. If I get my hands on her, I will do it myself. The murderous bitch!"

Torben kissed her tenderly on the forehead, squeezing her briefly. "Come on. Let's go and see the humans."

. . .

They walked into the stark room, the villagers looking up expectantly. Torben addressed Gemma and Caroline as they walked over, beakers in hand. "How are you all doing?"

"We're okay. We've done a headcount. We lost three people during the evacuation. I saw one die, the other two were an old couple. They may have been asleep. So, we're five people down from when we were abducted. Such a shame."

"Yes, it is. We are sorry for putting you through all this. And for what? A war is about to begin again."

"Oh fuck. What is happening?" Caroline asked.

"The leader of the resistance is responsible for an attack on an orbital station a few days ago. Millions were killed. Then the same leader set off a nuclear warhead on Biflux, our home planet. Kyra lost her parents and I lost my best friend and countless others that I have known and worked with for half my life."

"I'm so sorry," Caroline said, her shoulders sagging.

"We plan to take you home, Caroline. But first, we are to track their ship. They are making their way to Lundell, which is Biflux's moon. If they take control of the command post there, the war will be over before it has begun. All our lives will be over. The Lomogs are strong in technology, but weak when it comes to warfare. Their military is depleted, their resources scant. It will be over quickly."

"What will you do if it goes tits up?"

"Tits up?" Kyra asked, confused.

"Sorry. Earth talk. I mean if the resistance wins the war. Where will you go?"

"Honestly, we don't know. I still have the ship. The ion drive and singularity drive can take us anywhere we choose. But it's not that simple."

"Why not?" Gemma asked.

"You Earthlings are primitive when it comes to under-standing the universe. You have probably only scratched the surface regarding habitable worlds. Yes, there are billions out there. But it's not that simple. Many are still very primitive, with pack animals and no infrastructure. The advanced races, of which there are billions, may be hostile. The universe is a savage place. If we did have to leave, finding a new home would prove difficult."

"There is always Earth," Caroline said hesitantly.

Torben smiled. "I think not. We've plundered your planet, abducting several of its citizens, some of whom have died. That is on me. I am sure that your leaders would want my head on a block."

"But you were under orders. We would vouch for you," Gemma said, smiling at them both.

"Maybe. But we also have to think about the consequences of arriving at your world. I am sure that it would cause much upheaval."

Both women looked at each other, accepting the captain's words. "Yes. I suppose you're right. Earth is not ready for that revelation. There must be another option."

"There probably is. And if the worst comes to the worst, we will find that option. We both have much to live for, despite the events of the last few days." Kyra linked hands with Torben, placing her head on his shoulder. Both women knew there and then that the man and woman were an item. They could see the love and tenderness that they exuded towards each other.

"How long until we get to where we're heading?"

"A few hours until we reach the wormhole. Then probably about twelve hours to reach Lundell. The ship is almost at full velocity. We are making good time. I will speak to the crew, ask them to bring more food for you all. Along with something to sleep on. I'm sure we can accommodate you. After all, you're not prisoners, just guests. Could you relay what I've told you to your friends? I'm sure they want an update," he said, looking over at the villagers who sat watching the exchange.

"Will do. And thank you. I know we didn't get off to the

best of starts. But we know that you were just following orders," Caroline said, putting the record straight. Torben and Kyra exited the room, leaving the villagers sat in clumped groups as Caroline and Gemma gave them the latest update. And the hope of returning home.

THIRTY

"Just lie down. Both of you," Hugh said as he stood over Oscar and Finn. They were on their sofa, fluffy blankets trying to cover their bodies.

"Daddy, we want *Peppa Pig*."

"No, we don't," Finn said. "Can we have our *iPads?*"

"In a minute, guys," Hugh said as he placed the black bucket next to the sofa. "You both need to lie still. If you don't, you'll be sick again."

"Daddy," Oscar said. "I don't want to be sick. It not nice."

"I know, champ. Finn, I will get your *iPad* and headphones. Oscar can watch *Peppa Pig*. Okay?"

"Okay, Daddy," Finn replied. He returned a minute later, handing over the iPad and headphones for Finn, before putting a *Peppa Pig* series on the television. As Hugh walked into the hall, the door was rapped on twice. He opened the door, being greeted by two men. Another two men, looking official in dark suits with solemn faces.

"Mr Andrews?"

"Yes."

"My name is Spencer. This is Hargreaves. We'd like to ask you a few questions," the man said, producing a black warrant card. Hargreaves followed suit, two sets of identification on display.

Hugh looked at the cards, *MI-5* clearly displayed in the top left-hand corners. "Okay. But we need to talk here on the step. I have two sick boys inside. They both have the *Norovirus*."

Both men exchanged glances, Hargreaves taking a precautionary step backwards. "That's okay, Mr Andrews. We can talk here if it's more convenient, for now. I take it you know what this is in relation to?"

"My *tweet*?"

"Yes. I would like to know how you obtained the CCTV footage that you posted on the internet?"

"I'm not sure I want to do that."

"Why not? Your post has created quite a stir. Many agencies across the globe are analysing the footage. Our government are very keen to understand where the images came from. We're not here to make things difficult for you, Mr Andrews. However, having looked at the images, I could deduce that it came from a property in the village. It would not take us long to figure out the origin. You could just save us some time."

Hugh let out a sigh, leaning against the doorjamb. "I was walking around the field where the abduction happened. I noticed a gap in the conifers at the side of the field. That's when I spotted a security camera. So, I found the house and spoke to the owner. She's an old lady, guys, so go easy on her. She only had it fitted because she'd been broken into a few times."

"You can relax, Mr Andrews. We'll not cause her any concerns. We would just like to take a copy of the footage. Could you please tell us where the lady lives?"

Hugh gave them the road name, feeling guilty for doing so. "I wish I could come with you, to soften the blow. But I cannot leave my boys."

"That's understandable. But we'll take it from here."

"What do you think about the footage?"

"We cannot speculate as to the authenticity of the film at this point. It appears genuine, but until we have definitive proof, we would rather not disclose our opinion."

"Is there any news on my wife and the other villagers?"

"Nothing new, I'm afraid. Believe me, there are more people looking for them than you'd think. I'm sure we will find them. We may need to ask you further questions, Mr Andrews."

"That's fine. I'll be home for a few days by the looks of it."

"Okay. Good day."

The front door closed, both men heading out onto the pavement.

"I'm sure we'll find them?" Hargreaves said.

"I had to say something to keep him on side. We both know that they'll never be found, Nick."

"If the footage is genuine, there is no way in hell that they will be found. But where are they?"

"Who knows? They could be anywhere. The universe is a big place. Right, let's find out where the little old lady lives." They headed off along the pavement, the crisp autumn sunlight warming their skin. As they skirted the centre of the village they noticed the playground, devoid of life.

Hours later, Spencer's phone started chiming as the two men sat opposite the playground, as the sun touched the top of the trees near the field to their right. "Spencer," he said efficiently. He listened for a few moments, nodding in agreement with his superior back in London. He ended the call, blowing out a breath.

"Well?" Hargreaves asked impatiently.

"It's been confirmed. The footage has not been doctored."

"So, it could be an alien abduction?"

"They are calling it an unexplained occurrence at this point. That will be the official line. But we know it's probably is an extra-terrestrial encounter."

"Fuck. If this is ever confirmed, it would cause a world-wide panic."

"Maybe. It certainly would create a new way of thinking about religion. I'm sure it would cause unrest across the globe too. God versus Allah would kinda be a moot point. In a way, it may be a blessing. It's hard to blow things up for a cause that you believe in if the cause is proved to be false."

"I suppose you're right. What do we do now?"

"Head back to London. The Director-General is with the PM, briefing her on the events. He wants all operational heads back at Box 500 this evening."

"Traffic's going to be a bitch," Hargreaves replied, buckling his seatbelt.

"Believe me. Traffic is the least of our concerns," Spencer replied as the black Audi pulled away from the kerb, heading south.

THIRTY-ONE

THE BIFLUX SYSTEM

"They are altering course," Rex said.

"Significantly?" Torben responded, placing his graff in the cup holder next to his chair.

"No. I'm guessing that they are to rendezvous with the other ships that lie in wait above Lundell. So, they are heading around the moon to the far side."

"How far are they in front?"

"9,000 miles."

"Okay. Let's put our foot down. I want them in our sights by the time we reach Lundell."

"Okay, skipper," Rex replied, pushing the ion drive almost to its limits.

Torben activated his pilot. "Commander Spelk."

"Torben. Where are you?"

"A few hours from Lundell. We're gaining on the craft, which has altered course slightly. By the time we reach the moon, we'll be right on top of them. What news your end?"

"Not good. We sent up a few craft, in an attempt to scatter them. They destroyed them. They are heavily armed and prepared to fight to the death. The Lomogs have sealed off command with a ring of steel around them. Our greatest concern is that the craft you're tracking has a nuclear weapon on board. If that goes off, it's game over for all of us."

"Understood, Commander. I will call back when we have the moon in sight."

"Okay. Be safe, over and out."

"Over and out," Torben replied, breaking the connection. "Shit. They may have another warhead."

"That's not good. Like Spelk said if they detonate that on Lundell, it will wipe out the Lomogs and the Biflex people. The resistance will have succeeded."

"Let's try not to think about that. Let's catch them up and monitor them. The craft is a freighter, it will not be armed with anything that would harm us. Let's stick to them. It may make them do something rash."

"Fraken?"

"Yes, Commander."

"Hameda has made contact with us. She is demanding that our ships move aside, allowing her to access to the Lomogs' compound."

"And?"

"The Lomogs refused. It is down to us to stop the invasion."

"I'm coming up on Lundell. Their craft is now stationary, with several ships surrounding her."

"Okay. It looks like our craft are about to engage. It's going to get pretty hairy in there. I suggest that you move away to a safe distance and maximise your shields. Stand by, Fraken."

"Okay."

A few minutes went by, the static on the communication the only noise in the cockpit. Kyra walked in, sitting down next to Torben. "Any news?"

"We're standing by. Something is happening."

Before Kyra could reply, a voice crackled over the airwaves. "Fraken," Spelk said.

"Commander."

"They've just issued another threat. If we don't allow access they are going to crash into command, detonating the nuke."

"Oh no. Can your craft reach them in time to stop the attack?"

"Negative. The surrounding craft are laying down fire. Can you see that from your vantage point?"

"Just about. I can see flashes."

"We will not be able to stop them entering the atmosphere, should our crafts fail to take them out. Hang on. Many craft are moving, heading towards our orbit. I think they are going to try and break through the barricade."

"Shit," Rex said. "This looks like it could be the end."

"Commander, stand by," Torben said. "Rex. I have an idea."

"Many of the advancing craft have been taken down," Zowie informed Hameda. "However, they have Ion cannons on the ground. We will not stand a chance against them."

"Do you think we could land and penetrate the command post?" Hameda said, her voice edgy.

"I doubt it. There are hundreds of turrets, each aimed towards our position. Once we break through the upper atmosphere, they will unload on us."

Hameda pressed a virtual button on the display. "Brothers. This is Hameda. It looks like the Lomogs are going to try to stop us landing. I want all craft to descend. Take as many advancing craft as you can. And then take out their ground defences. Ankart. Your craft is to stay close to ours. Hold your position." Several voices came through the ship's speakers, all agreeing to engage. Hameda watched in rapt concentration as the resistance began advancing on Lundell, bright flashes emitting from their canons. Ullar and Zowie stared, frozen like statues as they watched many of the attacking craft. A shadow fell across the cockpit, blocking out the sun's ray as Commander Ankart's ship sat a few hundred feet above them.

"We've lost several craft, but so have they," Zowie stated, watching the heads-up display. "We're down to seventy-eight ships, all heading for command. Most of their advance party have now been taken out. But their ground defences are taking us out."

Hameda opened communications. "Aim for the ground cannons. Take them all out!" she barked. They all watched as explosions rocked the surface of the moon a hundred miles below them. Flashes of red and white peppered the surface as the resistance scored numerous hits to the ground defences. After ten minutes Hameda's last ship crashed into the mountain behind the command, engulfing the surrounding forest in flames.

Zowie looked up at Hameda, his face stricken. "All our craft have been wiped out, but most of their Ion cannons have too. I count three left, dotted around the command post."

"Very well. Commander Ankart. Head for the command post. Full fire on the cannons. We will shadow you." Hameda turned to Ullar. "Go to the warhead. Prep the timer for thirty seconds and stand next to it until I give the order. If we're going out, they're all going with us."

THIRTY-TWO

"Do you think it will work?" Rex said as he punched coordinates into the ship's computer.

"Not sure. I don't think anyone has ever tried it before. I was never told not to try it," Torben replied, the first flutterings of fear taking hold of him.

"How do we do this?" Kyra asked, gripping the armrests of her chair.

"Rex, Hameda's freighter is a few hundred metres behind the other ship. We need to do this quickly. You need to get directly above them, matching their speed. Then, engage the Singularity drive."

"Okay, here goes nothing," he responded, pushing the throttle forward.

"Hang on," Torben said to Kyra, taking her hand. "Things could get a little bumpy."

"Hameda. A ship is approaching our rear. It's moving fast."

"What kind of ship? Military?"

"Negative," the pilot replied. "It's an exploratory vessel."

"Then what the hell is it doing tracking us? Can we speed up and lose them?"

"No. It's coming in fast. If we speed up, we run the risk of hitting Commander Ankart's ship."

Hameda pressed a button on the console. "Commander, we have a ship approaching our rear. Can you take it out?"

After a brief pause of static on the line, Ankart replied. "Engaging our rear cannons now. Slow down, Hameda, so we have a better chance of destroying it."

"Slowing down," Zowie said, the ship's inertia making Hameda almost stagger forward. She gripped the seat in front of her, waiting for the Ion cannons ahead to unleash their power on the unknown ship approaching.

"Whoever you are, you've picked the wrong ship to mess with," she said, smiling. "See you in hell."

"Skipper, the attack ship is about to fire on us."

"Shields up, Rex," Torben said urgently, sweat peppering his brow. "Make evasive manoeuvres if you need to."

A white pulse appeared a few miles ahead, racing towards them across the void of space. Rex moved the controls to his left sharply, Shimmer050 veering out of the way of the onslaught. "They mean business, skipper."

"So do we. We have little time, Rex. We need to do this now. Whatever it takes, give it your best shot."

"Here goes," the hominid replied, closing the gap on the old looking freighter. He matched their speed easily, swerving the ship to its right as another bolt of cannon fire shot passed them. Shimmer050 moved upwards slowly until the two ships were almost touching.

Alert, alert! Proximity warning. Please alter course, a computerised voice rang out across the cockpit.

Rex's green fingers hovered over the holographic icon in

front of his face for a second as he said a silent prayer. He activated the Singularity drive, his stomach lurching as the ship
dropped violently into the vortex underneath.

"What the fuck's going on?" Caroline shouted as the villagers
staggered and slid across the room.

"I don't know," Gemma said, steadying herself against the
wall. An alarm sounded across the ship, the villagers looking
worried as they clutched their loved ones to them. Before
Caroline could reply, the ship lurched downwards, the Welsh
woman's feet leaving the floor as the ship jumped from one
side of the universe to the other.

The ship's alarm continued to sound for several seconds,
Shimmer050 spinning helplessly out of control until Rex
managed to engage enough thrust to slow them down to a
standstill. They sat in silence, watching as the old looking
freighter continued to spin in front of them, propelled by the
force of the wormhole's vortex. After a minute, the ship
floated a few miles from their position, facing them. "Rex,
open all communication frequencies," Torben said quietly, his
hand still gripping Kyra's.

They waited a few minutes until a voice crackled over
the airwaves. "Unknown craft. Who are you, and what the
hell have you done?" It was a female voice, loaded with
menace.

"This is Shimmer050," Torben stated. "We are under the
command of the Lomogs. You were about to destroy our
command post. I made sure that didn't happen."

"How? Where the fuck are we?"

"I made the jump, using our Singularity drive to transport
us to another point in space. You are now 13,000,000,000

light years away from Biflux. You are out of their reach. Your plan has failed."

The line went dead for a few minutes, the three of them waiting nervously for a response. "If what you say is true, then I order you to return us to Biflux."

"You have no authority over me. And you have no authority here. It's over, Hameda."

"So, you know who you're dealing with. Well, I have one more weapon at my disposal. If we are to die out here, you'll join us."

"Rex. Get us out of here," Torben said after he'd ended communications.

"Where do we go?"

"Head towards Earth. We can outrun them while we think of a plan to destroy them." Rex needed no further instruction as he engaged the ion drive. The ship shot forward, veering away from the other craft.

"They are following us, skipper."

"I expected them too. Increase to full power. We have to get some good distance between us. How long will it take to reach Earth?"

"Based on our velocity, just over a day," Rex said as he checked the ship's computer.

"Okay. Kyra. We need to speak to the villagers. Let's go."

She followed him out of the cockpit, her legs still trembling. "I cannot believe that worked."

"Nor can I. Remind me never to do it again though."

"How do we destroy them?"

"That's what I want to find out. I am sure that Earth can lend a hand."

They walked into the room, the villagers looking over expectantly. Caroline, Gemma and Sarah strode over, Caroline limping slightly. "What the fuck just happened?" she said, her voice strained.

"We made the jump. The ship that we were tracking was about to unleash a nuclear bomb on our people. We made sure that didn't happen. Sorry for the bumpy ride. Fortunately, we made the jump without any damage to the ship, just a few minor injuries. Are you okay?"

"I'll live. Twisted my ankle though, but I'm sure it will be okay. So, where are we?"

"Close to a red planet, not far from Earth."

"You mean Mars," Sarah said, her voice edged with excitement. Other villagers headed over, wanting to hear what was transpiring.

"Yes. We are about one day's travel from Earth. But we have a problem. The other ship is following us. It intends to detonate the bomb, destroying us all."

Cries rang out from the villagers. "You've got to do something," a woman yelled.

"We are doing something," Torben replied, trying to settle the group of humans standing around him. "Caroline, I need you to come with us."

"Okay, Gemma and Sarah need to come too."

"As you wish. The rest of you, stand by. I will arrange for more food to be sent through to you. The other ship is not as fast as us. We are already several hundreds of miles ahead of them. They have no other weaponry, just the bomb. If they detonate it now, we'll be too far away for any damage to affect us. Be calm. We shall give you an update when we have it." The five of them left the room, heading for the cockpit at the front of the ship. As they walked in, Rex turned, shocked by the humans that stood gawping at him. "Rex, this is Caroline, Gemma and Sarah."

"Hello," Rex said, switching to English seamlessly. "Welcome to the best view in town."

The three women smiled, liking the furry face that smiled

back at them. "Hello", they all replied, Caroline's eyes drawn to the hexagon on the hominid's chest.

"Rex is my pilot and a good friend." He turned to the women, his face serious. "The other ship contains the leader of the resistance, Hameda. She is responsible for the death and destruction where we've just come from. She dropped the bomb on Valkash, which nearly killed you all. If she has her way, she will destroy our ship, and everyone on board."

"So, how do we stop her?" Caroline asked tentatively.

"What weapons do you have on Earth?"

"We have loads," Sarah replied. "We have planes, tanks and ships. We also have nuclear weapons, although no one would ever launch one. It would result in a world war."

"Okay," Torben replied. "What do you have that flies?"

"Planes," Sarah responded. "We have fighter jets. Thousands of them."

"Would they be able to shoot a ship down?"

"I think so. What do you two think?" she said, looking at Caroline and Gemma.

"Definitely," Caroline responded. "We have over two-hundred countries on Earth. Our own country, along with America, has enough firepower to bring down most things. What are you thinking?"

"If that ship detonates the bomb, it will destroy us. We're stuck here now. I'm not going to risk another jump leaving Hameda in this solar system. She could wreak havoc. How many planets are there in your system?

"Eight," Gemma replied confidently. She looked at the other two, smiling. "Discovery Channel is amazing. Earth is the only planet that has life on it. The others are just lumps of rock, ice and gas.

"Okay. Does your planet have the technology to engage the other craft out here?"

"No," Gemma said. "We can barely make it outside our own orbit. We've only visited our moon a few times and that was years ago. If they are going to get involved, they need to do it on Earth."

"Planet coming up," Rex stated, making the others look out of the cockpit windows.

"Jesus Christ!" Caroline said. That's…Mars."

"Oh, my," Gemma said, her eyes widening. To think, we're the first people to ever see that. It's beautiful."

"Fuck," Sarah said. "I wish my phone had some charge in it. That would look amazing on Instagram." Caroline and Gemma looked at her, smiling. They all linked hands, watching in amazement as the red planet grew larger on their port side. Silence descended over the cockpit for a few minutes, Torben and Kyra also admiring the planet, an angry slash running across its surface.

Finally, Torben spoke. "Rex. Open up communications with Earth. See if anyone is reachable."

"Okay, skipper."

"I need you with us. If anyone answers, you will need to speak to them, telling Earth the situation. Can you do that?"

"Of course," Caroline said.

Rex opened up communication lines, sliding his fingers across the virtual display until static erupted inside the cockpit. It reminded Caroline of her childhood, trying to tune in her grandfather's shortwave radio. "There is no one on the line," Rex said.

"Caroline, I want you to relay a message. Hopefully, someone on Earth hears it. We have less than a day's travel. We need Earth to be ready for us." He pressed a button on the console, nodding at the woman.

"Err, hello. This is Caroline Dixon. I was abducted from Belbroughton a few weeks ago. I know this is going to sound crazy, but I am on the ship that took us, heading back towards Earth. We are in trouble and need your help. Please respond, over." Torben released the button, nodding in satisfaction.

"Over?" Gemma said, smiling.

"Isn't that what they say? Or is it over and out?"

"Doesn't matter, sweetie," Sarah said. That was great. If someone, somewhere hears it, they'll flush it up the system. We just need to sit tight."

"That's all we can do," Gemma said. "Sit tight and enjoy the scenery."

THIRTY-THREE

"WHERE ARE THEY HEADING?" HAMEDA SAID. THE SOLAR system around them had become a featureless void, only a bright star on the horizon offering them any vista. They had passed a large, red planet some hours before, marvelling at the striking features it offered before they ploughed on, chasing their quarry.

"No idea," said Zowie. "We are flying blind. I have no idea what is in this system. There are three planets out there, millions of miles away from us. They look too close to the main star to be habitable."

Ullar stood next to the door, a resigned look on her face. "Hameda. We've lost. There is no way back from this."

"Ullar," she said, feeling like she'd been punched in the stomach. "How can you say that? We're on the brink of a new order. Finally bringing peace to the systems."

"You heard what the man said. We're on the other side of the universe. There is no way our ship can return unless you force them to repeat what they've just done. And they won't do that. If we destroy them, it will be for nothing."

"I can't believe I am hearing this. From you of all people!"

"Look around. Where are we? Nowhere. We've lost. Most

of our ships were destroyed. The Lomogs and Biflex will rally themselves. They will restore their own order."

Hameda walked over to the other woman, a look of desolation etched across her face. "My dear Ullar," she said. "If you truly believe that, then I have no place for you." Ullar's eyes opened in shock as the older woman sank a blade into her chest, leaving it embedded to the hilt. She opened the cockpit door, motioning to the two guards who stood nonchalantly outside. "Put her in the airlock," she said defiantly. "I have no room on this ship for traitors." Two figures came through the door, dragging Ullar out of the cockpit into the corridor that led to the rear of the freighter. Hameda turned to Zowie. "Catch them. Whatever it takes. Catch that bastard ship."

"As you wish, Hameda," he replied, sweat trickling down his back, his hands shaking.

The two guards dragged Ullar easily towards the rear of the ship, flinging her into the wall next to the rear airlock. One aimed a kick at her jaw, snapping her head back into the wall, sending a few teeth skittering across the floor. One grabbed her breast, tightening his grip until Ullar cried out in anguish, not able to fend off the assault. They spoke in a language the dying woman didn't understand. They were not quite humanoid, their skin reptilian, with livid purple scales adorning their flesh. They both kicked her in turn, slapping her across the face with dry, calloused hands. The larger of the two reached down, grabbing her hair, twisting it in between his digits, making her cry out in pain once more as blood dripped from her mouth. The other sneered, aiming a kick between her legs that she managed to deflect with her thigh. The impact was ferocious enough to make her slip sideways onto the floor, retching in agony. They spat at her, issuing curses, their laughter echoing off the walls. Satisfied with their abuse, the guards walked a dozen paces towards the end of the corridor, a series of beeps and buzzers ringing out across the corridor. Through her fuzzy vision, Ullar could see that they were having trouble activating the inner doors, an argument brewing as one became frustrated with the other. She managed to drag herself into a sitting position, blood oozing from the blade still embedded in her chest. Every movement sent shockwaves of pain through her body, nausea hitting Ullar in waves, her vision blurry. She tried to take stock of her situation, her eyes falling on the door across the corridor. It was not marked, but she knew what lay inside. *The bomb*, she thought, peering back at the squabbling guards. As quietly as she could, she shuffled across the walkway, carefully opening the door into the darkened space beyond. The door clicked shut, Ullar knowing that she had mere seconds before they'd realise she was gone. The dark room was empty, save for a table in the centre. A table that supported a large cylindrically shaped device. On the other side of the door, she heard the arguing stop, a momentary pause as the guards realised they had been given the slip. Angry incomprehensible voices drew nearer, Ullar flailing across the room until she collided with the warhead. "I love you, Ragyi. See you on the other side," the woman said as she activated the countdown, four strong scaly hands dragging her back out into the corridor a split-second after. She landed in the airlock painfully, the goons smiling at her from the other side of the glass, completely unaware of what was about to happen. Ullar closed her eyes for the last time, waiting for the blackness of death.

Hameda sat in the chair, looking out as the cosmos sped past the cockpit windows. "What's taking them so long? she said, suddenly concerned.

"The airlock has not been activated yet," Zowie said, his brow knitting in confusion.

"They've been gone ten minutes. How long does it take?"

"Not that long," he countered.

Fear gripped Hameda as she levered herself out of the chair. "I'm going to see what they are playing at," she said, leaving the cockpit, heading towards the airlock. A few minutes later she came across them, her stride quickening as they closed the inner airlock behind them. She could hear them laughing, clearly enjoying their task. "What's taking you so long?" she said, peering through the airlock at Ullar. She looked serene, her eyes closed as if she were sleeping. Hameda looked behind her, noticing the door hanging open. Her insides constricted, a cold feeling washing over her as a faint beeping noise drifted through the doorway. "Oh no," she uttered as her vision exploded into a thousand Supernovae.

"Skipper. Explosion. Behind us," Rex stated urgently.

"How far?"

"Several thousand miles," the pilot replied, activating the rear camera. They crowded around the screen, watching as a ball of light lit the solar system, a silent aurora fanning out across the blackness of space.

"The ship has disappeared off the radar, skipper. I think it blew up."

"How?" Torben said edgily.

"I don't know. Malfunction maybe."

"Keep our velocity at this speed. I'm not taking any chances, Rex."

"Okay."

"How long until we reach Earth?"

"Twelve hours. I will need to slow before we reach the planet."

"Okay. Keep an eye out for our friends. Let us hope that

the ship malfunctioned and that we are in the clear." He looked at Kyra. "What do you think?"

"I don't know. I am hoping that you're both right. Maybe something went wrong on the ship."

They headed out of the cockpit, walking slowly back to Torben's quarters. Once inside, they collapsed onto the bunk, the man pulling the sheet over them. They lay there, feeling each other's heartbeat along with the steady thrum of the ion drive. It settled them gradually, Kyra falling asleep first. He succumbed to sleep quickly, all thoughts of death and destruction falling away into the blanket of space.

THIRTY-FOUR

EARTH

"PAUL, YOU NEED TO HEAR THIS," HENDRY SAID AS HE BUSTLED into the office, iPad in hand. Paul looked up, his eyes bleary, his chin dotted with grey stubble. He'd slept on the sofa the night before after a confrontation with his wife. Fireworks had ensued, Paul stating flatly that their marriage was over. He'd left the house at the crack of dawn, not bothering to shower or change his clothes. Fortunately, he kept a toothbrush and aftershave in his desk and was able to freshen up somewhat before the throng of staff arrived at *GCHQ*.

"What is it?" he said, his throat dry.

Hendry caught sight of his features, slowing down his stride. "Jesus! You look like shit. Did you sleep here?"

"Long story. Anyway, enough about me. What have you got?"

Hendry bustled over, swiping his tablet a few times. "This."

"Err, hello. This is Caroline Dixon. I was abducted from Belbroughton a few weeks ago. I know this is going to sound crazy, but I am on the ship that took us, heading back towards Earth. We are in trouble and need your help. Please respond, over."

"What the fuck! Are you winding me up?"

"No. It came through a few hours ago. Chinese satellites picked it up first, then the NSA. It appears genuine, the signal did not come from Earth. Our guys are trying to triangulate a position as we speak."

Paul looked at the clock on the wall. *Almost nine.* He was about to speak when his desk phone chirped into life. "Karen," he said. Paul listened for a few seconds before replying. "Yes, I've just heard the message…. Okay. We're on our way up." He turned to John. "The boss is calling a meeting. I will see you up there." Paul waited a minute, opening his drawer before spraying some more aftershave onto his neck. He straightened his tie, walking over to the mirror to check his reflection. *God. I look like death warmed up,* he thought, knowing that a quick trip to the bathroom was needed.

The office door opened, Sylvia peering through. "Good morning, Paul. What's going on? The place has gone mental."

He walked across to his desk, donning his grey suit jacket. "It looks like our abductees have been found."

"Really? Oh, that's good news. Where are they?"

"Heading towards Earth. On a spacecraft."

Sylvia checked herself, looking at Paul, her expression blank. "What?"

"Keep it under wraps for now. I will update you when I get out of the meeting, whenever that will be."

"Oh, okay," she said, standing before him.

"And if you're still up for that coffee, we should put a date in the diary?"

"Really?" she said, her expression brightening.

"Yes, really," he said, kissing her on the cheek. "It's time I started living my life again." He walked passed Sylvia, his aftershave enveloping her as she heard his footsteps receding out of the office. The woman turned, hanging her coat in the outer office before heading out to get her first coffee of the day.

"I reduced velocity an hour ago. We're approaching Earth's moon," Rex stated, holding a steaming cup of graff in his green paw.

Kyra and Torben looked at the blue planet on the horizon, marvelling at its vivid colour, tendrils of white cloud wrapping themselves around its equator. "Kyra, could you ask Caroline and her friends to join us please?" Torben said.

"Okay, skipper," she replied, smiling.

He grinned at her as she walked out of the cockpit. Torben turned to Rex. "How long until we get there?"

"Less than an hour. Coordinates are locked."

"Great," he said, sitting down next to the hominid.

"Do you want some graff?" Rex asked.

"I'd love some," he replied, his throat scratchy. "Any news on the other ship?"

"Nothing. We'd have seen them by now, skipper. I think they are long gone," he replied, before leaving Torben at the controls of his ship.

Rex returned minutes later, flanked by four females. "I brought enough for all of us," he said cheerfully, handing them out to Kyra, Caroline, Gemma and Sarah. They all thanked him, crowding inside the confines of the cockpit.

"Thank you, Rex," Torben said, taking a tentative sip of the herby concoction. "Perfect. Now, how do you want to do this?" he asked the three humans.

"How do you mean?" Caroline asked quizzically.

"It's daylight on your side of the planet. We can drop a cloak over us. No one would see us approach or land. It might make things run a little smoother that way."

They pondered for a moment, Caroline clearing her

throat. "Do that then. But can you remove the cloak when you actually land?"

"I suppose so, why?"

"Because our governments will try to cover this up. If people see the ship and take pictures and videos, it will be hard to deny it." She looked at the other two. "Do you agree?"

"Hell yes!" Gemma said. "It may cause a commotion at first. But UFOs and aliens have been covered up for too long. It's time the world knew the truth."

"I'm with you both," Sarah said. "Let's do this."

"Okay, Rex, initiate cloak."

"Initiated," he said with a flick of his wrist.

"Damn," Sarah said. "I miss my phone. Imagine that as your profile pic," she said, nodding towards Earth.

"It sure is a sight to behold," Caroline said. "God. All I want is a bacon butty and a cup of real tea. The rest can come later."

"A hot shower," Sarah said. "And a latte."

"A cuddle with my boys. And Hugh of course," Gemma replied, her eyes misting over.

"Ahh, hun," Caroline said. "They'll all be having plenty of cuddles soon. They'll have to prize you off them."

"Bring it on!"

Caroline looked at Torben and Kyra. "What will you do, once you've dropped us off?"

"Well, it's probably wise that we don't hang around. I am sure there would be many Earthlings who would like to ask us questions, and probably seize our ship. I'm sure we would not be allowed to leave your planet. So, as soon as your feet touch ground we will head off."

"Where?"

"Back to Biflux. We need to see what has happened. Hameda is no more, the resistance looks to have been wiped out on Lundell. Maybe we can piece it all back together again?"

"Let's hope you can," Gemma said. She stepped across to Torben, kissing him on the cheek. "We do not blame you for what has happened. You were following orders. Once we're back on Earth and can tell our story, we will make sure everyone knows that."

"Thank you," the captain replied, feeling humbled. "Could one of you please let your people know what we're about to do? Once we're ready to land, we will need them off the ship as fast as possible."

"Okay," Sarah said, heading for the door.

"Good idea. As soon as someone sees the ship, our air force will have planes in the air. But that will probably a while to organise. I'm sure you'll be heading home by that point." Gemma said reassuringly.

"Let's hope so," Kyra replied, linking hands with Torben.

Twenty minutes later, Sarah reappeared in the cockpit, her hair and makeup looking like she was ready for a night out. She smiled feebly at the other two. "I need to look my best if people are going to start snapping my picture."

Gemma and Caroline smiled. "I see your logic," the Welsh woman said. "I look like *Worzel Gummidge*, but who cares." Kyra and Torben exchanged a confused glance, not understanding the reference. But it did not matter. They were happy that their passengers were about to return home, to their loved ones. They knew that it had come at a price. People had died on Valkash, Torben and Kyra knowing full well the gravity of the situation. It would stay with them for the rest of their lives.

"The villagers are ready."

"Are they okay?" Caroline asked.

"Most of them are over the moon. Martin just stared at me. Kimberley too. I guess it doesn't really mean as much to them?" The cockpit fell silent, the words hanging in the air for all to digest.

"Rex," Torben said, breaking the spell. "Are we in position?"

"Coordinates are locked. Shall we descend, skipper?"

"Let's do this."

They all watched as they dropped into Earth's atmosphere, the three humans gazing in amazement as the vista opened up before them. "Oh my god!" Gemma said. "To think, I'd never even been on a plane before. That view is just spectacular."

"Isn't it just," Sarah said, her eyes taking in the spectacle unfolding before them. They dropped lower, the United Kingdom filling their view, the cloudless sky offering them an uninterrupted view of their home country.

"Perfect weather," Caroline said, to no one in particular.

"You have a beautiful home," Kyra said, squeezing Caroline's arm. "Such vivid colours. I am happy that you are all returning home."

"Thanks to you," Caroline said, smiling warmly. The green expanse of England filled the cockpit window, the network of roads and fields a welcome sight for its inhabitants.

"5,000 feet," Rex said, gently coaxing the controls, the invisible ship falling almost silently towards the small village of Belbroughton.

Torben pressed a button on the console. "This is Captain Fraken. Please move all villagers to the main ramp. We are ready to land. Rex. We're going to unload the passengers. I will be back in a few minutes. Remember. Remove the cloak just before we touch down."

"Yes, Captain," he replied happily, enjoying the landscape that the lush planet offered up to him.

"This way," Torben said, heading out of the cockpit. They walked steadily towards the outer door, Kyra pressing a button on the wall that made two white panels slide silently across, revealing the exit ramp. They stood there for a minute, waiting for the ship to land. Villagers began moving down the corridor towards them. Many were crying, tears of happiness falling freely. Others shuffled along, a low murmur building amongst them. Martin and Kimberly were holding onto each other, desolate faces staring straight ahead, their movements stilted.

"Are we really home?" Loz said, smiling at Caroline.

"We are," she replied, hugging him.

He turned to the villagers. "We're home guys," he called, cheers and sighs of relief drifting down towards them.

A minute later the ramp was lowered, green grass a welcome carpet at the bottom of the slope. Caroline, Gemma and Sarah moved to one side, allowing the villagers to head down the ramp into the field beyond. Not many regarded Torben or Kyra except Katie, who smiled warmly before carefully navigating the ramp. "After you," Torben said, smiling.

"Thank you, Captain," they all said in unison, making his face light up in a toothy grin. He linked arms with Kyra, following them down to the grassy space that the villagers called home. Many were already halfway across the field, urgently making their way back to homes and loved ones. At the far end a group of teenagers were standing, wide-eyed and open mouthed, staring at Shimmer050. One lad had his mobile phone out, videoing the unprecedented event, his hand shaking slightly. As the first of the villagers left the field, Torben could hear voices, and car horns tooting. He looked over at the entrance to the field as a car ploughed into a tree on the road that led through the village.

"Oh my god!" a young mother shouted, pointing at the spacecraft from the pavement. "Look. Aliens!"

"I guess this is goodbye," Torben said, addressing the three women.

"I guess it is. We hope you make it home. I know we didn't

get off to the best of starts, but we are grateful to you for saving our lives."

"Think nothing of it. It was the least I could do under the circumstances."

Caroline limped forward, kissing him on the cheek, pulling him down towards her. Gemma did the same, then embraced Kyra, squeezing tightly. "Thank you for returning me home to my family."

Tears stung Kyra's eyes as she held the woman. "Go and find them. They need you," she said, her voice faltering.

Sarah kissed them both, smiling at Kyra. "Love the hair by the way," she said, sauntering over to the other women who stood facing the ship.

"Stop. Police," a voice hollered from the entrance to the field.

Torben peered over, seeing a man dressed in black heading towards them. "I think it's time we made a departure," Torben said to Kyra, a watchful eye on the approaching human.

"W-what's going on," he said, suddenly unsure of what he'd stumbled across. The officer had been stood by the pub a few moments before, alerted by the people who'd hurriedly made their way past him. He looked at Torben and Kyra, then the spacecraft. "The villagers?" he said.

"They are home," Torben replied evenly.

"Who are you?"

"My name is Torben Fraken, from the planet Biflux. This is Kyra Zakx. We are returning your citizens to you."

Unsure of how to reply the officer tried to stall them, in hope that reinforcements would arrive. "I can't let you leave."

"I don't think you really have a choice," Torben replied gravely, as twin jets of steam expelled themselves from the ship's hull.

"You might want to take a video of this, officer," Caroline said, a few paces behind him. A black car screeched to a halt in the lane, two men dressed in black suits climbing out slowly. They regarded the scene in front of them, one of them slowly walking towards Shimmer050.

"You'd better make a move," Gemma said. "They may try and stop you leaving."

"I think you're right," Torben said. "Take care, all of you," he said, stepping backwards towards the ramp.

"Enjoy your lives," Kyra said. "We hope they are long and filled with happiness." The three women watched as the couple walked up the ramp before it rose into the hull of the ship. A few seconds later Shimmer050 rose into the air, gaining altitude quickly. Their eyes tracked the ship before it shot off quickly, the sound of low-flying aircraft filling their ears. They watched in rapt fascination as two fighter jets climbed almost vertically, trying in vain to catch the retreating craft. A domed shockwave appeared above them, the alien craft accelerating towards the heavens before disappearing into the upper atmosphere.

The two men appeared next to them, the taller one removing his sunglasses. "Was that what I think it was?"

"Yes. A spacecraft," Caroline said. "It's just dropped us off home."

"Were you amongst the villagers who were abducted?" he replied.

"Yes. We've had quite a journey. But we're home now," Gemma said happily.

"Who are you?" Sarah asked, smiling at the two men.

"Detective Sergeant Kemp, and this is Detective Constable Phillips," the man said.

Sarah decided to take the front foot. "Well, guys, we've had a fairly hectic day. I'm sure you'll want to ask us all sorts of questions. But for now, I need a shower, a vodka and a lie down."

The threesome walked past them, heading for the main body of the village. Caroline and Sarah stopped next to the pub, needing to cross the road. They hugged tightly, tears free-flowing. "It's been a blast, guys. I know we've been through hell, but I have made two new friends."

"Yes, you have, hun," Sarah said, sniffing back the tears that were threatening to erupt.

"Mummy," a voice said behind them. Gemma turned, her resolve crumbling as she saw Oscar and Finn running towards her, Hugh in tow. She could see tears in his eyes, her legs wobbling as the two boys made it to her. The woman dropped to her knees, gathering her sons into her arms.

"Mama," Oscar said, burying his face into her neck. Caroline and Sarah watched in silence as the family was reunited.

Hugh knelt down beside his wife, pulling her into his arms, his tears those of joy and relief. "Oh, babe. You're home. I saw all the villagers filing past and I just grabbed the kids and…" His voice trailed off, emotions overtaking him.

"I've missed you so much. All of you. Yes, I'm home. We're home," she said, smiling at her two new friends. They nodded before heading to their respective homes, their strides carefree.

"What happened?" Hugh asked, his voice shaky.

"Let's get home. I have a feeling that the world and his dog are about to descend on the village. And I need a cup of tea. A real one. An Earth one."

"Mummy," Finn said. "Can I show you my new *Captain America* costume?"

"Y'know what, baby bear, I can think of nothing better," she said tearfully, kissing both boys fiercely. They gathered themselves, walking back to their home, holding hands as sirens wailed along the country lanes.

THIRTY-FIVE

ONE MONTH LATER

SNOW HAD COME EARLY TO MIDDLE ENGLAND, LARGE FLAKES steadily settling over the landscape. Gemma walked the few hundred yards from her home to the Talbot Inn, the centre-piece of the village. She pulled her suede jacket around her neck as flakes began to invade her personal space. It was fully dark, even though it was not yet seven in the evening. *Good idea to head out early*, she thought, noticing the throng of humanity that was moving around inside the cosy pub. Houses and pubs were decorated in fairy lights, giving the village a festive feeling. Off to her left a detached house outshone all around it, an inflatable Father Christmas suspended halfway up the front wall, a large reindeer attempting to scale the roof. It was her first night out since she had volunteered to help out at the autumn fete. To Gemma, it seemed like a lifetime ago, even though it wasn't even two months since she'd woken up on the floor of an alien spacecraft, speeding away from her planet. A group of men stood outside the front doors, smoking and vaping as they attempted to ward off the cold weather. "That's one of them," a middle-aged man said as he puffed on his vape stick.

Gemma had accepted the fact that many of the villagers

were almost minor celebrities, paying little heed to the comments and questions that she'd fielded over the past fortnight. She smiled at the men, shouldering her way into the main lounge, before shaking flakes of snow from her coat, stamping her feet on the thick mat that had *welcome* emblazoned across it. "Over here, hun," a familiar voice called. She looked to her left, spotting Caroline and Sarah waving over at her. She weaved her way through the throng of humanity, averting her attention from the eyes and comments that the patrons levelled at her.

"Come and sit down, lovely," Sarah said. "Drink?"

"I'd love a pear cider," Gemma replied warmly. "One of those Swedish ones if they've got any?"

"Sit yourself down," Sarah replied, looking at Caroline. "Same again?"

"Why not," she replied. "I could do with a few tonight after the week I've had."

Sarah sashayed over to the bar, perching her elbows on the dark wooden top, her short skirt and knee-length boots drawing attention from most of the men and half of the women in the pub. Her blonde hair had been recently shaved on one side, reminding the approaching barman of a famous television presenter whose name escaped him.

"What can I get you?" he said, his friendly manner drawing a smile from Sarah.

"A pear cider, a *Peroni*, and a gin and tonic please."

"Ice in the cider and gin?"

"Why not. Let's live a little eh," she said, winking at the young man.

A group of lads stood to her right, appraising her through half-drunken eyes. The tallest of the group stepped towards her. "You're one of the villagers that were snatched, aren't you?"

"What if I am?" Sarah said coolly, noticing the leering sneers of the pack of young men.

"I've watched movies about stuff like that. Experimenting on us. Did they probe you?" The others sniggered, enjoying the moment.

Sarah smiled sweetly as the barman returned, placing two of the drinks on the bar, eyeing the youths warily. "I've not been probed in a long time, by aliens or by humans. Do you think you have what it takes?"

Suddenly unsure, the youth took a sip of his lager, trying to gain the upper hand. "Go on. You can tell us. Did someone boldly go where no other man has been before?" They all laughed, making some of the locals look up towards the bar.

"How do you mean, where no one has been before?"

"You know. Up your arse," the ringleader sniggered.

A passing barmaid stopped in her tracks, a look of disgust on her face. She was about to intervene when Sarah placed her hand on the youth's shoulder. "Believe me, sunshine, many a real man has already been there." She let the words hang in the air, the group of men falling silent. She turned, handing a crisp note to the barman. "I'll be back for the gin and tonic," she said, scooping the other two drinks off the wooden counter. She returned a few seconds later, taking the change from the barman. "Thanks, sweetie," Sarah said as she picked up her globe-shaped glass, the tonic fizzing and sloshing about.

"My pleasure. Are those guys bothering you?"

"Not at all. Just kids, trying to have fun." She headed back over to her friends, removing her black leather jacket, hanging it on the chair before getting comfortable. A crackling fire nearby cast a mellow glow across the lounge, Sarah enjoying the warmth on her bare, tattooed arms. "So, how was your month?" she asked Gemma.

"A blur. I've spoken to so many people. *MI-5, Ministry of Defence*, army doctors, reporters. I've been prodded, poked and examined, which was not entirely pleasant. I've even had a call from *ITV*, asking me to appear on one of their daytime chat shows. I may consider growing a beard and hiding out in the Clent Hills, with all the reporters I've had to dodge. It's been pretty intense." They both nodded, knowing what the young woman had been subjected to. They had been through similar routines, spending the first seven days after their arrival in a makeshift hospital that had been set up a mile away from their homes. More tears had flowed as loved ones had to say goodbye to the abductees as they were whisked away aboard army lorries, waving as they filed out of Belbroughton. Each villager had been examined and questioned, being kept in single isolated cells before the lorries trundled back into the village, happily reuniting them with their families. The village had become a hive of activity over the previous month, with various agencies and journalists setting up camp. The field where they had been abducted from was sealed off behind a tall metal fence, a convoy of white vans lining the kerb for hundreds of yards as policemen kept order.

"I've had someone call me from the *Sun*," asking me to sell my story," Caroline said. "They've offered me £50,000."

"Wow," Gemma said. "Are you going to take it?"

"Not sure. *MI-5* told me to refrain from talking to the media."

"Me too," Sarah said. "But how can we not? It's gone viral. I'm getting friend requests, marriage proposals, even pictures of guys dressed up as aliens, wanting to hook up. Plus, I've had reporters trying to snap pictures of me at my parents' house. My Dad lost it in the end, telling them to politely fuck off."

Gemma laughed. "Go you! My *Facebook* and *Twitter* have gone mental. I'm getting tagged by random people, I'm all *hashtagged* out!"

"How are the boys?" Caroline asked, changing the subject.

"Good. Really good in fact. They've never been this well-behaved. It was hard to say goodbye to them, so soon after returning home. But they knew it was only for a few days.

We've had them in bed with us every night since I got home. Poor Hugh has taken to sleeping in Finn's bed most nights. We need a queen-sized." She took a sip of her cider, the ice clinking around the rim of the glass. "How's your mum?"

"She's doing okay. Having me home has given her a much-needed boost. We got a doctor's appointment on Monday." Caroline took a swig of her lager, eyeing the patrons carefully. "She sends her regards to Hugh, by the way."

"Yes, he told me about the CCTV. He turned into quite the detective."

"That's nice though," Sarah added. "He never gave up on you."

"No. My knight in shining armour. How about your little boy? Is he okay?"

Sarah smiled before taking a measured sip of her drink. "He's fine. He's been in bed with me every night too. Mum and Dad have had their hands full with him over the past month or so."

Gemma and Caroline remembered what Sarah had told them on Valkash. that she lived in the village with her parents and son. "Do you have a partner?" Caroline asked. "With everything that we've been through, I never thought to ask."

"That's fine, sweetie. We've kinda had our minds on other things out there. I was seeing a guy from Stourbridge. Nothing serious. A bit like friends with benefits."

"Lucky you," Caroline replied. "I'd take any kind of benefit right now. Friendly or otherwise."

Gemma almost spat her cider out, wiping her hand over her mouth as she tried to regain her composure. "I know what you mean. Me and Hugh have not had five minutes to ourselves. I'm sure we'll get around to that. Maybe later, when I've had a few more ciders."

"I'm sure he'll think all his birthdays have come at once, hun," Sarah said, giving her a cheeky wink.

"So will I, hun," Gemma said, a warm smile spreading across her face.

A few hours later, Gemma walked through the front door of the house, sitting heavily on the stairs to remove her leather boots. She placed them next to the telephone table as Hugh walked to the lounge doorway. "No alien abductions?"

"Thankfully no," she replied smiling. "Lots of stares though."

"That's to be expected I guess. After all, it's not every day that someone gets taken to the far corner of the universe."

"True. Were the boys okay?"

"Yes, hun. They went to bed a few hours ago. Not heard a peep since. They are in our bed."

"That's fine. What have you been doing?"

"Watching *Question Time*," Hugh replied. You can guess what the subject matter was?"

"Aliens."

"Yes. It got quite heated. They had the head of the *Church of England*, along with a Muslim cleric and that physicist guy who is always on the TV. It almost boiled over into a full-scale brawl."

Gemma stood up, her legs feeling a little wobbly as she walked into her husband's embrace. She kissed him, full on the lips, before leading him over to the two-seater sofa. They got comfortable, Gemma draping her legs over Hugh's lap, reclining herself across the sofa. He rubbed her nylon-clad feet, drawing a smile from Gemma. "Hmm. That's nice, babe," she said, feeling relaxed and safe. "So, what was the consensus on *Question Time*?" she asked as fairy lights twinkled in the small tree next to the fireplace.

"Well, the physicist pretty much said that religion is now redundant, which angered the religious guys. Many of the crowd were agreeing with him. After all, how can God have created the Earth, knowing what we know? The Christian guy tried some lame attempt at saying God created the universe, and that this new development should not make people around the world question their beliefs."

"The Church would say that. They have nowhere to go now. Nor does Islam. We're not alone. I know that first-hand. I've seen the other side of the universe. God did not create all this. I can see a real shift in our humanity coming, hun. Maybe this will be the start of something good? How can you start a war over religion, when we know that their gods have been fabricated?"

"Let's hope so, babe. I suppose the *Flat Earth Society* are pretty fucked too eh!" She smiled, lacing her fingers into her hair. "Anyway, how much did you have to drink?"

"Err, probably more than I've had in a while," she said sheepishly.

"Well, it's nice to see you happy and relaxed. Maybe you and your friends can make this a regular thing? Girly nights out."

"Maybe. They're both really nice. To think, I would probably never have become friends with them, had we not been abducted."

"God works in mysterious ways. Sorry, I mean the universe works in mysterious ways."

She smiled at him, enjoying the constant kneading of her feet and ankles. She was now not only relaxed, but there was something else taking hold of her. "Enough talk. Take me upstairs and rock *my* universe."

"As you wish, my lady," he said, leaning over to kiss her.

THIRTY-SIX

PAUL LEWIS SWIRLED THE WINE IN HIS GLASS, NOTING HIS bare wedding ring finger. Not long after the discovery of his wife's infidelity, he had confronted her, which had turned into an all-out slugfest, without the actual slugging. His wife had gone on the defensive, blaming him for never being there for her. Paul had heard it all before, telling his wife that he wanted a divorce. He'd moved out two days later, renting an apartment on the outskirts of Cheltenham, as solicitors started to go through the motions of carving up their estate. He looked around the restaurant, its dark décor and muted lighting, combined with tasteful festive decorations, created a soothing effect on him as the woman approached the table. She sat down, placing her clutch bag next to her own wine glass, the ruby red liquid inside looking as inviting as the ambience inside the small Spanish restaurant. "You okay, Paul?" Sylvia said, taking a sip of her Rioja.

"I am actually. I was just people watching while you were away," he said, lifting the Albariño to his lips, enjoying the tart aroma. He took a sip, appraising the woman in front of him. Sylvia wore a long, red, figure-hugging dress, accentuating her curves. The red chiffon material on her arms clung to the skin, Paul drinking in the sight of her.

"I do that all the time. It's almost a fully-fledged hobby. Do you know what you're having?" she said, picking up the menu.

"I think so. I'll start with the Patatas Bravas and Albondigas, followed by the Fabada Asturiana. And you?"

"I quite fancy the Aubergine Parmigiana followed by the Spanish Bull Tail Stew."

"Sounds lovely."

"Well, this is effectively a tapas house, we can share if you'd like?"

"I like," he said, smiling. He removed his sports jacket, hanging it on the rear of the suede-backed chair, his dark shirt in contrast to his blue eyes and sandy hair.

"So. Have you heard from Claire?" she said, testing the water.

"Earlier today," he replied. "She called me with a list of items that she wants from the house. She's made quite an inventory."

"And?"

"And I am tired of fighting. Things like sofas and dining tables can be replaced. As long as I walk away with a fair settlement and my personal belongings, I am as happy as I can be."

"You're being very diplomatic?"

"That goes with the job I guess. We've been married for a long time. Truth be told, the last few years have been null and void. Once the boys started turning into men, our marriage started turning into a convenience. I've had a belly full of that. I want to live again. As you said, I'm not exactly collecting my pension, so why not start enjoying myself?"

"And are you?" she replied, testing the waters some more.

He reached across and squeezed her hand. "Very much so, Sylvia. Thank you for this. I'd probably be sat in the flat, tucking into a takeaway right now."

"You don't have to thank me. And I know that you'll need to get used to your new life. No pressure."

"I know. I've become almost institutionalised. I have no idea how to do this."

"You'll get there. Just enjoy being in your own skin - being Paul again – not just the subservient husband and dad."

"I intend to try. I also intend to scale back my work. Claire was right about one thing, I do work too much. I'm going to talk to Karen on Monday."

"What will you say?"

"That I want to cut back, which might not go down well. The last few months have been draining. The alien abduction, the long hours and the turmoil at home. I am ready to quit if she does not give me viable options."

"What would you do if you had to leave?"

"I don't know. I'm sure I will think of something though. One of my former colleagues runs his own security company. He's asked me a few times if I would like to work with him. I dismissed it at first, but looking at it now, maybe it's time for a change."

"Where does he work?"

"Bristol. He handles security systems, alarms and CCTV, along with consultancy for some lucrative clients. Footballers, celebrities and politicians. He's doing rather well."

"Sounds good. Maybe that's an option if Karen pulls up the drawbridge."

He smiled, liking her turn of phrase. "What about you? Are you still happy at *GCHQ*?"

"Yes. And even if you left, I would continue to work there. Although I'm sure my next boss would not be as hot as you, Paul."

He blushed, gazing into Sylvia's brown eyes. "Thank you, although I assure you, I am not hot. I'm a middle-aged father of two, who is about to become a divorcee."

"Believe me, you are hot. Have you not seen the women checking you out?"

"Where?"

"That table in the corner. The one with the six women? They look to be on a Christmas knees-up. A few of them have been looking over."

"Well, I never noticed. And anyway, I am here with you, and you are stunning. Why would I look anywhere else?"

She leaned over as a young female waitress headed over towards them. Sylvia kissed him softly on the lips, both sets of eyes closing as the world was shut off for a few seconds. "Thank you, Paul. You really are a wonderful guy."

"Have you decided yet?" the waitress asked, her West Country twang out of place in the muted restaurant. They ordered their meals, wine glasses refreshed as gentle Spanish guitar music filtered through the establishment. Conversation was easy, neither one trying hard to broach a subject. Paul sat there, rapt in attention at Sylvia's words, her smiles, her giggles. The evening moved into night, gentle snowflakes collecting on the window panes as plates were replaced and bills asked for. A few hours after arriving, the couple headed out onto the quiet side street, a thin blanket of white carpeting central Cheltenham.

"Thank you for a lovely evening, Sylvia," Paul said as he buttoned up his jacket.

"How far is your place?"

The directness of the question flummoxed Paul for a moment. Quickly regaining his composure, he pointed down the street. "A five-minute drive, or a twenty-minute walk. Why?"

"I thought we could open a bottle of wine back at your place, but only if you'd like to? No pressure."

"There is a taxi rank at the end of the street. Let's get out of the snow before we freeze."

"Sounds like a good plan," she said, taking the crook of his arm.

Sometime later, they lay in a tangle of limbs, half-consumed wine glasses on the bedside tables next to them. Paul gazed up at the ceiling, his breath and heartbeat starting to slow themselves. Sylvia lay with her head on his chest, her dress and underwear discarded on the floor next to the fitted wardrobes. The room was quiet, save for the noise from outside as the wind kicked up a frenzy, snowflakes battering the double glazing. "Weather's getting worse," Paul said.

"Hmm, yes. I guess I'll have to stay over."

"I'd like that," he replied, his fingers dancing lightly over her creamy skin.

They lapsed back into silence, each lost to their own thoughts before something came to Sylvia. "Paul, what about the alien abduction?"

"It's still raging on," he said. "Another reason to take a step back at work. I know that our focus will be pointed towards the stars very soon, instead of intercepting chatter from around the globe."

"I've been watching it on the news every night. There have been mass riots in the Middle East, along with demos in the United States and here in the UK."

"Well, that was bound to happen. Over half the world's population are religious, and they've just found out that extraterrestrial life exists. It's going to cause quite the shit storm."

"I've never really been religious. And I've never really thought about the possibility of aliens, but this has really opened my eyes. Has it opened yours?"

Paul moved onto his side, looking at the woman next to him. "Not really. It's been the dirty little secret for many years, since the fifties. There was the *Roswell Incident*, along with several well-documented sightings of alien craft around the world. This just confirms it all. And to be honest, it was only a matter of time until it was confirmed."

"So why the secrecy?"

"Because keeping it quiet maintains order. I don't know if you know this, but ancient civilisations talked about visitors from the stars. Some called them *Sky Beings*. Ancient Egypt was thought to have been visited by them numerous times. There has even been speculation about some of the ancient pharaohs being alien beings. There are many places around the world that we simply cannot explain. Stonehenge, Easter Island and the Nazca Lines. Maybe aliens have been visiting us for thousands of years. Maybe they have been linked to us more than we realise. But then, as religion took over, they either kept their distance, or we kept it quiet."

"Maybe," Sylvia said simply, pulling the duvet over her legs as she moved closer to him.

"I just know that things will now start to change, hopefully for the better. There may some initial chaos, but that will calm down. It's just incredible to think that a species came from the other side of the universe to Earth. The technology to do that is just mind-boggling."

"I will take your word for that," she said.

"I do know one thing. The last few months have made me think about life. I'm sure the people who were abducted are thinking the same."

"What's that?"

"To grab hold of life and enjoy it, before it's too late."

"Amen to that," Sylvia said. "Why don't you come and grab hold of me, so I can enjoy it," she demurred, removing the warm duvet from her body, letting his eyes take in exactly what was on offer.

THIRTY-SEVEN

LUNDELL

TWO MONTHS AFTER SPEEDING AWAY FROM EARTH WITH fighter jets following their ascent, Torben looked out of the cabin, across the calm sea. The ship had taken them home, coming through a wormhole a few million miles away from the planet of Biflux. They had been ordered to Lundell, Torben reporting to Commander Spelk, who had clapped him on the back as cheers rang out across the hangar, news to the captain's heroics was the main talking point for all Biflex people. They had spent a few weeks at command, answering questions and receiving warm wishes from all they came across. Then an invitation had been extended to Torben, who had reported to the centre of the command post, a huge stone throne room, a throwback to a bygone era. He stood, facing a dozen Lomogs, trying not to look at their emaciated frames as they imparted their thanks. He was branded a hero, single-handedly stopping untold devastation. The Lomogs had offered him anything he wanted. Riches, or a ship of his own in which to traverse the stars. His answer surprised them, beady eyes staring at him in disbelief as their metal bodies whirred and clicked. Torben asked for a cabin next to the sea to start with, that he would build. The Lomogs had agreed, telling Torben to find a place where he wanted to set up home. They would supply materials and equipment. They then informed him to return to command once he was settled.

They found an idyllic spot a few days later. Their craft had scooted across the equator, passing the settlement of Vasteras, a small fishing community next to the Sea of Sakarya. They had touched down, walking from the settlement along a gravel path that wound its way around the headland. After a short walk, they came across an open expanse of grass, framed on three sides by evergreen trees, the sea stretching out in front of them. Kyra had immediately fallen in love, Torben radioing his position to the Lomogs command. Less than a day later a sea craft had arrived, excavating machines rolling up the rocky beach towards the couple as they stood in warm clothing, braced against the stiffening breeze. Activity had been fast-paced, the workers felling hundreds of trees, while others dug out and set the foundations in place, and the Lomogs chief architect acted on Kyra's and Torben's exciting vision. Once the floor had cured, trimmed logs had been set in place, the cabin taking shape quickly. Kyra had visited Vasteras, leaving Torben to work with the architect, securing doors and windows as others fitted the timber roof. She returned back hours later as the sun was about to kiss the western sea, happy to have secured several items of furniture for their new home. Over the next few days, services were connected to the cabin, and a small Ion generator and solar-panelled roof tiles installed. They spent the weekend alone in the cabin, Torben building a boundary fence around the perimeter of the cabin, giving them some privacy, as Kyra spent most of the weekend back in Vasteras, talking to tradesmen who would apply the finishing touches to their new home.

. . .

He looked down at the table next to him, picking up his mug of graff, taking a sip as Kyra walked out onto the stoop. "Shall we finish the jetty today?" she said, wrapping an arm around his waist.

He looked down the grassy slope towards the sea, smiling at the half-built structure. Wooden pilings ran from the shore out into the water for fifty feet, a few roughly hewn planks screwed into place to give it some strength. "Great idea," he said, looking across the grass towards his newly built work-shop. "I'll just finish the graff and get the tools out of my den."

"Your den? Is that what you've called it?"

"I like it. Makes it sound cosy. I've already hung a hammock on the veranda looking out at the sea. I can relax there, while you bring me beer and graff."

"So, Captain. Is that how you see our future? Me being your personal assistant?"

He smiled, lifting her into his arms. "I have more plans than just food and drink."

"Is that so? I cannot wait to see what schemes you have dreamt up."

An hour later Torben was twenty feet out at sea, using a portable drill to screw the planks into place. Kyra was knelt next to him, making sure that both sides of the jetty were even as a figure came out of the trees a few hundred yards away. "Torben," she said, pointing up at the treeline.

"What?" His eyes tracked up the grassy slope, past the cabin to the gravel pathway that led to town. A lone man stood there, his hood covering his head. Torben placed the drill on the planks, standing up slowly before walking back to dry land, Kyra linking his arm. The man stood there motion-less as they approached slowly, Torben feeling the first prickle of danger, noting that the man was tall and rangy. "Can I help you?" he said, letting go of Kyra as he approached the treeline.

The man removed his hood, a shock of unkempt red hair standing out like a beacon in the morning sunlight. "You are one hard man to find," Ark Ramkle said, a huge grin splitting his face.

Torben's legs felt unsteady as he peered into the eyes of the ghost in front of him. He tried to speak, his words floundering like a fish on the rocks. "Ark?"

"Yes, my friend," he said, breaking into a jog towards his friend.

Torben staggered towards him, catching the younger pilot in a bear hug. "I don't understand. I thought you were dead?" They swung each other around, tears mingling with laugher as the woman approached, a bewildered expression on her face.

"So did I," he said, embracing Kyra warmly. "Quite a place you have here."

"Never mind that. How? I thought you were at Lomax when the bomb went off?" Torben asked, wiping his eyes.

"I will brew some graff," Kyra said. "You two get comfy on the stoop."

Torben grabbed his friend again, his emotions boiling over as he openly wept in his embrace. Ark, not one for emotional episodes, wept too, holding his friend tightly. "Long story. It's so good to see you, Torben. I never thought I would again."

They walked down to the cabin, seating themselves on the wooden bench, looking out at the sea. Kyra appeared a minute later, placing a brushed-steel tray on the table in front of them, letting the graff brew in a clay pot. She pulled up a chair, regarding the young man in front of her. "We thought you'd perished in the explosion?"

"I got lucky. I was underneath the port, with a young humanoid. Nothing was going on as such. We were just getting to know each other. Then, the whole place shook, much of the lower levels collapsing. We managed to make it to a bunker, one that was built in case of an invasion. They only dug us out a few days ago."

"How is Biflux?" Kyra said, her face neutral.

"Not good. Cantis and parts of Walvak were either completely levelled, or contaminated. When they found us, we were moved immediately into an irradiation chamber, staying in there for hours whilst they scanned our vitals. As we were leaving the planet, we could see the devastation. Many of the large glaciers high up in the tundra have melted, flooding many settlements further south. The place is a tomb." His words hung in the air, Kyra getting up to pour three mugs of graff.

"Kyra lost her parents. They lived in neighbouring Kiton."

Ark's face dropped, looking up at the woman who handed him his drink. "I am so sorry. I really am."

"Thank you, Ark." They would not have felt anything I'm hoping. They probably died in each other's arms. That is the only shred of comfort that I can take from it."

"I truly am sorry for your loss. So many lives lost. Such a fucking waste!"

"Are your family okay?" Torben enquired.

"Yes. Mother and Father were outside the blast radius. They are here on Lundell, to the east of command. We have family there, who are putting us up while the Lomogs figure out what happens next."

"I'm glad they're okay," Torben said as he took a tentative sip of his drink. "I still cannot believe that you made it out alive."

"Nor me. It was not much fun. Fortunately, the bunker was stocked with provisions. However, boiled red rice and rain-water is not what I would call exciting cuisine. But it kept us alive."

"So, who was the lady that you were stuck with?" Kyra asked as she tried to brighten the conversation.

"A young pilot called Ebrisa. She was staying over at Lomax, awaiting orders. We've kinda been inseparable ever since. She is checking us into a guesthouse in Vasteras. Once we were rescued, all we heard about was Torben, the saviour." He smiled a toothy grin that made the others follow suit. "Man! How did you pull that off?"

"It was not easy. I activated the Singularity next to their ship. It pulled us both through, depositing us in the solar system where we'd travelled to before. I could probably try that manoeuvre a hundred times and only succeed once. Not long after, Hameda's ship blew up, close to the planet where the abductees came from. So, we dropped them home and returned to Lundell. And here we are."

"Well, it's so good to see you, my friends." They both smiled, Kyra leaning over to give him a hug, planting a kiss on his forehead.

"We're so glad you made it. Torben was devastated."

Ark looked at the older man, a mischievous smile appearing on his face. "Aww. It's nice to know that you still love me," he said, hugging his friend.

"Okay, knock it off. I'm spoken for."

"I can see that. So, it looks like you two have made a nice place here. What are your plans now?"

"Truth be told, we're not sure, are we?" he said to Kyra.

"We've not thought that far ahead, Ark. Torben will go back to command soon, to see what they have in store for him. I'll report back too, although I am going to take a break. The last year has been difficult. But we have come through it, haven't we, Torby?"

"Yes, we have," he said squeezing her hand gently as the breeze whipped at the waves that lapped the shore.

"So, do you need a hand finishing that jetty?" Ark said enthusiastically.

"Don't you need to get back to your lady friend?"

"I will give her a call and ask her to join us, if that's okay with you two?"

Kyra looked at Torben, nodding readily. "Sure, my old friend," Torben said. "It will be nice to meet Ebrisa and tell her what a stand-up guy she's bagged."

They set to work, Kyra preparing a light lunch inside the stout cabin. She opened the windows, smiling as she heard the men's voices drifting across the grass towards her. *He looks so happy,* she thought as the younger man passed Torben an air hammer and nails. The wind was strengthening, ruffling the men's hair as they chatted and laughed. She opened the cooler, selecting an array of vegetables and a light dressing that she carried over to the counter. A few minutes later, the vegetables were diced and placed into a ceramic bowl with a good helping of dressing drizzled over them. Kyra walked back to the cooler, pulling out a dish of grallas. Firing up the griddle, she peeled most of the outer shells of the small crustaceans, splashing oil over them as they started to sizzle and spit. Pleased with her progress, she walked out onto the stoop as a young female approached from the pathway. "You must be Ebrisa?" Kyra said, her tone friendly and welcoming.

"Hello. You must be, Kyra?"

"Yes, I am. Welcome. I'm just preparing lunch. Would you like a drink?"

"That would be lovely. Walking from Vasteras has worked up a thirst."

"What would you like?" Kyra said as she appraised the young woman. She was slight of build, her head barely reaching Kyra's shoulders. Her long brown hair was wavy, seeming to bounce and shift whenever she moved. Her face was appealing, a light dusting of freckles sprinkled across her nose and cheeks. It was the eyes that Kyra noticed most. One was violet, the other a vivid blue. They seemed to sparkle when the sun's rays caught them, giving Ebrisa a magical aura.

"Anything cold would be great."

"We have beer, wine or juice. We're not fully stocked yet. Torben has big ideas to create a bar area out on the stoop."

"Men huh!" she replied, placing her slender hands on her hips. "A beer would do just fine."

Kyra walked over to the cooler, pulling two bottles of beer from the shelf. She handed one to Ebrisa, her fingers barely able to wrap themselves around the cool glass. "Cheers," she said, flipping the lid from the neck.

"Cheers," the smaller woman replied, popping the seal on her own bottle, taking a hearty gulp.

"Are you starting without us?" Torben said from the doorway.

Kyra turned to the two men, smiling. "I thought you two were hard at work. I was merely making our guest feel at home," she replied as Ark gathered Ebrisa into his embrace.

"Hello, you," he said, planting a kiss on her full lips.

"Back at ya," she said, wrapping an arm around his waist.

"Torben, this is Ebrisa," Ark said proudly.

"Pleased to meet you," he said, extending his hand.

She took it, matching his grip. "Likewise. I have heard many stories about Torben, the hero of the Lomogs."

"Stop it," Ark said playfully. His head is already starting to swell. We're gonna have trouble squeezing him back through the doorway."

Kyra walked over to the griddle, turning the grallas over, their shells blackened, oozing juice across the iron stove. She scattered some herbs across them, adding some more oil which sent a plume of smoke into the air. "Go and set up the table and chairs you two," she said to the men. "I will cut some bread with Ebrisa."

The two men complied, heading out of the kitchen,

bumping shoulders as they both tried to squeeze through the doorway at the same time. A few minutes later, Kyra placed the grallas salad on the table, Ebrisa placing a bowl of buttered bread in front of the men as the other woman headed back into the cabin. She returned a moment later, four bottles of beer held deftly between her fingers. "My kind of lunch," Ark said as he gratefully accepted the cold brew.

"You're not wrong there," Torben said, taking a swig of the heady liquid.

They settled down, each person helping themselves to a few large spoonsful of salad, the shellfish completing the dish perfectly. Kyra began peeling her first grallas, licking her fingers as she deposited slimy shells into a small bowl in the centre of the table. "So, what are your plans?"

Ark and Ebrisa looked at each other, both smiling. "We're not too sure. We'll spend some time in Vasteras, then we'll head over to my family."

"Have you met them yet, Ebrisa?" Torben asked before depositing a plump piece of grallas into his mouth.

"No. Not yet. I am looking forward to meeting them. And Ark wants to meet my parents too."

"Sounds like a good plan," Kyra said cheerfully. "Where are you from?"

"Originally, I'm from Hexagor. I grew up there, before my family moved to Biflux. We lived south of the Equator, in a small port called Kingsbain."

"I've heard of Hexagor," Torben said. "It's relatively close by, just a few light years away."

"Yes. It is a lovely planet, really verdant, with great weather and fabulous beaches. We only moved to Biflux because my father was transferred. That was almost fifteen years ago now."

"I've never been to Kingsbain," Kyra said. "Although, I know a few people who grew up there."

"It's really nice. Kind of isolated from the rest of Biflux.

Freighter ships use it as a way station, stopping there to refuel."

"What do your parents do?" Torben asked, the beer relaxing him, making him almost convivial.

"They are both retired now. They were teachers, working at the Kingsbain Academy."

Torben and Kyra nodded, both knowing about the renowned academy, where budding pilots and sea captains were schooled in warm, balmy surroundings. "Are they still there, after what happened in the north?" Kyra asked, her face dropping slightly.

"Yes, although they are on alert. If anything else happens, they will ship out to Hexagor. We still have family there, who would put them up." She took a pull on her beer, spooning grallas and salad onto a hunk of bread. She demolished the food, wiping her lips with a napkin. "How about you two? What are your plans?"

"Torben has yet to figure all that out," Kyra replied, winking at the man seated next to her.

"Kyra's right. We've both been through a lot lately. Kyra lost her family when the rebels attacked Lomax."

"Oh no. I am so sorry to hear that, Kyra." She said.

"Thank you. It's been a tough few months. But we're moving forward, making plans for the future. My parents liked Torben, and would be happy in knowing that we're both safe and settled."

"Well, let's raise a bottle to them," Ark said, hefting his beer into the middle of the table. They all clinked their bottles together, taking swigs of cold beer as a frigate appeared around the headland. They all watched it for a moment, its wake trailing behind it as it ploughed through the waters.

"Such a nice place to live," Ebrisa said happily.

"Yes, it is," Torben replied. "I could live out my days here, raise a family and grow old peacefully." He froze, realising what he had said.

Kyra looked at him, her expression inquisitive. "Raise a family?"

He blushed, taking a swig of his beer, hoping the cool liquid would reduce his temperature. "Well, isn't that what every man wants?"

"I suppose they do. Did you have anyone in mind to settle down and start a family with?"

He rose from his chair, pulling Kyra towards the timber rail that backed onto the grass. "I was hoping that you would be receptive?"

"Receptive?" Ark said. "Boy, you really have a way with words, man."

Torben blushed some more, looking out to sea. "Sorry. I'm no good at this kind of thing."

She took his hand, pulling him into her embrace. "Well, when you finally learn how to be good at that kind of thing, just let me know." Before he could reply, Kyra planted a kiss on his lips.

As they broke apart, he stared into her eyes. "I'll get learning. I'm sure Ark over there has a book on that kind of thing."

"Leave me outta this. You'll scare Ebrisa away."

"It may scare you away, Ark."

"How do you mean?" he said, suddenly confused.

"Well if you ever pluck up the courage to ask me to be your life partner, you'll have to run it by my Father. And he's almost three metres tall and weighs three-hundred keygrams."

"I'll bear that in mind," he said, smiling as Torben and Kyra came back to the table to finish their lunch, as a flock of birds scooted across the white-tops close to the shore.

THIRTY-EIGHT

EARTH

"No, I'm afraid she's not in. Can I take a message?" Hugh said, becoming increasingly frustrated by the tenacious voice on the other end of the line. "I'm her husband. My name? I thought you wanted to speak to my wife? My name is irrelevant." More grilling on the other end of the line made Hugh lose his patience, slamming the house phone onto its cradle. "Fucking stupid cow. Leave us alone," he said as he walked over to the kettle.

"Who was that?" Gemma said as she walked into the kitchen.

"Another crackpot, trying to get a story from you. We may have to go Ex-Directory."

"Or we could just get rid of the landline. We hardly use it. Why not just have it disconnected?"

"Because of the broadband, babe. We need the landline." A thought occurred to him. "I know what we can do. I will put the answerphone on. It will ring three times then go straight through to voicemail."

"You think of everything. Have I ever told you that you're a genius?"

"Not as often as you should," he said grinning. "Fancy a brew?"

"Why not. Could you drop a slug of whisky in it, please? I think I'm coming down with something."

"Oh no, we're only three days away from Christmas. You can't get sick now, babe."

"Believe me, it's not on my 'to do' list, hun."

"Okay. I will drop a wee dram in it, just for you."

"Thanks, babe," she said, kissing him lightly on the cheek. "I'll have this then head over to Caroline's."

"Okay. Say hi to her mum for me."

"Mister smooth. Fraternizing with an older woman. I'll have to keep my eye on you."

"Well. I am a genius, women tend to flock to them."

She playfully jabbed him in the ribs, walking over to the table to check her phone. "Oh god!"

"What is it?"

She walked over, handing him the phone. "This is becoming tiresome."

He looked at the phone, a figure on the screen dressed as *Doctor Spock*, naked from the waist down staring back at him. "Hmm. Do you think he's a real Vulcan? You didn't hook up with this guy whilst you were away, did you?"

Gemma burst out laughing, sitting at the table as tears formed in her eyes. "I'm sorry, hun. But that really tickled me."

"You've certainly become popular, even with aliens. Do I need to be worried?"

She rose from the chair, wrapping her arms around him. "Hun. You're the only man in the universe that I want, and that goes for Vulcans too."

Ten minutes later, Gemma pressed the doorbell of the cosy bungalow. Festive lights twinkled in the hallway beyond the frosted glass of the doorway. She stood there, the cold seeping into her bones as the door opened, Caroline standing there sporting a jumper with a red-nosed reindeer emblazoned across the front of it. "Hello, lovely. Come on in."

"Thanks, hun," she said, giving the Welsh woman a hug as she broached the threshold of the house. "Bloody hell! It's freezing out there."

"You're not wrong there. I wrapped Mum up well before she headed over to the village hall for choir practice."

"Bless. What time is she back?"

"Not sure. She's popping to the Horseshoe afterwards with a few friends. She probably won't be home until ten."

Gemma slipped off her suede coat, hanging it on a hook under the stairs before slipping her ankle boots off. "Is Sarah here?"

"Are you kidding? She's making herself comfy in the lounge."

"Good girl," Gemma said, walking from the hallway into the cosy living room.

"Hi, sweetie," Sarah said, rising from a small dark-coloured sofa. The women hugged warmly, Gemma getting a blast of perfume from the blonde woman.

"Love the scent. What is that?"

"Marc Jacobs, Decadence. Why not. I feel like living on the edge."

"I think you've done your fair share of that lately," she said as Caroline walked in from the kitchen.

"What can I get you?"

"Oooo. What's on offer?" she replied excitedly.

"Whatever you like. We're celebrating."

"What?"

"I've found a job."

"Woohoo," Gemma replied, walking over to embrace the other woman. "Tell me more?"

"Sarah. You fancy another?"

"Why not," she said, grabbing her empty glass. The two women watched as she padded over, adjusting her miniskirt. "It keeps riding up," she said meekly.

"You'll have all the men in the village chasing you, hun," Caroline said. "You've got legs to die for."

"Stop it. You'll have me blushing," she replied as they headed into the compact kitchen, the glow from the under-lighters a welcoming sight."

"So. Tell me about the new job?"

"It's in Kidderminster," she began, opening the fridge. "Wine, beer, or pear cider?"

"You read my mind. Cider it is." Gemma said happily.

Caroline cracked the lid on the bottle, pouring her drink into a large tumbler. Handing it to the younger woman, she filled Sarah's glass with a good slug of wine, topping it up with tonic water and a scattering of fresh raspberries. The blonde woman nodded her appreciation as Caroline continued. "Right. Yes. Kidderminster. Working in quality control. I did that a few years ago back in Carmarthen, so when I saw the job last week, I thought I'd throw my hat into the ring."

"Well, that's fabulous news. Cheers," she said, hefting her glass.

"Cheers," they both replied, clinking glasses.

"When do you start?"

"In the new year. Which suits me. It will give me chance to sort a few things out my end before I start work." She paused, smiling coyly. "There is one more thing too."

"Oh," Sarah said, placing her glass on the countertop.

"The guy who interviewed me was very flirty. He won't be my boss though. He's the Marketing Manager. We had a coffee after the interview, in their canteen. He was asking me about the alien thing, as he'd recognised me from the news."

"Get you, Miss Hottie! Talk about a fast mover!"

Caroline giggled, taking a sip of her beer. "I'm not normally like that, but he was rather yummy. So, I just played along a bit."

"How yummy was he?" Sarah said, suddenly very curious.

Caroline pulled her phone from her pocket, clicking onto *Facebook*. "I took the liberty of checking him out, just to see if he's married. Purely for investigative purposes, I'll have you know."

"But of course," Gemma replied as the Welsh woman handed her the phone. She looked at the screen, nodding her approval at the picture displayed. "He's a bit of alright. Is he with someone?"

"He's listed as single," she replied.

"My kind of guy," Sarah said. "I like a bit of scruff."

"Me too," Caroline added, her neck flushing. "The hairier the better. But I'll just concentrate on work."

"Yeah right," Sarah said. "I'm sure you'll be sharing coffee more often. Maybe he'll even take you to Greggs for lunch."

"Romance isn't dead after all," Caroline said sarcastically. "Right. I've got a few choices on *Netflix*. Shall we take a look, or do you fancy *X-Factor*?"

"*Netflix*," they replied in unison, the three women heading back into the lounge to get comfy as more snow started to fall outside.

Hugh came downstairs, happy that Finn and Oscar were sound asleep. He headed into the kitchen, retrieving a bottle of Scotch from the kitchen cupboard, along with a crystal tumbler before heading into the lounge. Flopping down into his favourite chair, he flicked on the TV, selecting *Sky News*. A red banner filled the bottom of the screen, white text filing across the TV from right to left as Hugh poured himself a large measure of Teacher's whisky. A female reporter addressed him and millions of others.

"We're about to go live from the emergency *G8* summit in Washington, where world leaders have gathered to discuss the recent alien abductions. President Wilson, along with Prime Minister Johnson, have been locked in meetings all day, but we're getting word that a statement is about to be made. We can cross live now to our correspondent, Lucy Banks."

"Thank you, Sophie," the news anchor said as she stood amongst other reporters, jockeying for position. "President Wilson is about to face the media, to hopefully give a definitive update on the recent events in Belbroughton, England. In fact, he's approaching the microphone as we speak."

Hugh took a sip of his whisky as the camera focused on a raised platform outside the White House, where a tall man and a slightly shorter woman walked out of white double doors. President Wilson, with his buzz-cut blonde hair and chiselled looks, smiled as he addressed the crowd of reporters. To his left, Prime Minister Johnson looked across the immaculate lawns, smiling as hundreds of cameras zoomed in on her, the odd flash making her flinch slightly. Her steel-grey hair matched the stylishly cut trouser suit that she wore underneath a black woollen coat.

"My fellow Americans, and citizens of our great planet, I can now say without absolute certainty, we are not alone."

He let the words sink in as cameras continued to flash on the dark Washington afternoon. He placed his weathered hands on the dais, preparing himself for the revelation that was about to come.

"On October 25th in a small village called Belbroughton in the UK, an advanced alien civilization abducted one hundred and seventy-two citizens, taking them to the far side of the known universe. Having listened to all the statements taken from these brave souls, we now know that they were taken to live out their lives on a planet called Valkash, which was some kind of alien theme park, harbouring creatures and civilizations from across the cosmos."

He paused, knowing that most of the planet would be hanging on his every word.

"They were returned to us a few weeks later, all except four of them, who sadly passed away whilst being held captive on that distant planet. Since they returned, our intelligence agencies from around the world have been gathering data to substantiate their story. However, aside from radar anomalies gathered by our friends in the United Kingdom, there are only a few pieces of genuine footage that captured the spacecraft leaving Earth. I'll open up the floor to a few questions at this time."

"Kelly Miles, *CNN*. Mr President, how was this able to happen? Why did no one spot this ship approaching Earth?"

"Well, this is the first documented event of this kind in the history of our planet. From what I have learned from *NASA's* Chief Administrator, the ship must have used a cloaking device, which could have made them invisible to our radars and cameras. The alien race that visited us have technology that has our top minds scratching their collective heads. Yes, Karen."

"Karen Voliva, *Fox News*. Mr President, what measures are you putting in place to guarantee the safety of the citizens of Earth in light of these abductions?"

"Good question, Karen. The *G8* have gathered here in Tokyo, with a plan to allocate our collective resources to look towards the stars. It will not be easy, but we need to do this. We will start to monitor movements across the solar system, hopefully detecting any future approaches from extra-terrestrial beings. We are already doing something similar to a degree, tracking asteroids and comets that could potentially strike Earth. We need to up our game, keeping an eye on as much as humanly possible. The safety of our citizens is paramount, whatever corner of our planet they inhabit."

"Joanne Barnes, *Sky News*. Prime Minister, four British Citizens are dead, two of them children. Will anyone be held accountable for their deaths?"

The woman stepped forward, the President moving to one side to allow the Prime Minister, Katherine Johnson, to take the podium.

"The short answer, Joanne, is no. The beings that abducted our citizens left the planet shortly after bringing them back home. They could be anywhere in the universe. We simply have no means of holding them to account."

"How about our security services? Surely they are answerable?"

"As the President said, this is an unprecedented event. Nothing like this has ever happened before. Any loss of human life is tragic, regardless of how it occurred. We will learn from this, ensuring that any future visitors are spotted before a repeat of this event can take place."

"But people are dead, Prime Minister," was the response from the throng of reporters.

"Yes, we are well aware of that. However, this could almost be classed as an act of God. Earthquakes and tsunamis have killed thousands of people across the world. But we can never fully predict when and where they will strike. We were simply not ready for this type of event, but we are now. And we will be ready if it happens again."

"Matthew Small, *Bloomberg News*. Mr President, do we know how this ship managed to travel to Earth from the other side of the universe?"

The President took to the podium, Prime Minister Johnson stepping to one side. "Having consulted with our top advisors, it is clear that some kind of wormhole technology was used to fold spacetime. I've been assured that this would be the only way to travel the 13,000,000,000 light years from their planet to ours. Thank you for your time ladies and gentlemen. We have no time for further questions at this point."

Hugh finished his Scotch, heading out of the lounge towards the kitchen at the rear of the property. "You'll be ready next time," he said as he popped two pieces of bread in the toaster. "Let's hope there isn't a next time."

THIRTY-NINE

KYRA STOOD ON THEIR NEW JETTY, LOOKING OUT AT THE ocean as the yellow star kissed the far-off horizon. Closer to the moon, the brown dwarf star was almost totally out of sight, just the top edge still visible before it finally set for the night. She pulled the sweater around her neck, taking a sip of graff from a small metal flask. A deep drone filled her ears, a breekin breaking the calm waters out at sea, its huge tail crashing down a few seconds later. Seconds later a relative silence returned to the shore, just a light breeze ruffling the evergreens behind the cabin. Kyra turned, looking up at Biflux above her. A single tear ran down her cheek, thoughts of her parents stirring her emotions as an approaching craft once more disturbed the quiet ocean. She watched as Torben brought the craft gently to the jetty, barely nudging the rubber buffers that ran its length. The glass-domed roof slid back soundlessly as he exited the craft, smiling at his woman. "Hi."

"Welcome home, Torby," she replied warmly.

"How long have you been stood out here?"

"Not long. I was watching the sunset."

He ambled over, wrapping Kyra into his arms. "Well,

you're the best thing I have seen all day," he said, before planting a kiss on her lips.

"Same here. Dinner is nearly ready. Shall we go and prepare?"

"Sounds good. The Lomogs are not exactly the best hosts when it comes to feeding their guests. Juice and fruit were all they offered me."

"Well, a ship's captain needs more than that to keep his strength up. Come," she said as she led him from the wooden structure back to their home. They walked into the kitchen, Torben heading straight for the chiller, pulling two bottles of beer from the top shelf. He cracked the seal on both of them, placing them on the countertop as Kyra pulled a large metal dish from the oven. She carried it over to the table by its bone handles, her thick gloves protecting her hands.

"Smells good," he said, his mouth starting to moisten.

"It will taste good too. I added some herbs to the meat from the garden. I cannot wait to get stuck in."

Torben pulled two bowls from the rack, placing them next to the steaming dish, handing Kyra a large metal serving spoon. "I'll set the table up on the stoop," he said cheerfully, leaving Kyra to serve the dark stew into the wooden bowls. A minute later she placed the bowls in front of him, placing some cutlery on the hessian table mat. "Thank you, it looks amazing."

"Well, let's not wait another minute," she said, raising her bottle.

He readily accepted, clinking glasses with her before taking a swig. "Good health."

"And to you." After a few mouthfuls, Kyra cleared her throat. "So, how did it go today?"

Torben nodded his head, chewing his way through the tender dark meat before replying. "Very good. They have issued me with unlimited credits, which will mean that we'll never have to worry about working again."

"Oh my," Kyra said. "That's amazing!"

"I know," he said, a smile spreading across his face. "They were trying to offer me posts in other systems, along with a promotion to Commander. When I said that I wasn't interested, they changed tack, offering me the credits instead. So, I took it, along with something else thrown into the bargain."

"What was that?"

Torben took a swig of beer, telling Kyra about his plan. She listened intently as the yellow star on the horizon finally disappeared from view, blanketing the land and ocean in darkness. Solar powered lanterns powered themselves into life, creating a yellowy hue outside the cabin and garden beyond. "Anyway, they agreed. So, the day after tomorrow, I will take one last journey in Shimmer050."

"Do you really think it's a good idea?" she asked.

"Yes. We need to redress the balance. Hopefully, this will do it. Then, when I'm home, we can start making plans for our future."

"Our future?"

"Yes," Torben said, rising from his chair. He walked around the table, kneeling in front of Kyra. "I love you. I think I loved you the first time I saw you, Kyra. I want my life to be entwined with yours. Would you consider becoming my life partner?"

He pulled a small black box from his pocket, handing it to the woman, whose eyes began misting over. She opened the box, her breath catching as she saw the small ring contained within. She deftly plucked it from its holder, holding it up to the light. It had twin platinum bands, held together by two gemstones, one blue, the other a sparkling magenta. "Oh Torben," she said, as tears formed at the corners of her eyes. "It's beautiful."

"So are you, Kyra."

She slipped it onto her finger, laughing as the gemstones shimmered in the lantern's glow. Kyra flung her arms around

Torben's neck, burying her face in his neck. "Yes, I would love to be your life partner," she said, pulling away before kissing him fiercely. "Thank you, Torby. You have made me the happiest girl in the galaxy."

Tears fell onto the man's cheeks as he kissed her hand. "I just love you. And I want to build a life here with you. And a family."

Beers were replenished as the young couple sat chatting on the steps leading down to the grass beyond. Kyra had fetched a warm blanket, draping it over their shoulders as they stared up at Biflux. Torben talked about extending the cabin, using the Lomogs credits to build them more rooms and outbuildings, along with a larger jetty, where more crafts could be moored. She sat listening, her head resting on his shoulder as she visualised their little enclave, surrounded by trees and the calm ocean. The pain and loss from the previous months began to slowly slip away, replaced by hope, love and excitement. She drank the feeling in as she sipped at her cool beer. She looked down at her hand, knowing that the ring on her finger would always be there. A part of her, just like the man who had changed Kyra's life forever.

"Hi, Rex," Torben said warmly as the hominid walked down Shimmer050's ramp.

"Skipper," he replied, accepting the captain's embrace. "It's good to see you."

"Likewise," Torben replied. He had left the cabin early, travelling the short distance to command post. The impressive conglomeration of buildings looked out over the ocean, flanked by snow-covered peaks to the rear, giving it a protected feel. Torben stood in a docking bay, peering out as light from the nearby star bathed the moon in a warm glow. "Where is Commander Spelk?"

"Onboard," Rex replied. "I'll bring you some graff. You'll find him in the cargo hold with his engineers."

"Thanks, Rex," the captain replied, heading purposefully up the ramp. A few minutes later, he walked into the cargo bay at the rear of Shimmer050. Three men were standing talking next to a large metal container, grey in colour with red markings. "Commander," Torben said, the three men turning towards him.

"Captain Fraken," Spelk replied evenly. "This is Morax, my chief engineer, along with Alfret, the Lomogs chief physicist. Your cargo is ready for dispatch. All the equipment and data you've requested is inside the container."

"Thank you, Commander. Let's hope it has the desired effect."

"I'm sure it will. I totally agree with this mission. I'm sure that it will be of benefit." He turned back to the two men, Torben taking his leave to make a call to Kyra.

"Hi," he said as her holographic face appeared before him.

"Hello, Torby. Are you ready to go?"

"Pretty much. Just waiting for the green light."

"You will be careful, won't you?"

"You can count on that. What time are you heading over to Vasteras?"

"In about an hour. I will visit the builder first, confirming an appointment as soon as possible. From there, I will spend some time at the outlets, getting a few ideas for the project."

"Well, have fun, my love."

"You can also count on that. I love you."

"I love you too. I will be back soon."

"Safe travels, Captain."

"You too, Officer Zakx."

. . .

An hour later Shimmer050 broke orbit, heading out past the host planet, with Rex handling the controls. "Okay, we don't need to worry too much about heading out to the safe zones. Just take us out far enough so we don't mess with planetary orbits."

"Okay, Captain," Rex replied. "Where are we heading first?"

"There is a binary star system close by. We will head there first, taking some images of planetary systems. Coordinates have already been uploaded. After that, there is a red dwarf, also close by. We will check out some more exoplanets. I think that will be a good head-start for them."

"Okay, Captain. As you wish. We can make the first jump in about two hours."

"Fine. I will take over for a bit. I will miss this ship. It really is something."

"Yes, it is."

"Do you know what post you will be taking next?" Torben asked.

"Yes. Commander Spelk has asked me to be part of a new project, codenamed Ezekial."

"I've heard about that. The multiverse theory."

"Yes. The Lomogs are convinced that they exist. Imagine that. Countless realities, within reach."

"It certainly is an interesting theory. Just take care, Rex. We have no idea what may lie beyond our own universe."

"True. But the chance to take part was too good to pass up."

"Well, when you return, come and find me. We will both be very interested in your findings."

"I will, Captain. Make sure you have plenty of beer."

"For you, Rex. Anything."

FORTY

ONE DAY LATER

"IMAGING UNDERWAY," REX SAID, AS HE STARED OUT AT THE planet orbiting the red dwarf star. It was nondescript, with mountains and oceans, but no signs of observable life. On the horizon, a dim star cast its glow across the solar system, two more distant glowing orbs of light increasing in luminosity somewhat, bathing the ship in a yellow glow. Shimmer050 hung in the planet's orbit, two-hundred miles from the surface, its numerous hull cameras collecting data as storms rippled across the planet.

"Okay, Rex. I'm going to check on the ship. Once you have all the data, upload it all to the cargo bay."

"Okay, Captain. Do you want some graff?"

"You stay here, my friend. I will bring you some."

"I could get used to this kind of service," the diminutive hominid said, winking at Torben mischievously.

Hours later, the ship came through the singularity, settling into the vacuum of space around it. Rex repeated the same procedure, taking images and collecting data of the large exoplanet nearby. Unlike the other planet, this one had vivid oceans, dotted with landmasses, cloud formations hugging the orangey surface. On the horizon a similar red dwarf to the one they'd just visited lit the surrounding solar system, a small moon clearly visible from their vantage point, trapped in the planet's orbit. "Lifeforms detected, Captain."

"Are they advanced?"

"Negative. Mainly single-cell organisms."

"Still. It's good data to capture. Upload to the cargo bay when we're finished."

"Will do. Do you want to visit the other systems? They are thirty light-years from our position."

"I don't think we'll need to. We have enough data for them. They should be happy with it."

"Okay, Captain."

Twenty-four hours later, Shimmer050 dropped through another planet's atmosphere, its cloaking device making the large ship invisible. It quickly plunged through the cloud layer, levelling out a few hundred feet above the surface. Snow was falling, the landscape blanketed in white as the craft touched down in a deserted area, nearby a small settlement. "Okay, Rex. We need to do this quickly. Contact the cargo bay, telling them that time is of the essence. We need to be on our way home in ten minutes."

"Okay, Captain," Rex said, his green fingers activating the ship's communications

"Cargo crew, unload the bay when we touch down."

"Affirmative," was the brief reply.

Torben and Rex sat in their chairs, looking out at the familiar sight, the captain flinching as a pair of headlights drove past the entrance to the field. "Come on. We need to be making a move."

They sat waiting as infrequent vehicles passed by their

position, the ship's cloak hiding them from view. After a few minutes, a voice came through the communication speakers. "Cargo bay unloaded. Closing bay doors."

"Okay, Rex. Let's go home." The ship ascended effortlessly, breaking orbit a minute later as Shimmer050 headed out into the void of space. In the deserted field, a large metal container with red markings sat there, becoming slowly covered in falling snow.

The following morning, the snow had stopped falling on the village of Belbroughton, a thin layer of white still carpeting the landscape. A black Agusta Westland helicopter landed at the far end of the field. Prime Minster Johnson exited the craft, being met on the frozen ground by Rupert Marshall, Secretary of State for Defence for the United Kingdom. Next to him, Oliver King, Chief Executive for the UK's Space Agency. As the Prime Minister's sturdy boots trudged through the snow, she could see numerous police cars, along with army trucks positioned around the large open space. A police cordon had been set up at the entrance, screening the field from prying eyes. "What's your latest update?" she said, pulling her black coat around her neck.

"The village is being evacuated, Prime Minister. Residents are being taken to Kidderminster and Worcester hospitals as a precaution," Marshall replied. Ahead of the threesome, a large metal container sat brooding on the ground, tendrils of steam seeping into the atmosphere. "*HAZMAT* crews have analysed the container and surrounding areas. Nothing remotely hazardous has been detected."

"Good. That's the last thing we need just after Christmas," she replied as they came to the alien object.

"It's one hundred and forty feet long, forty feet wide and

twenty feet tall," King announced as they came to two large steel doors.

"Has anyone tried to get inside?" Prime Minister Johnson asked.

"No, Prime Minister. We were waiting for you to arrive. There is a control panel just there," he said pointing. "It looks to have power, as you can see."

"Hmm," she said, walking forward.

"Prime Minister. I strongly advise that you fall back to a safe area whilst we open the container. It could contain an alien pathogen."

"Oliver. Open it please," she countered.

"If you're sure," he replied, extending his hand to the control panel. He placed his hand on the panel, a red line scanning his palm before the whole screen turned green. Steam billowed from the doors as they opened slowly, the threesome falling back a few paces until the doors were fully open. "Oh my god!" King said.

"Is that what I think it is?" Johnson replied, stepping inside the container.

"I believe it is," Marshall said as the metal confines lit up around them. Holographic heads-up displays lined the workstations and walls, displaying star maps and planetary systems.

Johnson waved her arm through one display, blue shimmering particles distorting until her hand passed through, returning the display to its normal state. They walked around the large object in the centre of the space, heading towards a map of their solar system, slowly rotating against the wall. As they approached, a holographic figure appeared, startling them. The Prime Minister regained her composure, walking a few paces towards the male figure in front of them. Despite the situation, she appraised the man. "Gosh. Not really what I expected. He's rather dishy isn't he," she said, the men stepping forward until they flanked her.

"My name is Torben Fraken. Captain of Shimmer050. I

recently visited your planet, abducting one hundred and seventy-two of your citizens. And for that, I am truly sorry. I was acting under the direct orders of the Lomogs, our bene-factors and commanders. I then returned them back home to you, except for four humans who sadly died whilst on the planet of Valkash. I am sending you this message, along with the contents of this container as a gift, from us to you. This idea was agreed upon by the Lomogs, who asked me to make delivery, which I am about to do at the time of broadcasting this message. I hope that what you discover is of great use to the people of your planet. We have no plans to return to Earth, so do not be troubled by the thought of another abduc-tion. We live on the far side of the universe, having everything we need to sustain us. Your planet is very special. Amongst the data I have given to you is information about two exoplanets, relatively close in proximity to Earth. If you're going to reach out to the stars, they are a good place to start. Captain Fraken, out." The image disappeared, leaving the solar system rotating next to it, the threesome standing in silence.

King broke the silence. "He's given us a spaceship."

"We need to keep this under wraps," the Prime Minister replied, walking over to the ship. She ran her hand across the hull, liking the slightly dappled feel of the dull alloy. "The only person I will inform is the President. If Russia and China knew about this, the shit would hit the fan."

"Understood," the Secretary of State for Defence said. "I will arrange for the container to be relocated to Hereford for now. We'll form a ring of steel around it, while King and his teams decipher exactly what we've been given."

"He spoke English," King stated.

"Yes, he did," the Prime Minister replied. "But let's not worry about that now. We've got a lot of work to do. We need to know how this ship works. And if it does work, what kind of technology it possesses."

"Understood, Prime Minister. Once it's in situ at Hereford, I'll have the smartest people on the planet poring over this."

"Good work. Looks like Christmas came a little late this year."

"You're not wrong," Marshall replied. "It looks like all our Christmases have come at once."

EPILOGUE

ONE YEAR LATER

TORBEN STOOD ON HIS NEWLY EXTENDED JETTY, LOOKING BACK at their home. The once compact cabin had increased in size dramatically. Guest quarters above a large workshop had recently been completed, the thatched roof on top of the wooden structure looking resplendent in the midday sun. A large wooden fence had been erected, forming a border around the property, giving them the seclusion and security they'd wanted. Their lives had settled into a happy routine, the couple growing increasingly close at the seasons moved on. Snows had arrived, bringing warm evenings in front of the fire, followed by spring, with its balmy evenings. The Lomogs had largely left them to it, occasionally asking Torben to visit command, with new propositions, which he kindly declined. All that he'd needed was right in front of him. He spotted Kyra walking out of the guest quarters, slowly walking down the stout wooden stairs at the side of the two-storey building. She saw him on the jetty and walked across the grass towards him, her gait not as loping as it once was. Torben smiled, his eyes drawn to her midsection, which had also dramatically increased over the previous months. "What have you been up to?"

"Just adding the last finishing touches to the guest wash-room. It looks really nice."

"You should be taking it easy. The physician told you that you should be resting."

"Torben Fraken, I am with child. I can still potter about the place under my own steam."

"Well, I am here to help you."

"I know. And I thank you for that, Torby. You've been working very hard over the past few months. Soon, our daughter will arrive. Then the real work begins."

Torben knelt down, placing his ear on Kyra's distended stomach. He felt a flutter inside, smiling up at his woman. "Hello, little star. It's your Father. I cannot wait to meet you, Elsor." At hearing her mother's name, tears pricked at Kyra's eyes. She let them form, then spill out over her cheeks, enjoying the tender moment with her family. "We're going to have such adventures." He kissed her midsection, standing up to wrap Kyra in his embrace.

"I like this softer side of you. When we first met, you were a different man to the one that stands before me today."

"Old age is mellowing me."

She giggled, playfully punching his shoulder. "It's love that has mellowed you, Torben Fraken. Love from me, and our little bundle. Talking of love, have you heard from Ark this week?"

"Yes. He and Ebrisa are back in Vasteras. Looks like they are getting quite serious."

"About time you pilots found good women and settled down. Let the youngsters explore the universe."

"You may have a point. My days of interstellar adventures are behind me. I cannot wait to be a father, putting our children in their bunks every night."

Kyra walked to the end of the jetty, a pod of sea mammals breaking the surface as they tracked their way across the ocean. "I love you Torben," she said. "I cannot wait for our baby to be born. I cannot wait to take your name and plan the rest of our lives here."

"I'll drink to that," he replied. "I'll drink for all of us."

"Just save me some. The thought of a cold beer is so good right now."

"Hold that thought, Kyra Fraken."

"Kyra Fraken. I like how that sounds," she said, a gust of wind ruffling her hair, the red lock shimmering in the sunlight. "Come. Let me show you the guest quarters. The washroom is complete and the bunks are freshly made."

Let's skip the washroom. Show me the bunks. I need to test their firmness."

"Hmm. Maybe it will speed things along," Kyra said as she took his arm, walking slowly with him across the stubbly grass. Towards their forever home.

Earth

Gemma stood with her sons as the bus pulled to a halt in the centre of the village. "Thanks, Des," she said, smiling at the bus driver.

"You take care. Bit slippery underfoot," the bus driver said.

"Bye Des, the boys said happily, drawing a beaming smile from the older man. He reminded Gemma of Santa Claus, without the beard, such was his rosy complexion and white hair.

"See you soon," he said, as they stepped off the bus onto the frosty pavement. They stood there, watching as the single-decker bus wound its way out of the village, towards Birmingham, the Christmas decorations bringing the sleepy village to life.

"Mummy," Finn said. "What are we doing tonight?"

"Daddy is going to watch a movie with you both," she replied as they crossed the quiet country lane. "Mummy is going out with her friends. You remember Caroline?" They both nodded happily. "Well, she is getting married soon and Mummy is going on her hen night later."

"What's a hen night?" Finn asked.

"Are there lots of chickens?" Oscar said?"

Gemma chuckled. "Yes, boys. There will be lots of chickens."

"Sounds fun. Can you take lots of pictures?" Finn said.

"Okay, my loves," she replied happily as they came to their home. Letting them inside the hallway, Gemma smiled when Hugh appeared on the landing. "Hello, hun."

"Hi, babe. Have you had fun?"

"It was nice. We rode the steam train all the way to Bridgnorth. Didn't we, boys?"

"Yes, Daddy," Finn said. And the driver tooted his horn when we got off. Mummy bought us hot chocolate too."

"Sounds fab. I'm very jealous," he replied, limping down the stairs, the cast on his leg making progress slow and painful.

"Steady, hun. You've already taken one tumble. Don't do it again."

"I'll be okay. Bloody thing," he said, looking at the cast. "I'll be glad when it's off. It itches like mad."

"Well, no more ice-skating for you, mister."

"You're not wrong there. That was the first and last time I do that. I'll stick to country walks and surfing the net."

"If you're okay to take over, I'll go and get myself ready?"

"Sure, babe. You go and do what you need to do. Boys, in the lounge, please. Daddy will cook you a pizza."

"PIZZA!" they cheered as Gemma started climbing the stairs, a broad smile on her face.

. . .

An hour later, she walked into the familiar surroundings of the Talbot Inn as the evening was getting into full swing. She bustled past revellers and a large Christmas tree, spotting a group of women in the far corner of the lounge next to an inviting fireplace that was gently crackling away, casting its heat across the pub. "You've started without me," she said playfully, smiling at Caroline and Sarah.

"Only just. This is the first round," Caroline replied jovially, standing to embrace her friend.

Sarah joined them, wrapping an arm around Gemma. "Hello, lovely. How's you?"

"Good," she replied, getting a whiff of the blonde woman's perfume. "We've been on the Severn Valley Railway today. Bloody cold though." She looked at the older woman sat next to the fire. "Hello, Margaret. How are you?"

The woman looked up, smiling warmly. "Hello. I'm good, dear. Caroline bought me a gin and tonic with raspberries in it. Bit of a change from sweet sherry."

Gemma chuckled. "Well, you enjoy. It's a special occasion." She looked over at the adjoining table, nodding at a few familiar faces. "Hello," she said politely, the women replying in a friendly manner as Gemma settled herself next to Caroline. "So, where's Tom this evening?"

"Probably knee deep in beer," Caroline replied. "He's not going mad though. He's meeting up with a few friends and colleagues in Kidderminster. He'll probably be home before me."

"Any news on the house?" Sarah asked.

"Yes. All being well, we'll be in after the honeymoon." Caroline had kept them updated about her impending house move, a three-bedroomed semi in nearby Blakedown - their new love nest.

"It'll need plenty of work," Margaret added. "No one's had the paintbrush out since 1976."

"Thanks, Mum. That's fine with us. It will give us chance to do a complete makeover. Put our stamp on it."

"Sounds very exciting," Gemma added as she suddenly remembered she'd forgotten to get a drink. "Anyone for a drink?"

"I'm okay, dear," Margaret said. "This will last me a while."

Sarah and Gemma nodded, Gemma knowing their favourite tipples. "I'll give you a hand, hun," Sarah said, standing up. Many pairs of eyes, both male and female looked her way as she attempted to straighten her miniskirt.

"Oh, to have legs like that again," Margaret said. "Make the most of it, dear."

Sarah smiled, blushing slightly at the compliment. "Thanks," she said awkwardly, before following Gemma to the bar. They returned a few minutes later, drinks placed on round cardboard beermats.

"Cheers," Gemma said. "To Caroline and Tom."

"Caroline and Tom," they repeated happily before each taking a sip of their respective drinks.

"Any news on the honeymoon?" Sarah asked.

"Nothing. He's still not letting on. I've been trying to find out for weeks. All I know is that I need to pack a swimsuit and not much else."

"You probably won't make it out of the bedroom, lucky sod!" Sarah said playfully.

"Well, here's hoping," Caroline replied, looking at her mother.

"I know what goes on, dear. I was young once. Your Father took me to Benidorm when we tied the knot. We had a lovely week, but I didn't get much of a tan, if you know what I mean."

"Mum," Caroline scolded. "Stop it. You'll scar me for life."

"Sorry, dear. I do miss your Father. He was a good man. But so is Tom. I know he'll take good care of you."

Caroline burst into tears, spilling some of her lager onto the floor. Gemma deftly took the glass from her as the Welsh woman embraced her mother tightly. "I miss him too, Mum. Every day. And I wish he was there to walk me down the aisle, well, registry office aisle."

"He'd be proud as punch, my love."

"I hope so. And you're right, Tom is a great guy. From the first time we met at the interview, I kinda had a feeling that something was in the air."

"Well it's all worked out well," Gemma said. "We have had an eventful year or so. Abducted by aliens. Involved in an interplanetary war before being dropped off home. That's a lot to put on your CV." She looked at Sarah. "How about you, lovely? Any gossip?"

"There may be."

The three women looked at Sarah, expectant expressions waiting to be updated. "Tell all," Caroline said.

"I've been seeing a guy from Bromsgrove. Nothing serious yet, we're just getting to know each other."

"Well, why don't you bring him to the wedding, hun? Then he can meet his extended family."

Tears formed in Sarah's eyes. "Really? Okay, thanks, hun. I will text him," she said, hugging the bride-to-be.

A few hours later, they all said their drunken goodbyes. Gemma smiled as she watched Caroline escort her mother gently down the road, the older woman swaying as she tried to navigate the pavement. Sarah gave her a kiss, sauntering off across the sleepy village, the sky above filled with distant stars. Gemma made the short walk home, stopping at her front gate, peering up at the blackness above her. She smiled, wondering where Torben and Kyra were, hoping they were safe and happy. Closing the gate behind her, she made her way up the path, towards her house. Her home.

Five years later

The ship slowed down, reverse thrusters deployed as it hung hundreds of miles above the ochre planet below it. Minutes later it was descending through the atmosphere, the heat shield protecting the hull as the ship headed towards the set coordinates on the planet's surface. A few hundred feet above the craggy landscape, landing legs appeared below the hull, readying the ship for its touchdown, gently settling on the hard rock a minute later. It sat there, flanked by dark-coloured mountains, lakes of water dotting the landscape. On the horizon a large star cast its light across the solar system, appearing much larger than what the crew were used to. Behind it another star lit the sky, appearing much smaller than the goliath that filled their view. Within the ship, feverish activity was underway, the landing party being readied and suited-up by crew members, just like how they had been prac- tising on the long journey from their solar system. Minutes later, the ship's ramp lowered to the rocky surface, settling almost silently. Two astronauts walked down the gradient, stopping shy of the surface as they looked at each other. One smiled at the other, patting him on the shoulder of his space- suit, giving him the go ahead. The man took a step forward, then another as the other astronaut followed suit. They stood there for a few minutes, taking in the strange vista, noticing the lakes and mountains around them. The two men took it all in, the smaller man scanning the surface with his atmos- pheric monitor. He checked the reading, satisfied that all was as it should be before placing the monitor on the dull, rocky surface. He unshouldered his pack, pulling out a metal staff that had a large swathe of material attached to it. The other man nodded to him, watching proudly as the man unfurled it before hammering it into a crack in the surface a few feet from the ship as jets of steam from the hull enveloped them. After a few well-placed taps with his steel hammer, the pole stood proudly, the flag fluttering gently in the breeze. It stood out against the dull backdrop, its red, white and blue colours vividly displaying themselves for the watching cameras. Thin clouds above the ship moved across the landscape as the two astronauts walked a few yards before turning back to their craft.

"I claim this planet for his Majesty the King, for Great Britain and the people of Earth. Command, we've made it. Astronauts Karl Hartley and Tim Bancroft are coming to you live from Proxima Centauri-B. It sure is beautiful up here."

"Another giant leap for mankind," Bancroft added, drawing a huge smile from Hartley.

"Jones," Hartley said into his intercom.

"Yes, Captain," replied the co-pilot from the cockpit of the ship, its name painted along the hull in bright yellow. Goldilocks-1.

"Gravity feels very similar to Earth's. Ground temperature is minus fifteen degrees Celsius, so I'm glad I didn't pack my beachwear. And there is definitely an atmosphere, clouds and water."

"So, we have a magnetosphere."

"Affirmative, although we can do all the technical stuff later. For now, Bancroft and myself are going for a hike."

"Be careful out there. We'll start unpacking."

"You do that. Over and out," replied Hartley as the two men began their first adventure, walking towards the rocky horizon, many new horizons, now within their reach.

THE END

ABOUT THE AUTHOR

Phil Price was born in Sutton Coldfield in 1974. He lived in various places until his family settled in Rednal, Birmingham in 1979. Growing up with and older brother and sister he always flirted with reading, as there were always books lying on shelves around the house. Then in 1997 he embarked on a travel expedition that took him from Greece to Thailand, via East and Southern Africa. Sitting in dusty bus stations in Kenya, Tanzania, and Malawi gave him the opportunity to ignite his imagination fully. Since those far off days he has never been without a book to read.

He toyed with the idea of writing a book in 2009. After writing a few short stories he caught a whiff of a story in his head. It grew and grew in 2010 until he had enough to begin his writing journey. Marriage and two children came along, with the story being moved to the back burner for periods of time. However, during those periods of writing inactivity the story continued to evolve until it just needed to be written down.

The book was littered with places that had influenced Phil's life. From the Lickey Hills in Birmingham, to the Amatola Mountains in South Africa with other locations, in-between and far beyond.

The book was finished sometime in 2014 and was left on his computer, until a chance conversation with an author friend made Phil take the bold step to publish his story, Unknown.

From there, Phil's love for the first book spurred him on, creating The Forsaken Series. A vampire/paranormal/horror trilogy, set in our world, and others too. His love of horror and all things supernatural, inspired by authors such as King, Herbert, and others, helped create the epic series.

Next on the horizon, is a science fiction novel, titled Zoo, which will boldly go where Phil has never been before...

Aside from his writing, Phil lives on the edge of a small town in Worcestershire, UK. A wife and two sons keep Phil happily occupied as he steers his way through life, playing husband, dad, and world creator in equal measure.

Zoo
ISBN: 978-4-86750-871-8

Published by
Next Chapter
1-60-20 Minami-Otsuka
170-0005 Toshima-Ku, Tokyo
+818035793528

11th June 2021